BRASS LIVES

BRASS LIVES

Chris Nickson

**SEVERN
HOUSE**

First world edition published in Great Britain and the USA in 2021
by Severn House, an imprint of Canongate Books Ltd,
14 High Street, Edinburgh EH1 1TE.

Trade paperback edition first published in Great Britain and the USA in 2022
by Severn House, an imprint of Canongate Books Ltd.

severnhouse.com

British Library Cataloguing-in-Publication Data
A CIP catalogue record for this title is available from the British Library.

ISBN-13: 978-0-7278-9088-7 (cased)
ISBN-13: 978-1-78029-811-5 (trade paper)
ISBN-13: 978-1-4483-0549-0 (e-book)

All Severn House titles are printed on acid-free paper.

Typeset by Palimpsest Book Production Ltd.,
Falkirk, Stirlingshire, Scotland.
Printed and bound in Great Britain by
TJ Books, Padstow, Cornwall.

For Julia Marlene Bedore Baldwin
1954–2020
The first American I loved.

ONE

Leeds, June 1913

'There's going to be a march,' Annabelle Harper said as she put down her copy of *Common Cause*.

'Isn't there always a march for something or other?' Tom Harper asked. 'What's this one about?'

She picked up the magazine again and opened it at the page she'd dog-eared. The suffragist magazine had arrived that morning and she'd worked her way through the articles between her other jobs – running the Victoria public house and arranging a series of information salons about democracy and Parliament for women.

'This one's different. It's going to be big. And it'll be national. People will be starting out in all different parts of the country and making their way to London. On foot, in caravans, then everyone will meet in the capital for a huge gathering. Thousands of us.' She smiled at the thought. 'They're calling it the Great Pilgrimage. A peaceful gathering,' Annabelle added pointedly, glancing at their daughter Mary, who was working on her business accounts, 'to show that the suffragists aren't like the suffragettes.'

'And the suffragists haven't achieved much in twenty years,' Mary replied without raising her head. But there was no sting in her voice. They both wanted the same thing: votes for women. The difference was the paths they took. Annabelle was old enough to believe that the violence of Mrs Pankhurst's women did little to help the cause. Mary had the bristling anger of youth burning inside her.

'You said "us". Are you going?' Harper asked.

'I might,' Annabelle replied with a smile. 'What do you think? It'll give you two the chance to be shut of me for a little while.'

'What, you, march all the way to London?' he asked, staring at her in disbelief. He couldn't picture his wife doing that. She'd gladly tramp around Leeds, but not two hundred miles to the capital.

'Don't be so daft. I'll drive.' She smiled. 'I can offer a lift to some others who don't fancy Shanks's pony.'

'Of course you should go.' They'd been married for twenty-three years and together almost every day of that time. A few nights away from him might do her the power of good. The Victoria more or less ran itself, and Leeds wouldn't fall apart while she was gone.

Annabelle had been a suffragist speaker in the town for a long time, up on the podium and making the case for women's votes. She'd earned the chance to enjoy the company of so many who thought the same way.

The weather was on her side, too, he thought; only June, but the summer had been balmy so far. Plenty of sun, warm, no more than a few showers of rain to help things grow. Perfect for a long trek.

'You're sure you don't mind?'

'Positive.' He nudged Mary.

'You go, Mam. Get some fresh air and see the country.' She lowered her head again to concentrate on the figures.

'Maybe I will. Go on then, clever clogs, how much profit did you make last month?'

'The business is doing very nicely, thank you.' Mary grinned. For the last three years she'd run a secretarial agency and school. Annabelle had put up the money and used her name to start the business as soon as their daughter turned eighteen. Mary had repaid her mother in full long before she turned twenty-one. Now she was of age, she'd officially taken over. Trade was brisk; there was no shortage of clients who needed typewriting performed, and word of mouth was constantly bringing more. With a flood of young woman eager to earn a living from office work, Mary had tapped into a boom.

It kept her busy six days a week, often late into the evening. But never on Sundays; that was her rule. Those were special. Whatever the weather, that was when Mary went out with the Clarion Cycling Club. It gave her a break from the agency, away from the routine of the office. It was good exercise in the fresh air, and above all it offered a chance to be with other young people. She'd take her Raleigh bicycle out of the shed in the pub yard and head up into the Dales or out to the Yorkshire Wolds and back, fifteen or twenty of them pedalling mile after mile. The Clarion was a political group, full of earnest young socialists and suffragettes; she'd made plenty of friends. But one lad in particular stood out: Len, from Cross Green. He was finishing his apprenticeship as a machine fitter, with the promise of a good job at Hunslet Engine ahead of him. For the last six months he and Mary been walking out together two or three times a week. It was more than a light romance, that was obvious; this was proper courting. Mary had gone to meet his parents, and he'd been over for his tea several times. Harper and Annabelle liked the lad. He was bashful and quiet, but who wouldn't be when your girlfriend's father was a copper?

The telephone bell put an end to his thoughts. He'd never cared for having the instrument at home, but it was a necessary evil, a part of his job. Much the same with the car and driver he had now. Since he'd been promoted again, rank demanded the honour. But it went against the grain, left him isolated. A copper needed to be out, walking around, hearing things and seeing them. Talking to people.

'Deputy Chief Constable Harper.' Almost two years now, and it still came as a surprise every time he said the words. Top brass in the police force of one of the biggest cities of the empire. Who'd have believed that was possible when he was pounding the beat round the courts and yards behind Briggate all those years ago?

Chief Constable Parker had persuaded him. Deputy chief was a new position, and Harper hadn't been keen to apply. He was happy running A Division, working out of Millgarth police station. He knew his manor inside and out, and he had a crack squad of detectives he'd spent years training. Why move?

'You'll be in charge of all the detectives in Leeds, Tom,' Parker said. 'I'll guarantee you can stay in plain clothes. Not many evening functions. And better pay.'

Finally, the chief had worn him down and he'd stood in his frock coat and top hat before the Lord Mayor to formally accept the rank. Annabelle was beside herself with pleasure. He wasn't so sure he'd done the right thing. He still wasn't convinced.

Harper listened with the receiver pressed tight against his good ear. Even that gave him trouble these days; his hearing had deteriorated again. He needed to concentrate on every word.

'No,' he said finally. 'That's Millgarth business. Drag out Superintendent Ash. Wait, make it Inspector Walsh; he can take care of it.' He shook his head as he finished the call. 'Honestly, ringing me about a burglary. For God's sake, that's why we have officers in the divisions.'

'A few years back you'd have been dashing out of that door,' Annabelle reminded him.

'More than a few,' he told her with a grin. 'And certainly not for something as minor as a break-in. And do you know what? I don't miss that part of things a bit.' He settled beside her. 'Right, you were going to tell me about this march . . .'

TWO

'Thank you for coming upstairs, Tom.'

Harper had received the note from the chief constable's secretary. Could he pop in for a quick word when he had chance? It was good news, he promised. All he had to do was climb the steps to hear it. These days, Harper had his office on the ground floor of the town hall. The building echoed with footsteps and voices. All the marble and shining surfaces of his new surroundings still felt foreign and uncomfortable, as if he was an imposter here. He'd spent his entire working life as a copper at Millgarth, next to the market. Noise was everywhere. Never mind, he told himself each day, he'd grow used to this sooner or later. He was still waiting.

'Something worthwhile, sir?'

'Oh, it is. It certainly is.' Chief Constable Parker of Leeds City Police was beaming and rubbing his hands together. 'You're definitely going to love this. We're releasing Lilian Lenton from Armley Gaol next Tuesday. You know who I mean? The suffragette.'

'Yes, sir.'

She was awaiting trial for offences in Doncaster. The court case had been all over the papers, but never a mention of where she was being held. He knew she'd been on hunger strike in prison. Lenton would be released under the Cat and Mouse Act so she could put on weight before they dragged her back to a cell and it started all over again.

'Here.' Parker slid a photograph across the desk. It was a candid shot of a young woman with her dark hair down over her shoulders, bundled inside a bulky coat. She looked as if she had no idea the picture was being taken. A brick wall stood in the background. 'That's her. They used a hidden camera at the prison.'

Harper's mouth hardened. Why had anyone felt the need to

do that? Secret pictures were supposed to be against the law. 'I see, sir.'

'I'm sure you'll be pleased to know there are rumours she'll try to run.' He ran his tongue around his thin lips. 'To make you even more cheerful, because of that danger, Special Branch have decided to handle the surveillance when she's released from prison. They've taken it out of our hands.' He grinned again; this time Harper joined him.

'A pound says she'll be gone two days before they even realize it.'

Parker shook his head. 'My money's on three. It'll take that long to dawn on them.' He gave a deep, hearty laugh. When he first took the job, at the start of 1909, he'd been a rigid, straight-backed man, hard enough to earn a reputation as a disciplinarian. But he'd eased up as he grew into the position. These days the men liked and respected him.

'I'll take that bet.'

'Their officers are arriving on Monday. I want you to go over everything with them.'

'Very good, sir.'

'And after that we can sit back and watch them make complete bloody fools of themselves.'

No ordinary policeman liked the Branch. They tried to be a force within the force, thinking of themselves as the elite, the chosen ones looking down on everyone else. The truth was a very different beast; they were nothing more than thugs with warrant cards, picked for their fists and their aggression, not for their brains.

He'd been back in his office for an hour, sipping a mug of tea and reading the daily reports from the divisions, when the telephone rang.

'Morning, sir. It's Superintendent Ash.'

The familiar voice made him smile. Until Harper's promotion, the two of them had worked together every day. Then Ash had taken over A Division and moved up in rank to run the station. The man wouldn't ring unless there was a good reason.

'Good morning to you, too. What can I do for you?'

'Something that might strike your fancy, sir,' Ash replied after a moment. 'I don't suppose you'd like your dinner at the café in the market, would you?'

'I imagine you could twist my arm,' Harper said. 'Your shout?'

'Of course, sir. Between one thing and another, I don't believe I've ever had a free lunch with you yet.'

He walked, glad of the exercise on a warm day. Briggate was thronged with Thursday shoppers crowding the pavements. Trams and lorries and carts bustled up and down the road. Harper cut through County Arcade, astonished as ever at its elaborate gilt and splendour, before crossing Vicar Lane, entering Kirkgate Market and climbing the stairs to the café on the balcony.

Ash was waiting at a table. He'd always been a big man, but now he looked broader than ever, the shaggy moustache over his top lip as grey as his hair. His face crinkled into a grin and he stood, hand extended.

'Thank you for coming, sir. I hope you don't mind that I went ahead and ordered; I know you like the cottage pie here.'

'That's fine,' Harper said, and it was. 'What's so important? Something wrong at Millgarth?'

The station would always have a special place in his heart. It was home.

'Nothing like that, sir. Something a little unusual, though.'

'What is it?'

Ash held a letter in his hand, written on thin onionskin paper. 'This arrived from America, sir. From the police in New York.'

That was enough to pique Harper's curiosity. 'What do they want?'

'It appears that one of their criminals is on his way here. He's probably arrived now.' Ash stopped and pinched his lips together. 'He's coming *back* here, that is. It seems he grew up in Leeds, moved to America when he was ten years old. Followed his mother. She went ahead and got herself settled.'

'Go on.'

'His name's Davey Mullen. Born on Somerset Street.' It was no more than three minutes' walk from where they were sitting, a row of run-down, hopeless houses. 'He's twenty-one now.'

Harper rubbed his chin. 'What's he done to make them write to us?'

Ash grimaced and shifted on his seat. 'It's more like what hasn't he done, sir. Quite a list, given his age. It took me by surprise.' He paused, just long enough to be sure he had Harper's attention. 'They're as certain as they can be that Mullen's murdered at least six people.' He let the sentence hang between them in the air. 'Four of them shot, the other two beaten to death. And two of those shootings were in broad daylight, with witnesses.'

'Then surely—' he began, then stopped when he saw the look in Ash's eyes.

'The witnesses decided to leave the city or refused to testify.'

Harper sighed. The old, old story. Fear and intimidation.

'Why's he coming here?'

'Recuperation. That's what he told people. He's a member of a gang. It seems some people from another gang found him on his own outside a dancehall and shot him eleven times.'

'Eleven?' Harper said in disbelief. 'Come on. Nobody can survive that.'

'He did, and he made a full recovery. He refused to tell the police who did it, but not long after he was back on his feet the bodies of some of this other gang started turning up. Now he's heading to Leeds until things cool down in New York.'

'What do they want us to do?' Harper asked. 'They don't have a warrant for him, do they?'

'No, sir.'

'Then unless he breaks any laws here, he's a free man.'

'They're tipping us the wink so we can keep an eye on him. His other reason for being here is to see his father. It seems he never made the trip to America with the rest of the family. It was just Mullen and his brother who followed their mother over there.'

'What's the father's name?'

'Francis Mullen. Goes by Franny. I had Sergeant Mason dig out his file. There's not much to him, really. Petty crook, in and out of jail. Loves his drink. Never held a proper job in his life. Parents came over from Ireland during the famine.' He shrugged and took a photograph from his pocket. 'The New York people included this, sir. It's Davey Mullen, from the last time they arrested him.'

Harper studied the picture. It showed the man's head, viewed full on. Thick, dark hair, glistening with pomade. A smile and straight, white teeth in a face brimming with arrogance, a young man utterly certain that the world belonged to him. On the back, someone had scribbled a few details. Mullen was a big man: six feet one, weight two hundred and ten pounds – fifteen stone, he calculated – carrying sixteen scars all over his body from knives and bullets. Next of kin was his mother Maureen. Mullen still lived with her, an address on West 47th Street. Behind it, in brackets, someone had added Hell's Kitchen. An apt name for any neighbourhood that was home to a man like him.

The waitress arrived with two full plates. 'They're hot, so don't you be burning yourselves,' she warned. 'I'll be back in a tick with your pot of tea.'

No talking shop while they ate; that was the rule. No spoiling the digestion. It allowed a few minutes for pleasure, a pause for thought. A constant roar of noise rose from the market, the conversation of shoppers, traders calling out their wares. Eventually, Harper wiped a slice of bread around the plate to soak up the last of the juices, swallowed the final mouthful and washed it down with a swig of tea.

'What did you have in mind for Mullen?' he asked.

'I thought Walsh and Galt could pay him a visit,' Ash replied. 'Just a quiet word, let him know his card is marked. Polite as a Sunday tea party. I'll put someone to watch him too.'

'The slightest breath of trouble, haul him in,' Harper ordered. 'We don't want any murderers walking round Leeds like they're God's gift. Keep a uniform on him too.'

'Not plain clothes?'

'No, let's make it blatant. We'll show him he's not welcome here.'

'I'll take care of it, sir.'

'Anything else I should know about?'

'Nothing much. Just the Boys of Erin trying to act up again.'

They'd been a growing thorn in the side of the police for a year, ever since Johnny Dempster became leader of the gang. Harper thought he'd crushed them more than twenty years ago, but they were slowly creeping back. They wanted to be a force again, to rule the Bank the way they had a generation before. It was the area of Leeds where the Irish had settled when they arrived. Once it had been desperately poor, dirty, a place where disease thrived. Even now it was bleak. Annabelle had grown up there, on Leather Street. Many still living on the Bank today could trace their ancestors back to Ireland.

'What have they been doing this time?'

'Tried a little protection on shopkeepers. We've taken care of it. I'm keeping a watch on them. Dempster's ambitious. I've a feeling he has big plans.'

'Time to stamp them down again?' Harper asked.

'Not just yet, sir,' Ash replied thoughtfully. 'I want to see what they have in mind.'

'Keep me informed.' He stood and patted his belly. They always served up big helpings in the cafe. 'And make sure this Mullen knows he's being followed.'

On Saturday morning he received a note from Ash.

Mullen was quite open and polite when Galt and Walsh went to see him. Claims he's come to see his father after all these years. The bobby watching him says he hasn't done anything suspicious. He's staying at the Metropole, flashing plenty of money around. Music hall and gin palaces in the evening. Spends part of the day with his father, but he already seems to have made several friends. Not exactly quality people – Dick Harrison, Bob Turnbull, Liam Byrne and the like. My guess is he has something going on, but I don't know what it is yet.

Harrison, Turnbull, Byrne: they all had long, long records for a string of mundane crimes. Not an ounce of imagination between the three of them, but they knew the jails better than most coppers. They were exactly the kind of characters to crowd round someone like Davey Mullen. They'd find a dangerous American exotic.

He put it aside. Nothing in there to worry him, at least for now. This suffragist pilgrimage that Annabelle had talked about would be stopping overnight in Leeds and he needed to arrange police coverage. An afternoon meeting in Roundhay Park, then another in the evening on Woodhouse Moor before moving on the next day. All the applications were in order. He'd have two detectives circulating in the park, then six at the big meeting later. The chief constable had already assigned the constables. It didn't look as if there'd be any real trouble.

Harper didn't even glance up at the tap on the door. Miss Sharp, his secretary. She was a pleasant woman, probably quite capable of handling most of his paperwork by herself. She'd quickly adapted to him, learned to speak into his good ear and made sure he had his tea first thing in the morning and in the middle of the afternoon.

'There's a Detective Sergeant Sissons here for you, sir. He doesn't have an appointment.'

'Send him in.' He'd brought Sissons into plain clothes himself, back in '99. The man had a quick mind, he could go far. But once he'd made it to sergeant he seemed quite content to stay there.

'You look like someone with things on his mind,' Harper said as Sissons gazed around the office, a little awestruck by his impressive surroundings.

Sissons nodded, his Adam's apple bobbing. Fourteen years in plain clothes and he still looked like a string bean; no one would ever take him for a copper, something that had served him well in the past.

'You know we have that American here, sir. The gangster.'

'Mullen. I was just reading Superintendent Ash's report.'

'Well, it appears we have another one in town, too. I was talking to the super and he sent me down here to let you know.'

'Oh?' Harper sat upright, alert and suddenly very interested. One American in Leeds was unlikely enough. Two was definitely more than coincidence. 'Sit down and tell me about it.'

'Rogers – he's a constable who started a few months ago—'

Harper had seen the man. He was impossible to miss. Big and bulky, he played prop forward for Bramley rugby club in his spare time. Sharp, intelligent eyes. He'd graduated near the top of his class in training. 'He heard someone with an accent and asked a few questions. All very discreet, sir.'

On his own initiative? That was enterprising for a man on the beat. 'How can he be so certain it's an American voice?'

'His uncle moved over there and did well for himself. Comes back and visits quite regularly. But he picked up the twang. That's why Rogers noticed it.'

Harper pursed his lips. It sounded plausible, as long as the constable wasn't one for fanciful stories. 'You said he made some enquiries.'

'Yes, sir. I can get him in here if you like. I brought him with me.'

'Good idea.' Better than hearing it second-hand, and if it seemed genuine he could give the bobby some praise.

Rogers was even larger than Ash had been when he was younger, well able to discourage any trouble with a sharp look. But for all his size, he was articulate and observant.

'He's staying in Mrs Hardisty's lodging house down off Kirkgate, sir.' The man stood to attention, helmet gathered under his left arm, the fingers of his right hand pointing straight down the side of his leg. He stared straight ahead, exactly as he'd been taught.

'You can relax, Constable,' Harper told him with a smile. 'You're not on the parade ground now.'

'Yes, sir, thank you,' he replied, but didn't move. Never mind; he'd learn in time.

'What have you managed to find out about him?'

'His name's Louis Fess. He's from New York, and he arrived here three days ago, sir.'

Three days. Not long after Mullen. 'You've seen him. What does he look like?'

Rogers narrowed his eyes for a moment. 'Tall, just a couple of inches shorter than me. Nowhere near as broad, mind. Fair hair, and he has a scar on his chin.' He indicated with a finger. 'I will say one thing, sir: the suit he's wearing didn't come from America. It was made down the road at Barran's, or my name isn't Harold Rogers. A decent bit of *schmatter*, but it's definitely not new.'

Now that was a very interesting piece of knowledge. 'How can you be so sure?'

A grin. 'My dad works for them, sir.'

'What about his shoes?' Harper asked.

'Boots, sir. They're in fair nick, but they're like the suit, broken in a bit. Before you ask, sir, it was Mrs Hardisty who told me his name. She won't breathe a word.' A quick smile. 'We have an understanding.'

Harper knew what that meant; Rogers would let a few minor offences slide at the lodging house.

'That's excellent work,' Harper told him, and saw the man's face light up. Exactly the same way his would have done all those years before, when he'd just started on the job. 'How did you come to pay attention to him?'

'I heard him asking someone for directions, caught the accent and noticed where he went. Later I saw him go into Mrs Hardisty's and stopped there an hour or two later.'

'Directions . . . Where did he want to go?'

'Somerset Street, sir. He was no more than two hundred yards from it at the time. That's what made me prick up my ears.'

Somerset Street. Where Mullen's father lived. No, this was definitely no coincidence.

'Very good.' Thank God for coppers who could think on their feet. 'Keep your eyes open. I might need you again on this.'

'Seems like it's connected to Mullen, sir,' Sissons said when they were alone.

'It has to be.' He rubbed his chin. This man Fess was trying to disguise himself with a second-hand suit from a local manufacturer and the kind of boots working men wore. Why would he want to do that? Maybe he believed he could hide his American accent.

Still, it meant he was keeping his own clothes somewhere, and that wouldn't be at Mrs Hardisty's. Nothing was safe from pilfering hands in that place. Where would he keep them?

'Go down to the railway station,' Harper said after a second. 'Talk to the left luggage office. Give them Fess's description and ask if he left anything.'

'And if it's there, do you want me to take a look inside?'

Harper grinned. 'Oh yes, Sergeant, I'd like that very much indeed.'

'Mr Fess has a travelling trunk with good leather straps and two locks at left luggage, sir.' Sissons said when he reported back an hour later.

Harper smiled. It had been a lucky guess. 'What's inside?'

'Three well-tailored suits with New York labels, four cotton shirts, two more in silk, handmade shoes, some ties with fancy labels . . . and he even brought an overcoat.'

'Curious that he'd prefer to look so shabby, isn't it? Let's have him in for a chat, shall we? Why don't you ask him to visit Millgarth and see what he has to say?'

'Gladly, sir.' Sissons smiled and stood. Then he continued, 'Fess had something else in his luggage, sir. A pistol and some ammunition.' The sergeant reached into his pocket and took out a small cardboard box of bullets. 'I thought this might be for the best, sir,' he added as he put it on the desk. 'I left the gun where it was. It's unloaded now, he won't be able to use it.'

'Good thinking.' Harper smiled. 'I don't imagine he has a licence for it. You've got a useful lever with that. And while we're at it, contact the New York police and find out about this man. Since he's already here, you'd better make it a telegram, not a letter.'

THREE

They sat with the windows open, a breeze softly billowing the curtains. There was nothing fresh or sweet about the air in Sheepscar, but it was still enjoyable as he sat with his collar and tie off and his suit jacket hanging on the back of the chair.

Mary was out at the pictures with Len, gone to see *Ivanhoe* at the Rialto, with the promise of supper at Fairburn's afterwards.

'She won't be back until eleven,' Annabelle said. 'Got to allow time for cuddling and kissing, too.'

'I don't know how she does it.' Harper shook his head. 'She's out of here by seven every morning and never back until late.'

'Young love,' she replied with a grin and a wink. 'You haven't forgotten what that's like, have you, Tom Harper?'

She'd herded him on to dangerous ground. If he said no, she'd want details of who he courted before he met her; if he said yes, she'd call him a spoilsport. Whichever way he answered, he couldn't win. It was safer to change the subject entirely.

'I was going over the details for when this suffragist march passes through town,' he said.

'The Great Pilgrimage,' she corrected him. 'That's the proper name. We're hosting the group making their way down from Newcastle. Mrs Renton and Miss Ford have roped me in to help. I'm arranging tea at the Mansion in Roundhay Park.'

'Very posh.'

'They'll have walked a hundred miles already. They deserve a slap-up spread after that.'

'Have you made up your mind whether you'll go to London with them?'

'I'd like to,' she answered after a moment. 'It sounds like it's going to be something quite wonderful. What do you think, Tom?'

He laughed. 'Since when did I have a say in things?'

'Since right now.' She jabbed him in the ribs with her elbow.

'You go. You've done enough for them over the last twenty years, you deserve it.'

'I'll drive.' Her eyes sparkled at the idea of the procession of women heading to the capital. 'It'll be fun. Who knows, we might even make a difference.'

They wouldn't. Deep down she knew that as well as he did. But he wasn't about to puncture her balloon. Perhaps it was just as well Mary was out; she'd have made some comment.

'Go on. We'll be fine. A break will do you good.'

'I think you're right.' Annabelle had never fully settled to anything since she stopped being a Poor Law Guardian, and that was a few years ago. She stayed busy enough, but the sense of vocation, of *passion*, had vanished. He'd be happy if she found it once more.

'Of course, without Muggins here to cook, the pair of you will probably end up eating out every evening.'

'Fish and chips.' He was smiling as he spoke. She knew her family far too well.

'So you haven't forgotten what young love is like?'

'Of course not.'

'Good. We can have an early night and you can show me you remember.'

Sunday morning and his car was parked outside the Victoria bang on half past seven. A Model T Ford; the uniformed driver let the engine idle until Harper was settled in the back seat.

'Town hall, sir?'

'Yes.'

People stopped to stare. Children ran after the vehicle. It was the same every day. A motor car was still a rarity, especially in an area like this. The only other one in Sheepscar belonged to Annabelle. The way people gawped always left Harper awkward and uncomfortable. He fussed and fidgeted until they arrived at Great George Street.

It wasn't a work day, but he often popped in for an hour or two. It gave him a chance to whittle away at the mountain of paperwork. Too conscientious, Annabelle called it. But he still felt as if he needed to prove himself in this job.

The report sat at the top of the pile. Sissons and Ash had questioned Fess. He claimed he belonged to the Gopher Gang in New York, just like Mullen; they'd sent Fess to England to watch over him. Not exactly a bodyguard, he explained, but to make sure nothing bad happened. Everything was on the quiet; even Mullen didn't know he was here, and he preferred to keep it that way. He didn't want to interfere in Davey's reunion with his old man. Fess wasn't here to cause any trouble. Just the opposite; he was there to make sure none began. Yes, he had a gun, but he'd been careful to leave it in his luggage. If any officer wanted to go with him to the station, he'd gladly hand it over.

Everything had been painstakingly typed up by a constable who couldn't spell too well, with a scrawled note at the end in Ash's writing: *He sounds convincing, but I don't believe a word of it. We don't have enough to hold him.*

Paperclipped to it all was the brief telegram sent by the police in New York.

Louis Herman Fess. Age 27. Member of Hudson Dusters gang. They shot Mullen 11 times. Known gunman. Violent. Dangerous.

Short, simple, and to the point. Underneath, a little more from Ash: *This arrived an hour after we let Fess go. He's vanished from the rooming house, the men are searching for him.*

Dammit. An American gunman loose in Leeds. Someone who probably wanted to finish the job his friends had started with Mullen.

By the time he left the town hall there was still no word of Fess. Harper had passed the word to every division. With his accent, an American shouldn't be too hard to spot. If they hadn't found him by morning, Harper would take charge of the hunt himself. Get Fess off the street before any trouble began.

He'd finished his supper and poured the last cup of tea from the pot when Dan the barman came up the stairs to the parlour.

'I'm sorry to bother you, Tom, but there's a man downstairs asking for you.'

That was unusual; people rarely sought him out at home. 'Not one of my lot, is it?' he asked. Maybe they'd found Fess. No, couldn't be, Harper thought; they'd have telephoned.

'This one's definitely not a copper.' Dan frowned. 'You ask me, he's got the smell of crime about him. Young and big. Talks strange, too. Like he's from Leeds but with something else on top that I don't recognize.'

Harper gave a grim smile. Mullen had decided to come to the Victoria.

'Thanks, Dan. I'll be down in a minute.'

Annabelle was watching him. 'You know who it is, don't you?'

'I can take a good guess. It's that man I told you about, the one from New York. Mullen.'

'The one who's killed people.'

'Yes.'

'Here. In my pub.' She glared and started to rise.

'Give me a minute before you come down,' he asked. 'Don't worry, I'll make sure he doesn't cause any trouble.'

'He'd better not.'

Mullen was sitting at a table with his back to the wall, a pint of beer in front of him. He had the handsome, dark Irish looks that he'd shown in his police photograph, wearing an expensive grey suit that fitted him flatteringly, with a soft collared shirt and a brilliant red silk tie fastened with a gold pin. Flaunting his money in his clothes.

He sat with his legs crossed, shining black shoes catching the light, looking at faces and assessing their eyes for danger as Harper settled across from him.

'You're safe enough in here. From the customers, at least.'

A dip of the head in acknowledgement.

'This must be different from the places you're used to at home,' Harper said.

Mullen grinned and showed his good, even teeth. 'A bar's a bar, doesn't matter where you put it. *Sláinte.*' He took a long drink of bitter. 'I'll tell you this, though: the Americans have a long way to go before they can brew beer like the English.' He stared at the glass. 'And Leeds is home, after a fashion.'

'Some parts of it might be. But not this place. What brings you out here?' Harper's voice was sharper, his face hard.

'A man told me that you lived above a public house. I was curious to take a look and see what kind of deputy chief constable would do that. Anyway, it's only a short stroll from Somerset Street. Perfect for a summer's evening.'

Harper saw the man's gaze shift and his smile broaden.

'This is the woman who owns the public house,' he said.

'Mrs Harper.' Mullen stood. For the briefest moment, he looked awkward and self-conscious, as if he wasn't quite sure how to act around a woman. 'A pleasure to meet you. You have a very welcoming pub here.'

She sat, never taking her eyes off him. 'Are you enjoying your visit to England, Mr Mullen?'

'I am, ma'am. I'm enjoying being back and seeing my father again.' Dan was right, Harper thought; there was still a definite trace of Leeds in his voice, somewhere deep in the bedrock. But much of it had been overlaid by the nasal New York cockiness. 'I got to say, it's changed a lot in ten years.'

'How is your father?' Harper asked, as if he hadn't seen a report on Francis Mullen just the day before. The man spent the better part of his time drunk. He'd been kicked out of two beershops for trying to start fights.

'Happy to see me,' Mullen replied after a moment.

'I don't know if you've heard, but there's another American in

Leeds at the moment. Someone called Louis Fess. He's from New York, too. Maybe you know him.'

He'd dropped the name to see Mullen's reaction. It was a pleasure to watch the way his face shifted: anger first, then worry, and finally a snapped-on grin of bravado. All in the course of a second or two. Interesting; he hadn't known that Fess was here.

Mullen ran a hand down his jacket, smoothing the material. 'No,' he said, 'it don't mean anything.'

Maybe that worked on the American police, but it wouldn't fool any copper in Leeds. He knew exactly who Fess was, and he wasn't pleased to hear the name. No surprise, since he was from a rival gang.

'A suggestion,' Harper said as the man drained the rest of his pint in a single swallow. 'Actually, it's more like an order. You're going to take out that gun very carefully and leave it with me.'

'Why?' The man's body stiffened, as if he was preparing for a fight.

'First of all, you spent a lot of money on that suit and it's ruining the cut. It's also illegal under the 1903 Pistols Act. Do you have a licence for the weapon?'

'I didn't know I needed one.'

It was a lie, it showed in his eyes. He wanted to be challenged.

'If the barrel is shorter than nine inches, the law says that you do. Since you're a visitor here, we'll let that pass as long as you leave the weapon here.'

For a moment, Mullen didn't move and Harper could feel the tension grow around him. Then he reached into his pocket, brought out the gun with the barrel between his fingers and placed it on the table.

'Satisfied?'

'For now. Thank you.'

The outside door opened and Mary entered, waving before she disappeared upstairs.

'Is that your daughter? Mary, right?

Annabelle turned her head to stare into his eyes. 'I tell you what, luv, now it's my turn to make a suggestion.' Her voice was iron. 'Only mine's an order, too. You're going to forget you ever knew her name, or that you saw her. And if you show your face in here again, I'll bounce you out on to Roundhay Road by the seat of your fancy trousers before you can say Jack Robinson.' She stalked away.

Mullen glared but said nothing. Harper watched as the man stifled his anger. No one would dare talk to him like that in America; he'd tear them apart for the sport of it. But New York was half a world away. He was in Leeds now. The rules were different and he was powerless.

'I think your wife has taken against me.'

'Very perceptive, Mr Mullen. There are plenty of other places to drink in town. You'd do better in one of those. I'm sure you can find your way back to where you're staying. The Metropole, isn't it?' He stood. 'I'll wish you goodnight.'

The constable following Mullen was standing outside the Victoria, watching his quarry stride furiously away. Harper stood next to him. 'Make sure you don't let him out of your sight.'

Monday, the beginning of a new week. Early brightness outside the curtains, the hint of another pleasant summer's day ahead. Harper lurched awake as the telephone bell started to ring, and hurried through the living room to snatch up the receiver. A hair after five o'clock.

'Sorry to disturb you, sir.' Ash's voice. For once his calmness and composure were missing. 'But I thought you needed to know about this. We found Fess an hour ago.'

From his tone, there was more to come. 'Where?'

'Down in the arches under the station. A night watchman discovered him. He'd been shot.'

A few hours after Mullen had been in the Victoria. Interesting timing. 'Is the body still there?'

'I had it sent over to Dr Lumb in Hunslet. I'm at Millgarth—'

'Stay there. Tell them to send my car and I'll collect you.'

He glanced at the table. Mullen's gun lay there, the metal black and dull.

FOUR

'**A**long here, sir.' Inspector Walsh guided him down from Neville Street, into the arches. The Dark Arches, people called them, as black as pitch at night. A good place for the prostitutes to do business. And for a shooting.

Farther along, torches lit up the floor and the vaulted brick ceiling as constables searched the area. Small businesses used the railway arches for storage, turning them into cheap warehouses.

'No doors forced that we can find,' the inspector continued. 'His body was right here.'

All that remained of Louis Fess was a chalked outline on a concrete floor. A bullseye torch showed the bloodstain where his life had slipped away in a foreign country. Not much of a memorial. He looked at the detectives around him: Ash, Walsh, Sissons, Galt. His old squad. Better at their jobs than any of the flash devils at Scotland Yard.

'What do we know? *Facts*, please.'

'A watchman was making his rounds and came across him around half past three,' Sissons said. 'He alerted a bobby. As soon as Superintendent Ash arrived, he recognized him. Fess wasn't carrying any identification. No wallet. He'd been shot at close range in the back of the head. So far we haven't managed to come up with any evidence.'

'How long ago did it happen?'

'After midnight, we believe. Dr Lumb should be able to say more.'

'Turned up any witnesses yet? Anyone who heard the shot?'

'No, sir,' Galt answered. 'They'll all be long gone by now. We'll keep asking and come back again tonight.'

'Fess was a gang member,' Harper said. 'He'd killed people. He was probably here to murder Mullen. He was a professional, yet someone managed to come close enough to shoot him. That's food for thought, right there.'

'We'll be spreading the word among the informers,' Walsh told him.

'Do we know where he went after he ducked out from Mrs Hardisty's?'

'We haven't managed to trace him yet,' Sissons replied.

'Get busy on that.' He brought Mullen's pistol from his pocket and explained how he'd taken it. 'The man's not an idiot. He'd make damned sure he knew the law, and he was banking on me confiscating his gun. Seeing this makes me wonder why he brought it to the Victoria in the first place. And why he came when he did. He acted surprised when I told him about Fess being here, but maybe he knew. It's all too convenient.'

'I'll bring him in,' Ash said.

'Send a pair of uniforms to the Metropole for him, and make

sure they don't treat him with kid gloves, either. Let him stew for
a while before you talk to him. He'll have been through it all
before, but not the way we do.' Harper took out his pocket watch.
Not long after half past five. 'Let's work out where we go from
here and get to business.'

They had a plan, Harper thought as he walked up East Parade
towards the town hall. Walsh and Galt would try to trace where Fess
had been staying and who he'd seen. Sissons would talk to the
uniforms who'd been shadowing Mullen and find out his movements.
He was their main suspect. He had to be. Two Americans over here,
a pair of killers with a history of bad blood between their gangs,
the murder attempt and revenge in New York. Then there was the
matter of Mullen carrying a gun. The bulge in the suit pocket had
been obvious; he'd even touched it. That wasn't an accident or
carelessness; he'd done everything but hold up a sign. The man
wanted Harper to spot it and take it from him. He had a reason.
     Ash and his men would break all that down. He knew them,
he'd trust them with his life. Meanwhile he had a meeting with
the chief constable and two officers from Special Branch.

Freshly-made coffee, biscuits from the bakery in St James's Square;
Parker was pushing the boat out for his visitors, but they didn't
seem to notice. They gobbled and slurped as if they hadn't been
fed for a week. Inspector Cartwright and Sergeant Gough. Brutal-
looking characters, unsmiling, with hard eyes and slit mouths.
     'As we all know, Miss Lenton is being released tomorrow,' Chief
Constable Parker began. 'A doctor has determined the hunger
strike has weakened her to the point where being kept in prison
will be detrimental to her health.'
     'They need to force feed the lot of them,' Cartwright said. 'That's
what I'd do.'
     Parker's gaze flickered to Harper then back again. His expression
showed nothing.
     'Maybe so, but we don't determine the rules, Inspector.' He
continued to read from the paper in front of him. 'She'll be released
into the care of Mr and Mrs Rutter. He's the director of the art
gallery in the city and we know full well that he's a supporter of
women receiving the vote. They live in Chapel Allerton. Now, how
many men do you have with you, Inspector?'

'Six, sir. Enough to keep watch on the house twenty-four hours a day. Good men, too, I picked them myself,' he said with pride. 'She won't have the chance to slip away.'

'That's fine,' Parker said. 'Tom?'

'The Rutters live on Westfield Terrace,' Harper began. 'That's a small private street of villas set back from the main Harrogate road. You won't be able to stay inconspicuous while you watch—'

'We want her to know we're there,' Gough told him.

'—and the area beyond the back door is overgrown. Difficult to observe.'

'Don't you worry about my men,' Cartwright said. 'They're resourceful. My job is to make sure she doesn't escape, then haul her back to prison as soon as the quack says she's fit.'

'Then I wish you luck, gentlemen,' Parker said. 'Ask if you need anything else.'

Once the pair had gone, Parker poured more coffee for himself and Harper. 'Still sticking with two days, Tom?'

He pursed his lips. 'After that performance I'm tempted to switch to one.'

'I don't blame you. Dear God, what a pair of pompous idiots.' He rolled his eyes, took a cigar from its case, then cut off the tip and enjoyed the ritual of lighting it with a match. 'With that lot around, if the woman doesn't run, she's either very poorly or she's got no spirit about her.'

'She'll go,' Harper said. 'She's not a fool. But we have something more important that doesn't concern the Branch. A murder last night. An American gangster. He was shot in the head. And we have another of them in town . . .'

'Da?'

Harper looked up from his desk, astonished to see Mary standing in the doorway of his office. She was smartly dressed in a dark burgundy jacket and pale pink blouse, her skirt just above her ankles, button boots polished and shining. He sat back and looked at her.

'You must want something important,' he told her. 'I think this is the first time you've ever come to visit me at work. Certainly since I moved to the town hall.'

He knew he'd hit the mark when she blushed. 'I have an hour and I thought I'd take you out for your dinner.'

He cocked an eyebrow. 'All right, now I know something's going on. Offering me a meal? Are you paying as well?'

Reddening even more, she nodded.

With a wink, Harper said, 'Well, I can hardly refuse that, can I?'

There were plenty of cafés to cater for the workers from the town hall and all the nearby financial offices. Mary tucked her arm in his as they crossed Victoria Gardens, then the Headrow, and down Park Row.

The owner greeted him like royalty and made a fuss over Mary as he showed them to a table at the back of the room, away from the window and the noise.

Harper waited until she'd ordered.

'Right, what is it? Is something wrong? Some problem with the business?'

'Of course not. It's doing very well, Da,' she answered with a smile. He noticed she wore a small enamel badge on the lapel of her jacket. Green, purple, and white: suffragette colours. 'We're so busy that I'm taking on more typists. No need to worry on that score.'

As soon as she began to talk about work, he noticed the way her face became thoughtful and serious. She'd been like that from the time she began the company. Mary had worked hard and it had paid off handsomely, more than enough to put money in the bank as well as keep her in new clothes and hats. She was just like her mother in that way; she couldn't resist fashion.

The food arrived and he tucked into a chicken pie, mashed potatoes and peas.

'If it's nothing to do with the agency, then it must be romance. You and Len?' Her look told him that he was right. 'You haven't thrown him over, have you?'

She coughed so hard he was worried she'd choke. Finally a swig of tea calmed her.

'No, no. Honestly, it's nothing like that. Da, you're sweet.' She treated him to another warm smile. 'Sometimes you're very clever—'

'That's probably why I'm the deputy chief constable.'

'But you're a *man*.' She stared at him and finally the penny dropped. 'My God. He's proposed.'

Beaming, she nodded. 'The night before last.'

He should have guessed; he was supposed to be the detective in the family. The signs were right there, he'd only needed to look: the joy in her eyes, the way her steps seemed to be light as air. She was bursting with the news, one of the biggest things she'd ever know in her life. He was a fool for not noticing what was right in front of his face.

'That's absolutely wonderful.' He knew he was grinning. He probably looked like an idiot, but he didn't care. 'Does your mother—?'

'Oh, we've already talked about it,' Mary said as if it was nothing. 'She's over the moon. But I want your blessing, too.' She stared at him. 'You know that, don't you?'

They were some of the most beautiful words he'd ever heard. Pure poetry. She wanted his blessing. This girl he'd helped to make loved her father. What more could any man ask in life? Of course Annabelle was thrilled. She was probably already coming up with ideas for the trousseau. The wonder was that she'd been able to keep quiet that morning.

'I couldn't be happier for the pair of you,' he said. 'Honestly, I mean it. You know how we feel about Len. He's a good lad, just right for you. He's solid, he has a good future.'

She laughed. Her eyes were sparkling. 'You don't have to convince me about him, Da. I can give you chapter and verse about him if you really want to hear it.'

He shook his head with a rueful grin.

'Of course. I'm . . .' He couldn't find a word that came anywhere close to the feelings coursing through him. They'd make an ideal couple, loving, tender, both of them clever and willing to graft. Yet underneath his joy there was also the tug of loss. Mary was a woman, but she'd always be his little girl and now she was leaving him. Better to say nothing at all than put his foot in it. 'Are you going to have a pudding? We ought to celebrate.'

He was smiling. He couldn't stop. Miss Sharp raised a questioning eyebrow when she saw him, but he didn't say a word. It was still family news. He wasn't about to spread it until he'd talked to Annabelle.

Suddenly all the paperwork in front of him seemed mundane. He'd known there would be much more of it when he accepted the position, but he hadn't anticipated this amount. Still, he'd been ready for something different, and the chief had persuaded him that running CID for the whole of Leeds would test him. So far, though, there'd been little to offer a real challenge. Maybe this shooting would change that.

The telephone rang and Ash's voice was in his ear.

'I thought you'd want to know, sir. Dr Lumb confirmed what we knew about Fess. Death occurred between midnight and three; he doesn't want to be more precise than that. What he did say is that the killing made him think of an execution. The modern equivalent of a beheading were his words.'

Interesting, Harper thought. And worrying. 'Have you brought Mullen in yet?'

'He's still waiting in the interview room, sir. Had him there for quite a few hours now.'

For a moment he was tempted to go down and handle the interrogation himself. He missed all that. But this was Ash's case. It had taken place on his manor, and he knew how to run a tight investigation. Harper took a breath. 'Let me know what happens.'

'Very good, sir. I talked to the man following him last night. After the Victoria he went back at his father's place on Somerset Street for half an hour. Then he walked over to his hotel. The lights went out in his room by half past ten. Our constable left after that. We had no reason to believe we needed someone on him every minute. Of course, there are plenty of ways out of the hotel.' A small cough. 'And we didn't know he was armed. No sign of a weapon when we searched his room, of course.'

'No.' A reproof, and completely deserved. As soon as he'd taken the weapon from Mullen, he should have informed Ash. 'My fault. Lean on him.'

'Don't you worry, sir. I plan on it.'

The rest of the day passed in a flash; he could barely recall a moment of it. The first thing he really knew was his driver parking in front of the Victoria. Then Harper was through the doors and hurrying up the stairs.

Annabelle stood in the kitchen, taking a casserole from the oven for their tea. She turned and saw the expression on his face.

'Mary told you, then?'

'She even took me out for my dinner. All grown up, *and* she paid the bill. How long have you known?'

'She told me yesterday, but it's been in the wind for weeks now. The poor lad just needed to pluck up his courage and ask her. He's as bad as you were before you popped the question, all that pussy-footing around.'

'When are they going to get married? I was so caught up in it all that I never thought to ask.'

She dished up the food on two plates and handed him one. As they sat at the table, she said: 'It'll be a while yet. He still has two months on his apprenticeship. I know Hunslet Engine have said they'll take him on, but he'll want to have his feet under the table and put a few bob away before they walk down the aisle. I expect they'll be engaged for a year at least.'

'And a big church do after that?'

She stared at him, sighed, and shook her head: 'Honestly, what do you think? *Of course* it'll be big. We'll have a proper service and a slap-up meal afterwards. And don't you dare imagine you can go cutting corners, Tom Harper. We have the brass and we're going to spend it. She's the only child we have. We're going to give her a wedding day she'll remember the rest of her life.'

Annabelle had made up her mind; there was no point in complaining or protesting. Not that he would. Just like her, he wanted Mary to have the very best. At least he didn't have to dip his hand in his pocket yet; it was still a long way off.

'Where is she tonight?'

'Having her tea at Len's. They're breaking the news to his parents. And he's coming here tomorrow, so you'd better make sure you're on your best behaviour.'

That was him warned. He spent the evening going through the *Mercury* and the *Post*. News of Fess's murder had come too late to make the early editions. Not that there was much to tell, and Ash would handle any reporters who wanted details. For now, at least, they'd keep Mullen's name out of it.

FIVE

'Good morning, sir. It's Kersey over at D Division.'

Harper smiled and pressed the receiver close to his ear. He'd known Bob Kersey for far too long; they'd been cadets together, back in the mists of time. Three years ago he'd been promoted to superintendent and put in charge of the area around Armley, Wortley, and Bramley. A good man for the job.

'What can I do for you, Bob? As long as it doesn't cost a penny, it's yours.'

'The governor at Armley sent me a note. He's releasing the suffragette today. Miss Lenton. A taxi's booked for noon.'

With everything else that was happening, it had slipped his mind. 'Thank you for reminding me. At least we're not involved in this one; Special Branch is keeping an eye on her.'

'The government must want her to slip out of the country.'

'The chief reckons she'll be gone in three days. My money's on two.'

Kersey laughed. 'Is that how our top brass spend their time now? Making book on when a criminal will scarper?'

'If you prefer, Superintendent, I could come over there and spend a few hours inspecting your detectives . . . have them on parade all togged out in their top hats and best coats.'

'No, that's fine. I'm sure you all know exactly what you're doing at the town hall . . . sir.'

He wasn't going to worry too much about Lilian Lenton. It had become Branch business, nothing to do with Leeds CID. He followed up on reports of a string of burglaries in Hunslet, wanting to know what progress they were making, and dealt with all the memos and correspondence that Miss Sharp piled on his desk.

Harper blinked as he stood by the lion on the town hall steps. The sun seemed too bright after the dimness of his office.

'I'm glad I caught you, sir.'

He blinked once more and saw Walsh on the step below him. The inspector had aged well; there were still plenty of traces of the bright young constable he'd put into plain clothes sixteen years before.

'That sounds ominous,' Harper said with a smile and glanced up at the clock. 'I'm going for my dinner. Why don't you come with me?'

The Kardomah on Briggate was busy, the air rich with the smell of coffee. Upstairs, women ate at tables and a few businessmen gulped down a sandwich or an omelette. They were lucky; a mother and grown daughter were leaving and they took the window seat, where they could look down at the street.

Harper studied the faces passing below, looking for any he might recognize. He knew Walsh would be doing the exact same thing; no need to ask. It was copper's habit. But there was nobody. Leeds had grown so large and spread so wide that sometimes it seemed as if it had become a city full of strangers.

'You might as well tell me about it,' he said as he cut up his cheese and onion tart. 'The Fess killing?'

'Yes, sir. We pressed Mullen as hard as we could, but he didn't give an inch. Pointed out that he'd been at the hotel all night. Our own man had followed him there. And he couldn't have shot anyone because you'd taken his gun.'

'Too clever by half,' Harper said.

'Exactly, sir. As if he'd arranged the whole thing. A double bluff, perhaps. We searched his room from top to bottom. Then his father's house on Somerset Street, with the old man cursing up a blue streak. Nothing at all. Exactly as you'd expect. We've had some of the people Mullen's been spending time with in, too, but so far we haven't come up with anything at all.'

'What about Fess? What had he been up to?'

'Sissons and Galt are looking. Superintendent Ash suggested I come and see you, in case you fancied stepping out from the office and helping us.'

Harper threw back his head and laughed. 'Go on, then. Which one of you came up with that one?'

Walsh blushed, the colour rising up from his shirt collar. 'When you were the superintendent at Millgarth, you always used to complain that you spent too much time behind your desk. I imagine you hardly poke your nose out at all these days, sir. And you have to agree that this is interesting.'

It was certainly that. The kind of case he used to relish. Now, though, he had too many responsibilities. All of Leeds was his manor. He had to keep an eye on plain clothes officers across the city.

'I'll do what I can,' he said as he poured the last of the coffee from the pot and stirred in some cream. 'I can't promise to give it much time, but you're right, it's intriguing.'

Walsh grinned with pleasure. 'It'll almost be like the old days, sir. The super thought you'd want to be involved, given that Mullen showed up at the Victoria.'

'I haven't forgotten about that,' Harper said. 'Keep me up to date on everything you find. That's your job; Ash has the whole of A Division to run.'

'I will, sir. Every day, more if something happens.'

'Good enough. You know how to reach me in the evenings, too.'

'Yes, sir. And thank you for dinner.'

'Just don't expect it to become a habit.'

They shook hands and Harper strolled back to the town hall. Almost one o'clock. In his office, he picked up the telephone receiver and asked the operator to connect him with Chapel Allerton police station.

'Inspector Douthwaite.' The man always sounded posh, as if he was speaking with a plum in his mouth, but he was a solid, reliable copper.

'Harper here. I just wanted to check that Miss Lenton showed up as expected.'

'I watched the taxi drop her off half an hour ago, sir. Two Special Branch men were right behind it the whole way. They're parked on Westfield Terrace now.'

That was what he wanted to know. Now he could really set it all aside and let the Branch botch the job. More paperwork, interrupted by Miss Sharp bringing a cup of tea at three, and finally some letters to dictate. Five on the dot and he was outside, climbing into the Model T and settling on the leather seat as the driver started the engine.

Traffic was heavy on the journey out to Sheepscar. More of it every year, Harper thought. Horses and carts, lorries, trams, motor buses and motor cars: the roads seemed as if they were bursting with them, everything going slower when it was designed to move faster and faster.

It wasn't just the roads; for God's sake, there were even people up in the skies now. Flying, as if they wanted to be birds. He'd been amazed when he read about Bleriot flying across the Channel – what was it, three, four years ago? Just a few months later, he and Annabelle had driven up to Soldiers Field to watch a Leeds man fly an aeroplane he'd designed and built himself. A chap called Blackburn, an engineer who'd started a business selling them from a workshop on Benson Street, just the other side of the river. And it was impressive, no doubt about that. Breathtaking. It was the future. The world was changing right in front of his eyes, something new every day, and Harper understood he didn't have a hope of keeping pace with it.

'Here we are, sir,' the driver said as he pulled on the handbrake. 'Usual time in the morning?'

'Yes. Thank you.'

Upstairs, Annabelle was waiting, looking him over with a critical eye as he stepped through the door. 'Go and put on a fresh collar,' she told him. 'That one's all grubby.' She licked a fingertip and wiped at a mark on his cheek as if he was a child. 'Wear your red tie, too, Tom. The dark red one, not the scarlet. It goes better with that suit.'

He did as he was told; life was easier that way. A few minutes and he was sitting in the armchair reading the *Evening Post* while Annabelle worked in the kitchen. Just before six she came out, apron off, and checked her own appearance in the mirror before inspecting him once more.

Two minutes after the hour, Mary arrived with Len right on her heels. She was still talking nineteen to the dozen as she hung up her coat and took his cap.

Poor Len, Harper thought. The lad never looked completely comfortable here, as if he was worried he might say the wrong thing. He was big, awkward at times, still growing into his body. Gawky; he seemed to lope as he moved. That would all change in a year or two. This evening he appeared more nervous than ever. He didn't even relax as they ate, barely speaking a word as Harper asked him about the apprenticeship. But he seemed more at ease once they moved on to the job waiting for him at Hunslet Engine.

'Did you know they do business all over the world? Africa, India, almost all the Commonwealth countries. They've promised they'll give me the chance to better myself, too,' Len said with a smile.

'Better yourself?' Annabelle turned to stare at him. Like a hawk, she'd picked up on the words. He hesitated before he replied.

'Yes, Mrs Harper. They told me I have real potential and they'll help me study for an engineering degree while I work.'

Now, that would definitely be something, Harper thought. Mary was brimming over with pride, and he didn't blame her. University was for people with money. Len must have true talent if the company was willing to do that for him. Still waters, he thought as he looked at the young man. Len was an ordinary-looking lad, not especially handsome. He had unruly fair hair that he'd pomaded and brushed into faint submission, the remnants of a few youthful spots on his cheeks, blue eyes that darted around. Big hands with thick calluses on the palms. Nothing to mark him out at all. Just a regular working man.

Len had turned down a third slice of cake. Mary and Annabelle
had cleared away the plates and the tea had been poured. Harper
could have sworn that his daughter was nudging her young man
under the table.

'I think Mary's already told you,' Len began. 'I asked her to
marry me and she said yes.'

He stopped, as if he wasn't sure what else to say. But he appeared
so completely happy. Mary rested her head against his shoulder,
looking as content as he'd ever seen her.

Harper looked at him. 'We'll be proud to have you as part of the
family.'

'We'll be buying the ring soon,' Len continued.

'This needs more than tea,' Annabelle announced. She picked
a bottle of whisky and four small glasses from the sideboard and
poured them each a tot. 'To love and marriage and years of
happiness.'

'We couldn't be happier for the pair of you.' Harper toasted
them. He looked at Len. 'She's picked a fine young man, and
you've got the best girl in the world.' As he opened his mouth to
add more, the telephone rang.

'Harper.'

'It's Inspector Walsh, sir. I know you're off-duty—'

Not *now*, he wanted to say. But he stopped himself before the
words slipped out, keeping his voice pleasant and even. 'I told you,
any time is fine, if you have something to report.'

'It's nothing definite,' the man began. 'But I talked to the super
and he said I should let you know.'

'Well, what is it?' Make it quick, he thought. 'Don't keep me in
suspense.'

'I heard a whisper a couple of hours ago. From a man who's
usually reliable. He said there's another American around Leeds.'

'What?' He almost bellowed the word, aware that Annabelle and
the others had turned to stare at him. 'A third one? That's not
possible. Are they sure it's not Mullen? Or perhaps he saw Fess
before he was killed?'

'He's positive, sir. According to him, this one's quite small.
Completely different to the others. That's all we have on him.'

Harper was silent. He had no idea what to make of it. Walsh's
voice intruded as his thoughts raced.

'It's just a rumour, nothing to back it up.'

'It doesn't matter, you did right to tell me. Pass the word. Let's get everybody looking for him.'

'Very good, sir.'

'If anything else comes up, let me know immediately.'

He sat down again, but the mood was broken. Five more minutes and the youngsters left to see a variety show at the Empire. As they were going, Len handed Annabelle an envelope. 'My mam said to give you this.'

'They've asked us to their house one evening,' she said as she read it. 'Listen: *As we're going to be in-laws, it seems only proper we should meet, so we'd be glad of your company. Yours faithfully, Mrs Edna Robinson.* Isn't that lovely? I'll drop her a line in the morning and make the arrangements.'

'Yes,' he agreed. But his mind was already elsewhere.

SIX

Nine in the morning and the heads of each division had gathered in the chief constable's office for the monthly meeting. Harper sat to one side, half-listening. Little of the conversation so far involved him; CID was his real bailiwick, not the drudgery of rotas and assignments.

His moment came at the end, bringing up several cases and asking how investigations were progressing. Before setting his notepad aside, he said: 'You've very likely heard about our dead American and the main suspect.' They nodded their acknowledgement. 'It seems there's word going round that we might have yet another Yank here. A third.' He gave the brief description. 'Remind your men. We'd like to talk to him. Be careful, though. I don't know, but he might be dangerous.'

'Is he a possibility?' Brian Duncan from B Division asked.

'I'm not even sure he actually exists.' It made them all smile; they'd all experienced their share of phantom culprits. 'But yes, if he's real, he's a possibility.'

As the meeting broke up, he walked downstairs with Ash. Their footsteps echoed off the high ceiling and marble walls.

'Anything fresh this morning?'

'Very little at all, sir. No trace of this third man, and we don't have a prayer of breaking Mullen's story. He's been through this kind of thing too often before. I let him go last night.'

'People watching him all the time?'

The superintendent nodded. 'I have a man posted inside the hotel at night now.'

'Good, good.' It was all they could do.

'We're following up every lead on Fess, we might have something today. And this third Yankee . . .' He shrugged. 'I'll have them beating the bushes, but he's just a rumour. For all I know, we could be looking for a ghost. Something about the story doesn't feel right to me.'

'Nor me. But check.'

For a few hours, Harper forgot about dead Americans. He lost himself in the routine of memoranda and preparing a report for the Home Office about the effectiveness of plain clothes policemen. It felt like a pointless exercise, something to make a civil servant in London feel important; that was why he'd put it off until the last minute.

By three o'clock he was close to the end. As he was blotting the final page, the telephone bell began to ring.

'Harper.'

'Da? It's Mary.' She didn't sound like herself. Instead of the cheerful cockiness, she seemed . . . worried? Scared?

'What is it?' he asked quickly. 'Has something happened?'

'A man came.' Her voice seemed to quiver. 'That American you and my mam talked about. The one who was at the Victoria.'

'Mullen? Has he gone now? What did he want?' He was already on his feet, ready to dash over there.

'Yes.' She took a breath and started again, more composed. 'Yes. He was only here for a minute. Came in and said, "You must be Mary Harper. You're even prettier up close. I can see why your father is so protective." Then he just looked at me like . . . I don't know and left.'

'I'm coming down right now. Are you sure you're all right?'

'Yes,' she said, still unsteady and afraid. Then again, more firmly. 'Yes. I'm fine. The others are here, the girls.'

'Lock the door and don't let anyone in until I arrive.'

He disconnected, then asked the operator for Millgarth police station.

*　　*　　*

63 Albion Place. Before he entered, he glanced up at the windows. Mary's business was at the top, with the company name painted on the glass. He climbed the steps to the second floor. The corridor was neatly swept, a shining brass spittoon sitting on the landing.

Ash was waiting, his face as dark as a storm. He'd known Mary her entire life. Harper had a good idea what the man was thinking.

He tapped on the door. 'It's me.'

A key turned and he put his arms around his daughter. She was strong, very independent and determined. They'd brought her up that way. But she was still young and the world could be a harsh place.

'Don't worry, it's fine now,' he said, stroking her hair. She trembled a little, face buried against his shoulder. 'Talk to the rest of them,' he told Ash. 'Let's put together a statement.'

Mary kept him close for a full thirty seconds before she finally pulled away and wiped at her eyes. She tried to smile and reached into her handbag. 'I must look a mess.'

'Don't be daft. You look wonderful.'

'Da, you can't lie to save your life. Give me a minute.'

Ash had everything in hand with the women, softly asking his questions and noting down their replies.

When Mary returned, she'd brushed her hair, powdered her face and put on fresh lipstick. Her back was straight, as if she was in charge of everything. In control again. A lie, of course, and he knew that as well as she did. But it was a useful pretence.

'Do you want to leave early? I can take you home.'

She shook her head. 'No. We have too much to do and I'm not going to run away because of any man.'

That was the girl he knew; just like her mother.

'Then let me arrange for a constable to escort you to the tram.'

'He wouldn't dare do anything with people around.' But even as she spoke he saw she was gripping her handkerchief tight, fingernails digging into her palms.

'No,' he agreed. Mullen would choose somewhere quieter.

'We'll keep the door locked here. And if I have to go out, I'll take one of the girls with me.'

It was sensible. It shouldn't have to happen, and he'd make

damned sure it never occurred again. But in the meantime, she was doing all the right things.

'I can always get Len to come here for me if we're going somewhere.'

Len. He'd forgotten about him. The last thing he wanted was for the lad to go after Mullen. That wouldn't be a contest; it would be slaughter.

'Don't tell him,' Harper said. 'Please.'

Her eyes flashed. Her mouth set with anger. 'But he's my—'

'Look, I know you don't want to keep anything from him. But the man who came here, he's killed people in New York. Shot them and beaten them to death. If Len starts something with him . . .' He let his words sink into her mind. 'We'll handle it,' he told her. 'He won't be back again. I promise.'

Mary took a deep breath and nodded.

'Will you be all right?'

'Yes.' She glanced over her shoulder. Ash was putting away his notebook. 'And Da . . . Thank you for coming.'

'Of course,' he said and squeezed her hand. 'Any time, any time at all. What do you think a father's for?' You looked after your own. You protected them if you can. And you hurt anyone who tried to do them harm.

Back outside, the air felt heavy and sticky with all the smells of the city. Engine fumes and smoke. He stared at the crowds of people and traffic moving up and down a few yards away on Briggate.

'The constable following him probably didn't realize your daughter had a business here,' Ash said.

'No,' Harper agreed.

'We'll talk to Mullen.'

'I'd like to be there.'

'Better if you're not, sir. What you don't know can't come back to hurt you.'

The man was right. But he wanted to beat seven bells out of Mullen and leave him bruised and bloody. No one did that to his daughter. No one.

'Maybe.'

'Don't you worry. He won't be giving her any problems in the future.'

'Thank you.' Thank God for good, loyal men.

*   *   *

'He did what?' Annabelle exploded. By the time he reached her, she'd torn off the apron and was halfway across the room. Harper grabbed hold of her arms before she could reach the door.

'It's being handled,' he said. She tried to pull away, but he kept a firm grip on her dress.

'It's being handled,' he repeated, staring into her face until she understood. 'It won't happen again.'

'I'll kill him myself.'

'No one's doing that.'

Anger flared in her eyes and faded again. 'If I see him . . .'

'Don't worry. Mary will be fine.' He hesitated. 'Best not to tell her what's going to happen, though.'

Her mouth was set hard, but after a second she nodded her agreement.

Mary was safe enough now, he felt sure of that. But in the morning he cancelled his driver and took the tram into town with her. He walked to Albion Place and checked the stairs and her office before he left. She said nothing, but once she saw everything was clear, the strain left her face. She kissed him on the cheek and for once he felt he was on the side of the angels.

A tap on the wood and the chief constable stood in the doorway.

'Mind if I come in, Tom?'

'Help yourself, sir.' He gestured to one of the empty chairs. 'Miss Sharp, could we have some tea, please?' He looked at Parker. 'Something important?'

'Yes and no.' He puffed on his cigar and leaned back to watch the smoke drift towards the ceiling. 'Have you heard anything more about Special Branch and Miss Lenton?'

'Only that they followed her from Armley to Chapel Allerton. Would you like me to check?' He picked up a pen.

'No, there's no need.' He waited until the tea sat in front of them. Lilian Lenton wasn't the reason he'd come downstairs, Harper thought. Parker wanted it to seem that way, but it was just the prelude. The main act was about to begin. 'My neighbour is a doctor at the infirmary. He stopped in for a drink on his way home last night and told me about his final patient of the evening.'

Harper felt the small crawl of fear rising up his spine. But he kept his face blank and said nothing.

'An American who'd taken quite a beating. Two teeth gone, a mass of cuts and bruises. Lucky that nothing was broken. From the description, he sounds like the one you told me about.'

'Mullen. Did Mr Mullen say what had happened to him, sir?' Harper held his breath as he waited for the reply.

'No. Refused point blank to say a word about it. Doesn't Ash have a man following him?'

'He does, sir. On my orders.'

'Then find out what happened, Tom. We can't have visitors to Leeds assaulted like that.'

'Absolutely not. I agree.'

Parker downed his tea in a single swallow. 'You wouldn't know anything about it, would you?'

'This is the first I've heard, sir.' He could say that with some measure of honesty. It *was* the first he knew that the beating had happened. 'I'll get to the bottom of it.'

'Please make sure you do.' He smiled. 'We don't want it happening again.'

The man knew. He might not have had any proof, but Parker had pieced it together. The visit was a warning, and Harper didn't need to be told twice.

'I talked to the constable following him,' Ash said over the crackle of the telephone line. 'After Mullen left your daughter's office, he went back to the Metropole and didn't leave again before our man went off-shift at six.'

'What about the night men?'

'We have several off ill at the moment, sir, so I could only spare one man outside the hotel. The first he saw of Mullen was when a taxi dropped him off around nine last night, all bandaged up and walking very gingerly. As far as he was aware, Mullen had never gone out. He was shocked and asked what had happened, but Mullen said he wasn't going to discuss it.' Ash's voice was steady, even, utterly bland.

'I see.'

'If he wants to make a complaint, I'll follow it up, of course. In the meantime . . .'

'Yes, yes. The chief wants us to make sure nothing else happens to him. You'd better let me have your report in writing.'

'I shall, sir . . .'

*   *   *

Friday morning, half past eleven. Harper sat in the chief constable's office, listening to Inspector Cartwright of Special Branch. Beside him, Sergeant Gough's face was so red with anger that he looked as if he might explode.

'None of my men had seen any sign of Miss Lenton, so I knocked on the door first thing this morning and asked to see her. I wanted to know if she was well enough to be returned to Armley Gaol.' Cartwright spoke as if he was reciting from his notebook in court.

'Go on,' Parker said. He clamped down on the cigar in his mouth to hide his amusement.

'The maid told me that she wasn't there. My men searched the house from top to bottom and the information was correct. She was not there.'

Parker studied the rising smoke. 'Have you discovered what happened?'

'She escaped, that's what happened.' Gough was close to shouting.

Harper raised an eyebrow. 'How?'

'As best as we can ascertain, sir, she was in disguise,' Cartwright continued, avoiding their eyes as he stared at the wall. 'She arrived on the Tuesday. Late that afternoon a delivery van appeared on Westfield Terrace. It was driven by a young man. He had a boy with him. We observed the boy eating an apple and reading a copy of *Comic Cuts*. The driver called out "Groceries." A servant opened the door and said, "All right, it's here." The boy took a basket into the house through the back door.' He went silent for a moment, glaring at the sergeant. 'Shortly after that, the delivery boy reappeared with an empty basket, returned to the van and it drove away.'

'The delivery boy who came out was Lilian Lenton in disguise?' Harper asked.

'Yes,' Cartwright said through clenched teeth. 'That's what we've managed to discover. I talked to the grocer. He told me everything as soon as I threatened him with prosecution. Miss Lenton was taken a mile away to' – he consulted his notebook – 'Moortown, where her friends had a taxi waiting to drive her to Harrogate. We're pursuing our enquiries from there. At this point we have every reason to believe she's fled the country.'

'That's very unfortunate,' Parker said. 'And it makes the Special Branch look pretty poor.'

'Yes, sir, it does.' Cartwright was staring daggers, but he had to sit and take it. His men had messed up. They'd allowed the woman to escape as they sat and watched. 'You can help us, if you'd be so good.' He looked as though they were the hardest words he'd ever had to speak.

'What do you need?' Harper asked.

'If you could ask the force in Harrogate to talk to people they know and discover where she's gone, that would be a great help. The sooner we can find out the better, of course.'

'We will.'

'Thank you, sir.' The men stood.

Before they could leave, the chief said, 'A word to the wise, Inspector. I'd advise you not to prosecute the grocer. If this comes out in court, you'll look an utter fool.'

Cartwright gave a quick, angry nod and the door closed. Harper reached into his wallet, took out a pound note and placed it on the desk.

'Three days. You were spot on, sir.'

Parker sighed. 'I'll take your money, Tom, but I can't say I'm happy about it. If your men had been watching, she'd have never slipped away.'

He hoped not. He expected more from them than that. But he'd never know the answer.

'I'll give Harrogate a ring.'

'Make sure they know the Branch was responsible. Let's see if some real coppers can pull their irons out of the fire. Now, I hope you have some leads on the killing of this American.'

He didn't. Ash's men were still digging, but so far they'd come up with nothing. No idea where Fess had stayed after he'd left Mrs Hardisty's rooming house. No hint of the people he'd seen. As if he'd completely vanished until his body was found.

'I know it seems impossible in a place like Leeds, sir,' Ash said. His thick hair stood like wire as he ran a hand through it. 'An American ought to stand out. But we can't find a thing. Sissons thought he might have run out to the suburbs to stay, but that doesn't make sense either. Not if he wanted to watch Mullen.'

'What about this third American?' Harper asked. 'Any sign of him yet?'

'No, and the more we look, the more I'm inclined to believe he doesn't really exist.' He shook his head. 'But honestly, sir, the way things are, I'm not sure of anything right now.'

'What about Mullen? Is he keeping his head down?'

'Spends his days with his father. They're either in the house on Somerset Street or off to the pubs. In the evening he goes out for a meal or meets one or two people. A very quiet life.'

'Not been seen close to Albion Place again?'

The two men smiled at each other. 'Nowhere near, sir.'

It wasn't his case; he had to keep reminding himself of that. He had too many other things on his plate. But it had become personal as soon as Mullen showed up at the Victoria. Even more so when he'd gone to Mary's office. The man was playing a game of some kind. That was obvious. So far one man had died because of it. But where was it going and how would it end?

It wouldn't be good; he was certain of that.

He'd finally settled into the routine of a warm summer Friday afternoon, the world outside the window looking so much more appealing than the one within, when Miss Sharp announced his two o'clock appointment.

'Show them in, please.'

Three women, and none of them intimidated by his office or his rank. They were all well dressed, not young, from money but with no need to flaunt it.

He knew Isabella Ford. They'd met many times over the years. She was a friend of Annabelle's, the woman who'd turned his wife into a suffragist organizer and speaker.

'Sit down, please, make yourselves comfortable,' he told the women, and waited until they settled.

'Deputy Chief Constable,' Miss Ford said. 'Congratulations on your promotion.'

He acknowledged it with a smile and a dip of his head.

'I don't believe you've met Miss Meikle. She's from the West Riding Federation of the National Union of Women's Suffrage Societies.'

'How do you do?' The woman looked polite and reserved, but the fire of belief burned in her eyes and her mouth was pursed and ready for debate.

'And this is Mrs Renton. She's the secretary of the Leeds Women's Suffrage Society.'

'Ma'am.'

They probably both already knew Annabelle and that he was sympathetic to women having the vote.

Tea arrived on a tray with four Viennese slices. Apparently Miss Sharp approved of the cause, too.

'I trust you know that we'll give the march all the help we can,' Harper told them. 'The police want everything to go smoothly.'

A quarter of an hour and he was standing at the door, ushering them out. Miss Ford was the last to leave, shaking his hand and thanking him.

'Annabelle tells me she's going on the pilgrimage,' she said.

'Yes. She's probably packing right now.'

She kept hold of his hand and a wistful look came into her eye. 'I wish I could go with her.'

'Why don't you?' Harper asked. 'She'll be driving, you could go with her in the car.'

She gave a sad little smile. 'I have too many responsibilities here, I'm afraid. Next time, if it's still necessary.'

He was close to finishing for the afternoon. Saturday tomorrow, just a morning of work. After that, perhaps he and Annabelle could take a drive into the country. Skipton, maybe, and a stroll around the ancient castle, or up to Fountains Abbey where monks had once lived so far out in the wild. Somewhere away from here.

Harper was still daydreaming when the telephone bell sounded.

'Detective Chief Constable Harper? It's Inspector Richards in Harrogate. You rang earlier looking for information about Lilian Lenton.'

'That's right.' He sat straight, the receiver pressed close against his good ear, a pencil in his hand.

'I put my men on it. Turned out to be quite straightforward,' Richards told him with a touch of pride. 'The taxi driver thought there was something fishy about the two young men he brought here. He believed they were girls. But they paid the fare so he wasn't too fussed.'

'Where did he drop them?'

'Right by Valley Gardens, sir. But there's more. Another taxi driver received a request to take two young women to Scarborough.'

'That's quite a distance.'

'Exactly, sir. Of course, he wasn't going to turn it down; it's a forty-mile trip, it'll have made him some good money. We're just trying to find him now.'

'Excellent work, Inspector,' Harper said. 'Have one of your men take a statement from the driver and forward it to me, please.'

'Of course, sir. We already have one from the man who brought her here.'

Another call, waiting for the operator to connect him to the Scarborough police station. But there was only a sergeant on duty. It took fully two minutes to make him understand the importance of it all, and the fact that an escaped convict might be enjoying the sea air.

One final conversation, this time with Inspector Cartwright of Special Branch, passing on what he'd learned.

'That's very quick. I appreciate it, sir. I'll despatch some of my men to Scarborough immediately.' He sounded properly grateful and humbled, Harper thought.

'Good luck to you.' He'd need it. The suffragettes obviously had a good network. Lilian had probably been bundled on to a boat days before. Now she was free on the Continent or on a train to some distant part of the United Kingdom. If the Branch ever found her, it would either be through betrayal or sheer good fortune.

He spent a quiet evening with Annabelle. Mary had gone to the pictures with Len. Always out, but why not? They had the money and the energy. And all the stories on screen in the cinema offered a few hours' escape.

He was deep asleep when Annabelle nudged him hard. 'Telephone,' she said.

By habit, he glanced at the clock. Five past three. The middle of the night. It had better be important or some constable was going to get a roasting in the morning.

'It's Ash, sir.' He snapped awake. The man would never ring at this time unless it was an emergency.

'What's happened?'

'A fire, sir. Albion Place. It's the building where your daughter has her business. I thought you ought to know.'

SEVEN

Harper tried to organize his thoughts into some kind of sense. 'Send a car for me.'

'On its way, sir. And I've ordered them to bring Mullen in.'

He had to shake Mary's shoulder to make her stir. But as soon as he told her, she was out of bed and gathering her clothes. Two minutes and he was dressed, waiting in the parlour. He'd done this so many times in his life. But only another thirty seconds passed before she was dashing out of her room, clutching a coat and pulling a wool hat over her unbrushed hair.

They didn't speak on the journey into town; he could feel her tension and see the way she knotted her hands together. With no traffic on the road it only took them five minutes to reach Briggate. The car hadn't even stopped before she was out and running across the street.

One of the firemen put his arms around her to hold her back. But it looked as if the blaze was already done. All that remained were wisps of smoke rising up into the night sky.

Ash was talking to the fire inspector, who saluted as Harper approached with Mary at his side.

'It looks worse than it is, sir. We'll make sure once it's daylight, but I reckon we caught it early enough to avoid any damage. The copper on the beat spotted it and blew his whistle. We arrived before it had a chance to take hold.'

'How did it start?' Mary asked. 'Do you know yet?'

For a moment, all the man could do was stare at her in surprise. That wasn't a woman's question. But she was a copper's daughter, she'd grown up with all of this. He glanced at Ash before answering. 'The glass in the street door was smashed and someone poured petrol in. I smelled it straight off. It's arson, no two ways about it. The first flight of stairs will need to be replaced, and new plaster on the walls. But everything above that looks fine. Probably not even much smoke damage.'

'Thank you.' She smiled at him. 'To you and your men.'

'Mullen will be at Millgarth by now,' Ash said. 'Do you want to question him, sir?'

Harper thought for a moment, then shook his head. It was safer to stay clear of it all. Things had become too personal; they'd been that way since Mullen turned up at the Victoria.

'No. It's your case.' He started to turn away. 'Make sure you ask whoever brought him in whether Mullen smelled of petrol at all. Check all the garages in the area; it was bought somewhere. And let's not assume the motive was to destroy my daughter's business. There are plenty of other companies in there.'

Ash smiled. 'They'll be on it in the morning, sir.' He raised his hat to Mary and began to stroll back to Millgarth.

Harper gazed at the building, raising his eyes from the door to the second floor.

'You won't be doing any business tomorrow.'

'I still have to be here when the girls arrive, Da. I need to talk to the landlord, too.' She was already making a list in her mind as the driver took them back to Sheepscar.

At home, Mary brought a notebook into the living room and began writing.

Should he let Annabelle sleep? He stood by the bedroom door, weighing the thought. Better to wake her; she'd want to know. As soon as she was up, she began to bustle around, making tea and cooking breakfast for them all.

'Do you think it was him?' she asked as they ate.

He wanted to say yes, but something stopped him. Mullen was a bully-boy. He was a killer. The history with his gang in New York showed that. He was ruthless, violent, and he didn't have a conscience. But he wasn't stupid. He must have known that he'd be the obvious suspect. Maybe it was his idea of revenge for the beating he'd been given. Perhaps he believed he could brazen it out.

Either that or someone was doing a very good job of setting him up for a fall. This mysterious third American, perhaps. If he even existed.

'I don't know,' he told her finally. 'It's Millgarth's case.'

Annabelle gave him a sharp, questioning look then turned back to her food.

Finally, at twenty-five past seven, washed, shaved, and dressed in a light wool suit, he walked down the stairs and through the pub. Mary followed on his heels.

'Ready?' he asked.

With a sigh, she nodded.

He had the driver wait on Albion Place as he tried to assess the damage. A constable stood at the entrance to the building to keep people out, but he let them through into the vestibule.

There wasn't much to see. Blackened walls, the stairs turned to charcoal and crumbling. Nobody would be going up until they were replaced. He'd been to the aftermath of enough fires to know the damage was light. Lucky.

Lucky *this* time, he corrected himself.

Harper had settled with his morning cup of tea, put on his spectacles, and was reading through the first of the CID reports when Parker tapped on the door and strode in.

'I heard about the arson.'

That was inevitable. The fire brigade was part of the police force; its senior officers reported to the chief constable.

'I was out there during the night, sir, and back again this morning. It's not as bad as it first looked.'

'Even so . . . your daughter's office is in that building, isn't it?'

The chief knew the answer; he wouldn't have bothered with the question – or any of this – otherwise.

'Yes, sir. Ash has pulled in Mullen.'

A nod. 'Just make sure he doesn't have any more accidents.'

Then he was gone again. Harper sat back and thought. The visit had been to let him know that Parker was on top of things and that he was concerned. A way of offering some tacit support. And that was very welcome. With the hint of a warning in the tail.

He ached to go down to Millgarth, but he forced himself to stay at the town hall. Ash would be in touch as soon as he had something to report. Harper had trusted him when they both worked out of the same station. The least he could do was bloody well let him do his job now.

At noon he wished Miss Sharp a pleasant weekend and stepped out into the hazy sunlight. With all the smoke and the smuts from the factories, the air was never clear and clean around Leeds. It didn't matter; the warmth still felt heartening.

For a second he considered telling the driver to go to Albion Place. But Mary could handle that herself. She was capable. He didn't want her to think he was fussing. How did you strike a balance between caring and interference?

'The Victoria,' he said.

Dinner was a slice of ham, some lettuce and tomato with a couple of slices of buttered bread. But no questions about the fire. Curious, he thought.

Once they were done Annabelle put on a pale blue broad-brimmed hat and tied it under her chin. She was dressed for a day out, in a white blouse with a bow at the neck and an indigo skirt that stopped above her ankles to show off a polished pair of button boots.

'Skipton?' she suggested. 'Somewhere we don't have to think about . . .'

He grinned. 'You must have been reading my mind.'

'That's hardly difficult, Tom.' She shook her head pityingly. 'After all, you're a man.'

So much countryside. Living in the city, it always took him by surprise when the buildings disappeared and there was nothing but fields and farmhouses. They passed through Ilkley, with the crags towering high above the town, and up into the Dales.

Annabelle was a confident driver, overtaking all the slow, creaking farm wagons and carts on the roads. Twice they saw other motor cars, but otherwise it was easy to imagine they'd been thrown back a century or more. Men were working in the fields. A small herd of cattle gathered under the shade of a tree. The miles dropped away behind them until she found a place to park close to Skipton Castle.

They'd visited a few times over the years, but the place never palled. So much history, all there in front of him. The huge, thick walls of the gatehouse offered a hint of the power that must have dwelt here once, and the yew tree in the courtyard still stood after all these centuries.

Even more, though, he loved the market along the main street. The stalls offered things so different from Leeds. Fresh cheeses, butter straight from the churn, ice cream manufactured in a local shop.

Annabelle took his arm as they strolled and brought her head close to his. 'Now, what's going on with this fire? Did he do it or not?'

'I don't know. I told you, Millgarth is taking care of it.'

'That's not an answer, Tom. Come on, it's your own daughter.'

'And that's precisely why I'm keeping my distance.'

For a moment she was silent, pursing her lips and frowning. Then her expression cleared as she understood.

'Still going on the pilgrimage?' Harper asked.

'I was. With all this going on, I'm not so sure now.' She stopped to examine the decoration on a shawl, bargaining with the woman selling it until they found a price that left them both smiling.

'Go,' he told her as they moved slowly along. 'You might as well. There's nothing you can do to affect things.'

'I know, but . . .' She stopped and stared at him. He could see the uncertainty in her eyes.

'If anything happens, I can send a telegram and the coppers can find you. You could be home in a few hours.'

'Yes,' she agreed. 'Daft, isn't it? I wouldn't think twice if it was anyone but Mary.'

He squeezed her hand. 'I know. Believe me, I know.'

Sunday morning. All around Leeds, the church bells were ringing. But each year the congregations dwindled. When men and women all worked so many hours, who could be surprised? They needed time to rest, time to see to all the jobs at home, time to themselves before the new week came around all too soon.

Harper was in his top hat and formal suit at St Peter's in Kirkgate for the monthly church parade by the police cadets. Outside, with the hymns still ringing in his ears, he dismissed the driver. Perfect weather for a walk back to the Victoria. With a couple of stops along the way.

Workmen bustled in the building on Albion Place. He watched them for a minute. The new stairs were already in place, completed the evening before. This crew was re-plastering the walls. Tomorrow or Tuesday, everything would be open for business again. Never a delay when there was profit to be made.

Millgarth was quiet, the parade ground hot and summer dusty. Sergeant Mason saluted as Harper strode through to the detectives' room. No sign of Walsh or Galt, only Sissons in his shirt sleeves, writing up a report.

'Did you squeeze anything from Mullen about the arson?'

He shook his head. 'Not a thing, sir. It wasn't for want of trying.

Our man in the hotel hadn't seen him leave. No stink of petrol on him or his clothes.'

'How long did you keep him?'

'Eight hours. We took it in turns to question him.' He shrugged. 'After that we didn't have any grounds to hold him longer.'

'Very well,' Harper said, but the words were pure reflex. If Mullen wasn't behind the fire, then who'd done it? Why? 'Is the superintendent in?'

'Sorry, sir, Mr Ash is up on the Bank. The Erin Boys had a scrap with another gang.' A wan smile and a forlorn look at the weather beyond the window. 'I'm the one holding the fort.'

'Do you have any clues at all about the fire?'

'We've taken some fingerprints but I've no idea if they'll help. There are plenty of offices up there, sir, and people in and out all the time.' He shrugged. 'Nothing to indicate they're from the arsonist at all.'

'What about the Fess murder?'

'Same, sir.' He shook his head. 'We've had a few whispers, but they all turn out to be smoke. No idea where Fess was staying or who he was seeing. He vanished. We're beginning to feel like we're banging our heads against a brick wall. And before you ask, sir, not even a hint of this third American.'

'Of course not.' Every possible frustration. He'd experienced it himself often enough in the past. 'Keep at it.'

There was no need to say it; he knew they'd keep burrowing away to find answers. Using their informants, following up on everything. They had a reputation and the pride to keep it intact.

One final visit before the walk to Sheepscar. Somerset Street, a couple of minutes away from the police station. A place where people lived who'd been broken by the years. Rotted window frames, gutters that sagged and drooped. Glass missing from half the windows. Neglected and desperate. The type of street the illustrated papers showed when they wanted to describe poverty. But this wasn't an illustration. It was all too real for the people who lived here. He'd known streets like this his entire life. They'd still exist long after he was dead. The old order would persist.

Walking home didn't bring any fresh ideas; it offered nothing more than a sheen of sweat on his skin. Mary was out. Even a fire wouldn't keep her from cycling with the Clarion Club. Just a short outing today, though. She was back in time for tea, crumpets and jam, followed by a slice of sponge cake. Afterwards she washed the pots, and Harper stood in the kitchen and told her what he'd seen on Albion Place.

'The landlord promised me it would be ready tomorrow,' she said as if it was what she'd expected to hear. 'I warned him if it took any longer I'd start withholding rent. There are too many empty places in Leeds right now and I've been a good tenant.'

'They haven't managed to pin it on Mullen.'

For a moment she was like a statue, not moving at all. Then she put down the last clean plate and wiped her hands on her apron.

'He won't bother you again,' Harper said.

She turned and looked at him. 'Are you sure, Da? You promised that last time, before the fire.'

'I know,' he admitted. 'He's been warned off. If he tries to come anywhere near you, the constable following him will make sure nothing happens.'

Her mouth tightened. He could read the expression in her eyes. Then she smiled.

'I need to go over some things for tomorrow. We're going to have to catch up on all that work and make sure nothing's damaged.'

Dismissed, he thought as she closed the door to her room. Well, maybe he deserved it. But who was ever truly safe in this world?

EIGHT

Monday. A busy week ahead. Seven more days and the women on the pilgrimage would arrive in Leeds; he needed to go over the fine details with the appropriate divisions. Follow up with Special Branch and Scarborough police to see how they were progressing in their search for Miss Lenton.

And there was Louis Fess.

That one was the puzzle. The rest was information and order. Murder sold newspapers, and the killing remained on the front page; lower, now, below the fold. But as soon as there was any new information, it would be the headline once more.

Nothing fresh in Ash's report from Millgarth. He knew exactly what that meant. The men were working and coming up empty. But he also understood what he had to do. No choice but to put them under the cosh to come up with a result. It wasn't a pleasure, but it came with his job.

He was considering how to word his note when Miss Sharp tapped on the door and closed it behind her as she entered. Strange, he thought; she wasn't usually so secretive.

'There's a gentleman outside.' Her voice barely rose above a whisper and he had to strain to catch what she said. 'He wants to talk to whoever's in charge of the Fess case. The chief constable is out today, so he wants to speak to you.' The smallest pause. 'He's American. Says he's from their embassy in London.' She placed a calling card on the desk. *Charles Armstrong, third secretary, Embassy of the United States of America, 4 Grosvenor Gardens, London.* It all sounded very impressive.

'You'd better bring him in.'

Armstrong was younger than he'd expected, still in his early thirties, a brawny man wearing a well-cut lounge suit with four buttons and a soft collar on his shirt. A heavy moustache, small spectacles and hair cut short like the pictures Harper had seen of Teddy Roosevelt, the American president. The type of firm handshake intended to establish that he was in charge.

'You must be here about Louis Fess,' Harper said.

'That's right.' The man took a handkerchief from his breast pocket and used it to polish his glasses. 'Our ambassador asked me to come up and discover what you're doing to find his murderer.' The faintest hint of a smile. 'After all, he's one of our citizens.'

'We're doing everything we can. The same as we would for any killing.'

'I'm sure you are, Deputy Chief Constable. But you have to understand, we look after our own.'

'As you should,' Harper agreed. 'Tell me, though, what do you know about Mr Fess?'

'More than you might expect,' Armstrong replied. 'I did a little checking before I caught the train.' He stopped as Miss Sharp placed a tray on the table. 'I'm well aware he was a criminal. That doesn't mean he shouldn't receive justice, no matter where he was killed.'

'He brought a gun with him. It was in his luggage. We talked to him before his death and he lied to us. Said he'd come over to watch over another of your gangsters, a man called Davey Mullen.'

Armstrong frowned. 'I remember reading stories about him. He was shot about a dozen times and survived. It was in all the papers.'

'He grew up in Leeds and left for New York when he was ten. His father remained here. Mullen claims he's visiting him. Fess was a member of the gang that shot him.'

'You've had Mullen in for questioning?'

'Of course.' He wasn't about to mention the arson or the man's intimidation of Mary. 'And we've found nothing to indicate he's guilty. The men on the case are some of our very best. They used to be my squad.'

'I'll be honest with you, Mr Harper. Normally I wouldn't be sent up here to ask questions about a case like this. We'd write a letter or make a telephone call.'

'Why the difference this time?'

He looked embarrassed. 'One of our elected representatives from Manhattan – that's where Fess lived in New York – has been putting pressure on the State Department to investigate.'

Interesting, he thought. Wheels within wheels. 'What does that mean, exactly?'

'In blunt terms? I'll tell you, but if you quote me, I'll deny I ever said it. The representative is bought and paid for with criminal money. They financed his election and rigged votes to put him in office. Now they want their money's worth, so they tell him to get us involved.' He shrugged. 'The State Department talks to the ambassador, and I end up sitting here.'

'Politics,' Harper said.

'Politics,' Armstrong agreed. 'It makes the world go round.'

'I'm afraid you've had a wasted journey. I meant what I said, though; there's very little I can tell you.'

'If it's not this Mullen, is it someone local?'

'Not that we know. My men have excellent sources and they've come up with nothing.'

There was hesitation on Armstrong's face. He wanted to say something but wasn't sure how. Unusual for a diplomat.

'I have a request.'

'Whatever I can do to help, of course.'

'Might I see where it happened?'

Harper was taken by surprise. He hadn't expected that. 'If you like. I'll warn you, though, there not much to see.'

'I've always enjoyed sensationalist novels.' Armstrong kept his voice low, as if he was confessing a sin. 'This is the first chance I've had to see anything real, and I might never have another.' His face flushed deep crimson.

'Then we'll go. And I'm sure the City of Leeds can treat you to luncheon afterwards.'

People, he thought as he watched Armstrong climb into his railway carriage. You never knew what to make of them. He hadn't looked like a man with a taste for the gruesome, but he'd wanted to know all the gory details.

None of it had spoiled his appetite. He'd cleared everything on his plate and a pudding before collecting his case from the Queen's Hotel.

A whistle screeched loudly. The locomotive for the London train gathered steam; another minute and it would leave the platform.

'I'll be in touch as soon as we make an arrest,' Harper promised.

'Thank you.' Armstrong smiled. 'And I appreciate you indulging me. I know it must have seemed odd, but I appreciate it.'

As he strode up Park Row, he shook his head again. People.

Half past four and the afternoon felt as if it would never end. A fly droned around his office, landing in front of him and buzzing away before he could swat it.

Harper tried to concentrate. There was a pile of papers on the desk that needed his attention, but his heart wasn't in the work. It was one of those days when he ached to be out there, asking questions and trying to discover who'd killed Fess and set the fire.

Finally he picked up his hat and left. No need for a driver, it would do him good to walk home. Traffic was backed up on the Headrow. A carthorse had collapsed in its traces. Men tried to pull the huge animal away while the trams and motor lorries waited. The old world holding up the new. A constable, a fresh recruit from his nervous look, was trying to bring some order.

Millgarth was strangely quiet. He exchanged a few words with Sergeant Mason, then strode through to the detectives' room. Empty. Ash was in his office.

'All of them out slaving away?'

'Thank your friend Mr Mullen for that, sir.'

'Why?' he asked sharply. 'What's he done now?'

'Went back to his hotel after dinner. Our man spotted him creeping out and rang it in. Sissons and Galt are following him. I sent Walsh to take another poke around in his room.'

'If he goes anywhere near Mary . . .' Harper said, but Ash was already shaking his head.

'He won't have chance, sir. I can promise you that. I have someone watching her office.'

'Very good. Anything new on the arson?'

'I talked to the investigator. All he could confirm is what we already knew on Friday night. Someone broke the glass on the door, tossed in some petrol and set light to it. There's nothing to give any indication who's responsible. We haven't turned up anything to tie Mullen to the blaze. We're still searching for someone who might have bought fuel in a small container, but we're probably on a hiding to nothing with that.'

'What about Fess's murder? I had a visitor from the American Embassy today.'

Ash sighed and ran a hand through his hair. 'Still nowhere on that, too. I know Mullen is the obvious suspect, but we haven't found any witnesses or evidence. None of our narks have come up with a name.'

'This third American?'

He shook his head. 'No. I'm as certain as I can be that he's a figment of someone's imagination.'

'So we've got damn all?'

'I'm sorry, sir.'

'Never mind. It's happened before. You'll get there in the end. What was the problem with the Erin Boys?'

'Something and nothing. A fight over territory. I had the constables crack a few heads; that should take care of things.' The smallest of hesitations. 'What do you want us to do about Mullen?'

Harper thought for a few seconds. 'Nothing, unless he looks like causing a problem. He's probably testing us, to see what we let him do. When the time's right, we'll slap him down again.'

'Very good, sir,' Ash agreed. His face stayed impassive but his eyes showed his real feelings. He wasn't a happy man.

A good walk to Sheepscar. A chance to idle along, to see things up close rather than hidden away in a motor car where he passed so quickly. All the smells and sounds that made up Leeds. Kosher food cooking in the Leylands, sauerkraut and chicken and the constant hum of sewing machines in the sweatshops. The malt from Brunswick brewery. The hot stink of iron rising from the foundries and the sewage stink of chemical works and tanneries up Meanwood Road. Little of it was lovely. But all of it was his. It was home.

Harper was crossing Manor Street, no more than a hundred feet from the Victoria, when he caught sight of the figure coming out of the shadows. For a second he hesitated, waiting until the man showed himself in the light.

Davey Mullen. He stood with his arms spread. 'Mr Harper,' he called. 'Can I talk to you?'

'What do you want?'

'All the things that have been going on. I'm not behind any of them.'

He had bruises on his face from his beating, the colours turning to greens and purples, and he moved with cautious stiffness. Harper saw Sissons and Galt running down the road. Impressive; Mullen was slowed by his aches and pains, not on his home turf and he'd still managed to give them the slip. Harper lifted a hand for them to keep their distance.

'All right,' he agreed. 'Where?'

'Your pub's over there.' He pointed over his shoulder.

He shook his head. 'My wife's pub. And you're barred.'

Lizzie's café was still open. The woman was cleaning up at the end of the day; grudgingly, she agreed to serve them.

'Twenty minutes, Mr Harper, then I'm turfing you out. And I'll warn you, a cuppa and a teacake is your lot.'

'Thank you, Lizzie, that'll be plenty of time.' He turned to Mullen. 'You heard her; you'd better say your piece.'

The man stared down at the table for a second, then raised his eyes. He was wearing a clean shirt and a red and black striped tie with a four-in-hand knot. A steel-grey suit with a collar on the waistcoat.

'When I told you I didn't know Louis Fess, I was lying,' he began. 'I knew exactly who he was. But I had no idea he was in Leeds. I swear to that. I couldn't believe it when you told me.'

'And he was shot in the head just a few hours after that,' Harper said. 'I'd already taken a pistol off you that you just happened to be carrying when you came into the pub. No, you need to do better to convince me. And don't tell me you didn't know the law about guns.'

'I knew,' Mullen agreed with a nod.

'Why? Where did you get the weapon?'

'I was checking, seeing how sharp you were, what you were like. I brought the gun with me from the States. In case I needed protection.' He paused. 'Someone set me up for that killing.'

Harper leaned forward, resting his elbows on the table. Lizzie brought two hefty mugs of tea. 'Let's say they did. Who was it? Why would anyone do that?'

'You want to know what I think?'

'Isn't that why we're here, Mr Mullen?'

'The Hudson Dusters couldn't finish me off with bullets back in New York, so they're trying something different over here. If you convict me for murder, I hang, right?'

'Yes. But Fess was one of the Dusters. We know that. Why would they let one of their own be killed?'

Mullen shrugged. 'He'd proved himself, but he was a nobody. They sacrificed him.'

'Fine.' It was ideas, all in the air. And unlikely. 'If that's the case, who pulled the trigger?'

The man looked him in the eye. 'I don't know. Maybe they hired someone over here. Or maybe there was another one of them that Fess didn't know about.'

A third American . . .

'If anybody local was involved, I'm sure the police would have heard,' Harper said. 'No, it's not going to wash. And what about you intimidating my daughter and the arson at her office? Maybe those are nothing to do with you, either?'

'OK, I stopped in to talk to her. I've never denied it. Why not? She's pretty, she's got something about her. But she gave me the bum's rush. Fair enough. And your guys made me pay for it.' His voice took on a harsh edge. Anger? Desperation? 'I had nothing to do with that fire, Mr Harper. You've seen my record. Think about it for a minute. I don't destroy property; something like that just isn't my style.'

'Then who did it?'

'You've had your cops watching me every day. Two of your plain clothes men are standing outside right now. You ever thought there might be someone else watching me, too?'

An interesting thought. 'I'll ask you again, Mr Mullen: who?'

'Someone from the Dusters, maybe, or somebody they've hired. It has to be. It's the only explanation.' He brought his palm down on the table and the slap reverberated around the café.

Harper leaned back in his chair. 'Or all this could be a very clever trick of yours to divert suspicion from yourself.'

'It's not.' He shouted the words, then pulled himself up. 'It's not,' he repeated quietly, 'I'm telling you the truth.'

'We'll see, Mr Mullen. We ought to go, Lizzie's waiting to lock up.'

Outside, Mullen stared at him then turned to make his way back towards town. Galt shadowed him. Harper waved Sissons over.

'Where did he lose you?'

'Near Somerset Street, sir, by his father's place.'

That made sense. It was where he'd grown up; the area was imprinted on his mind.

'I want you to send a telegram to the New York police. Ask if Mullen's ever been a suspect in an arson.'

'Yes, sir. Do you want me to follow him first?'

'No need. Galt can handle it. I think he came out to talk to me. I don't imagine he'll give you any more problems today.'

He'd made Mullen think that he didn't believe a word. But the man had given him plenty to consider. It was all *possible*, that was the damnable thing. Mullen could be innocent of murder and setting a fire. But he could just as easily be guilty as sin.

NINE

He sat, swirling the tea in the cup and thinking.

'That must be stone cold by now,' Annabelle said.

'It doesn't matter.'

'What's bothering you tonight?'

'Work.' He didn't want to be more specific, to bring up Mullen's name and see her anger flare. 'It'll pass.'

'I went to the Mansion at Roundhay Park today,' she said, and he was grateful for the change of topic. 'To arrange tea for the marchers when they arrive. We'll have the meeting afterwards.'

'No problems?'

'We're not expecting too many to make it here. A couple of dozen at most.'

The mention jogged his memory. 'They started out today, didn't they?'

'Yes. I had a message earlier.'

'And are you still planning on joining them?'

She smiled. 'I am.'

He grinned. 'My men will be ready when the women are here. We'll make sure there's no trouble.'

'We're the suffragists, not the suffragettes,' she reminded him. 'We don't cause trouble.'

'I was thinking about men, not you.'

'We can look after ourselves.'

'The police will take care of things in Leeds.' He stared at her.

'Yes,' she agreed. 'Of course.'

'Galt gave me his report,' Ash said. Harper sat in the visitor's chair in the office at Millgarth. He'd been back here often enough since his promotion, but it was always a strange, disorientating experience. He was so used to being on the other side of that desk. 'Seems Mullen led them quite a dance.'

'He knew where he was going. He wanted to see me. He claims he's being set up for Fess's murder and the arson at Mary's office.'

'Do you believe him, sir?'

He sighed. 'That's the thing. I don't know. Everything he said was plausible enough . . .'

'But you'd trust him as far as you could throw him?'

'More or less.'

'Sissons sent that telegram to New York. We received a reply. Mullen has no history of arson at all. They've never even suspected him of it. He might be telling the truth about that.'

'It still leaves a killing, and Fess's was definitely his style,' Harper said. He held up his hands. 'I know, we don't have a scrap of proof.'

'I was going to ring you about that this morning, sir. We've managed to find out a little more about Fess. That constable, Rogers, the one who spotted him in the first place. He was covering a beat over by the river last night and asked questions in a few rooming houses. Fess had stayed in one of them.'

'I thought the constables had gone around them all and asked questions as soon as he vanished.'

'They were supposed to,' Ash replied, and darkness rippled through his voice.

'What did Rogers discover?'

'Fess must have scarpered off there as soon as we let him go. The landlady doesn't read the newspapers, she didn't hear about the killing. When he didn't come back, she took his things to sell and let the room again.'

'He can't have had much.'

'Just a change of clothes, by the sound of it. She'll have gone through the pockets and kept any change she found. He'd already left everything else when he ran, and he didn't dare return to left luggage for his trunk. We have that down in the evidence room.'

'We need to know who he saw, who he talked to.'

'I've put Rogers on it, sir. He seems to have the knack of picking up on things.'

'Have you put him in plain clothes yet?'

'Started this morning. We could use some fresh blood in CID.'

That was true. Every one of Ash's squad had plenty of experience, but the job needed new men, younger, eager.

'Let me know how he does. He seems like a bright spark. What are we going to do about Mullen? He came up with something interesting – maybe someone else is following our copper who's trailing after him.'

'I don't see it, sir,' Ash said as he shook his head. But his eyes were full of questions.

It was close to five when the telephone rang. He pushed the receiver against his ear.

'Deputy Chief Constable Harper.'

'This is Inspector Warren in Scarborough, sir.' Even on a poor line, he could hear how apologetic the man sounded. 'You talked to my sergeant about a woman named Lilian Lenton. The suffragette who escaped.'

'I remember.'

'I thought you'd like to know that we haven't found any trace of her and neither have the men from Special Branch. There's a rumour she was smuggled on to a yacht going to the Continent, but it's nothing more than talk. I haven't found anyone to confirm it, let alone anyone who'll admit to having her on board.'

'Is the Branch still stymied?'

'Yes, sir.' He paused. 'I want to apologize for not being here when you rang. My daughter was ill in hospital.'

'Improving now, I hope.'

'On the mend, thank you. Forgive me for asking, sir, but weren't you a friend of Inspector Reed in Whitby?'

'I was, yes.' The images flashed through his mind. Poor Billy, dead for five years after keeling over with a heart attack. 'That's a while ago now. Did you know him?'

'Only briefly, sir. I was a sergeant here when he was around. He seemed like a nice chap.'

'He was.' The memories were flickering in his head like an evening at the cinema. Time to pack them away again; they never did any good. 'Thank you for letting me know, Inspector. Keep me informed if you learn more.'

'Yes, sir.'

A bittersweet way to end the day, he thought. Tossed back through the years. He and Reed had worked together twenty years before. They'd been good friends for a while. Annabelle still kept in touch with his widow, Elizabeth; just cards at Christmas and birthdays these days. They'd grown apart over time. Life and distance.

He was waiting for his driver outside the town hall when a clerk came rushing out of the building.

'Sir,' he called. 'Sir.'

Harper turned. The man was running towards him. All the colour had vanished from his face.

'Are you looking for me?'

The man gave a frightened nod. 'They want you down by the Metropole Hotel, sir. Someone was firing a gun.'

A gun? It was the middle of the afternoon. What in God's name was going on?

'Do you know who—' he began, but the man was already shaking his head.

'As soon as my car arrives, send the driver over.' With all the carts and trams on the road, he'd be quicker on foot.

Harper dashed down towards King Street, dodging and swerving between the afternoon crowds on the pavements, pushing people aside. His chest was tight. No one dead, please. Not that.

The Metropole. Mullen was staying there. This wasn't a coincidence. Had he been shot? Or had he been shooting? Harper moved faster, skidding around the corner.

Policemen directed the traffic away, leaving the road empty in front of the hotel. He saw Rogers and Galt poking through the gutter with sticks. An ambulance was pulling away from the kerb. Ash stood on the steps. As soon as he saw Harper, he broke away from a man in a frock coat who'd been talking to him.

'Someone took a shot at Walsh, sir.' His face was grave.

Harper felt the panic rising in his chest. 'Is he—'

'Missed him, sir. Not even close. He's inside, shaken.'

'Who was hurt?' Harper asked. 'I saw the ambulance.'

'They wounded one of my guests,' the man next to Ash said. The hotel manager, Harper guessed.

'Who?' His pulse was racing and his throat was dry. 'How bad?'

'A woman out with her husband, walking a dog, sir.' Ash's voice was calm and steady. 'There were three shots. Looks as if one blew off a fragment of brick and it hit her in the leg. Doesn't seem like more than a cut, but I had the ambulance take her to the hospital, just in case.'

Good. Ash was in control. But for Christ's sake, things like this didn't happen in the afternoon in Leeds.

'What was Walsh doing here?'

A small hesitation before he replied. 'Mullen had slipped away from the constable again. Walsh had come looking for him.'

'Mullen's out running free and someone takes a shot at one of our men?' He turned away and took a few paces, trying to steady his fury.

'I have everyone hunting him, sir. The whole division.'

He nodded. 'And you're positive Walsh is fine?'

'He was already inside when it happened. But go and talk to him yourself.'

He could feel the beating of his pulse. 'Tell me exactly what happened.'

'Walsh had just entered the hotel, sir. According to witnesses, one of the shots broke the glass' – he gestured at the shattered window at the front of the hotel – 'and a second caused that injury to the woman. The third must have gone wide.'

'Look, I—' the manager began, but Harper cut him off with a hand on his arm.

'I understand your concern, sir. For your guests and your hotel. But I need to talk to the superintendent here and get the investigation moving. I'm sure you can appreciate that.'

'Yes, I . . . yes,' he replied, clamping his mouth shut.

'One of my men will be in to take your statement soon. Please assure your guests that they're absolutely safe. We'll keep a constable outside the hotel.'

After a moment, the manager nodded and disappeared through the door. As soon as he'd gone, Harper said: 'Mullen.'

'We'll find him, sir.' There was venom under his words. 'And he'll wish we hadn't.'

'When did he evade his tail?'

'About two hours ago, sir. Went in the Pygmalion to shop, ducked through the people and nipped out through another door.'

An old, old trick at a department store, and the copper with him had fallen for it.

'How long ago did the shooting happen?'

Ash pulled the watch from his waistcoat. 'We received the call twenty-five minutes ago.'

By then, Mullen had enjoyed an hour and a half of freedom. This was a complete bloody mess.

'Where was the gunman?'

'Over there.' The superintendent gestured towards a ginnel between two buildings on the other side of the street. Most of the area was in deep shadow. The perfect place to hide, Harper thought. 'No cartridges, so it looks as if he was using a pistol.'

Just as well it was only a handgun. At that distance a rifle would have been deadly.

'How many witnesses do you have?'

'Three. One of them was delivering across the street.' He sighed. 'Not that they saw anything, sir. By the time anyone plucked up the courage to go and look, he was long gone.' Ash peered into the distance and lowered his voice; Harper could barely make out the words. 'The chief's here, sir.'

A shooting was bound to draw Chief Constable Parker. With innocent people around and a policeman as the target, he had to be seen to be taking charge. Harper turned and saw him, a couple of reporters dogging his footsteps and making notes as they walked.

'Tom. Superintendent.' He glanced around, taking in the scene. 'Shots from over there?'

'Yes, sir,' Ash replied, and Harper let him give the summary.

'Walsh is unhurt? Not a scratch?'

'Right as rain,' Ash told him. 'I made sure of that, sir.'

'I'll go inside and see him, then down to the infirmary to visit the lady,' Parker said. 'Tom, I want you to supervise this. No offence, Superintendent, I know you're very good, but it's going to be all over the papers. We have to deal with it at the highest level. The mayor will be asking questions. We've had one man shot dead; now this, and in the middle of the day. Are they connected?'

'Impossible to say yet,' Harper answered.

'Then find out.' His voice brooked no excuses. 'I'm not having this in Leeds. I want a result soon.' No need to say more than that. They both understood what he meant.

'Mullen,' Harper said. 'You know what to do.'

TEN

Walsh sat in a corner of the bar, out of sight of any window. Five cigarette ends lay in the ashtray, but the drink on the table looked almost untouched.

'Did the chief have much to say?' Harper asked.

'Wanted to make sure I was fine.' A grin. 'I told him I'd never felt better.'

'You were lucky.'

'I know.' He reached for another cigarette and lit it. At least his hands were steady. 'It's funny, I don't normally smoke, but . . .'

'Calms the nerves.'

'I've never been shot at before,' Walsh said thoughtfully. 'All kinds of things, but not that.'

'You were already in the hotel when he fired?'

A nod. 'I'd just come through the doors. Then there were three shots, one right after the other, *pop pop pop*. I can still hear them.' He pursed his lips and cocked his head. 'It must have been Mullen, mustn't it?'

'We'll know more when we find him. I want you to take the rest
of the day off—'

'Sir?'

'Call it medical leave. Report back first thing tomorrow, bright-
eyed and bushy-tailed. That's an order.'

'Very good, sir.'

'We'll have Mullen in custody by then.'

He just hoped he could keep that promise.

Ash was waiting outside on King Street, pacing around on the pavement. There was relief in his eyes, a grin plastered on his face.

'We've got him, sir.'

'Where?'

'Round the corner. He was walking along, on his way back here,
happy as you please.'

'Where is he now?'

'They're putting him in a wagon to take to Millgarth.'

Harper thought for a second. 'No. Bring him here. Up in his
room. I'll talk to him.'

'Are you sure, sir?'

'Positive.'

There was something about all this that just didn't feel right.
Mullen had a history of using guns, and he was a killer. No doubt
about that. He knew full well how to handle a weapon. If he'd
wanted to hit Walsh, he'd have pulled the trigger before the
inspector was through the door. Scare tactics? That was possible.
But what would be the point? He simply didn't buy it.

This reminded him of the arson at Mary's office. Something
intended to make Mullen look guilty. In his mind, Harper ran
through the possibilities.

The man could be responsible and trying to brazen it out. He
certainly wouldn't put it past him. And yet . . . Mullen had come
to find him by the Victoria, purely to insist he wasn't guilty. That
had felt as if it came from the heart.

He sighed. 'Keep a man on the door outside his room. Just in
case.'

'Very good, sir.'

Mullen looked shocked. He sat on the bed, drawing on a cigarette
and taking nips from a small silver flask. He'd been searched. He

hadn't been carrying a gun, he didn't smell of cordite. There was nothing incriminating in his room. But that didn't prove a thing.

'I didn't do it,' he said. His face was pale and drawn. It heightened the colours of his bruises.

'You say that every time we meet,' Harper told him. 'I could fill a book with all the things you haven't done.'

'I mean it. For Christ's sake.' He raked a hand through his hair. 'Why would I do something like that? I might as well just point a finger at myself.'

'I've been a copper long enough to know that criminals do plenty of stupid things.'

'Not me.' He took another sip.

'Handy that it happened when you'd got rid of the man following you. Or is that a coincidence?'

'I don't know.' He looked up. 'I mean it, I don't.'

'Where did you go?'

'I . . .'

'If you want me to believe you had nothing to do with the shooting, you're going to have to tell me. And you'd better have witnesses. Reliable, honest ones.'

Mullen was quiet, smoking and studying the cigarette between his fingers. His legs were moving, feet tapping out different rhythms on the carpet. He didn't seem to notice.

'Well? I'm waiting for an answer.'

'A woman.'

'Who?' Harper asked.

'She's married.'

'Who is she?' He wasn't going to stop pressing until he had an answer.

It took time and patience, but finally he had the name.

'Wait here.'

Ash and Galt were at the front desk.

'Anything from Mullen, sir?' the superintendent asked eagerly.

'A woman named Anthea Morton.'

'Jigger Morton's wife?' Galt asked and began to grin.

'That's her,' Harper said. 'Mullen says he slipped off to see her. Didn't want anyone to know.'

'Especially her husband, I bet. Jigger has a right temper.'

'Go and talk to her. And make sure she tells you the truth.' He glanced around. 'Did Walsh leave?'

'Gone home, sir. He still looked peaky, mind,' Galt said.

'Can't blame him, can you? Let's find some answers on this.'

Back upstairs, the hotel room felt warm. Oppressive and close.

'Let's just suppose for a minute that you're telling me the truth—'

'I am,' Mullen told him.

'*Maybe* you are,' Harper said. 'That leaves a big question: who in Leeds would want you dead?'

'Nobody.'

'Someone does,' Harper said. 'I think you'd better come up with a few names.'

The man stared into the distance. 'Maybe there's one,' he answered after a while. 'There was a fellow who was giving my old man problems over some money he owed. I told him to back off.'

'Told him how?' Harper asked.

'I was polite at first.' Mullen shrugged and gave a fleeting smile. 'But he didn't want to listen, so I had to be more forceful.'

'You have money. Why didn't you pay the debt?'

'Because my da said he didn't owe it.' He could hear the pride and anger in the man's voice.

'What did you do?'

'I hit him. Only a few punches. Nothing too bad, broke his nose, probably a couple of ribs when I kicked him. Enough to make sure he knew, that's all. So he'd keep his distance from my father.'

'What was his name?'

'Some guy called Barney Thorpe. He's given my old man a rough time.'

Harper rubbed his chin, feeling the rough stubble against his hand. Thorpe was a man who made the honest part of his living buying and selling things. But most of his income came from lending money at high interest. Intimidation and violence were second nature to him. He was a man who'd relish his revenge.

'When did all this happen?'

'A couple of days after I arrived. My da told me about it. He had a couple of bruises and I asked him what had happened . . .' Mullen left it at that.

'Was this before Fess died?'

'Yes.'

'You should have told us back then. It might have saved all this.'

Mullen shrugged once. Harper stood.

'How did you manage to get close to Thorpe? He usually has a bodyguard.'

'It was in a pub. I waited until he went to the toilet. That's usually a good place to catch someone.'

Ash stood outside on the steps, still surveying the scene. 'Galt's gone to talk to Mrs Morton.'

'We'll see what she says. In the meantime, here's another name for you: Barney Thorpe.'

He raised an eyebrow. 'How did you come up with him?'

Harper explained, seeing the superintendent frown as he listened.

'I never heard a word about Thorpe taking a beating.'

'I daresay he decided to keep it quiet. Something like that would make him look weak.' He paused. 'Who's his protection these days?'

'The last I heard, it was Bert Jones. You know, used to box middleweight.'

'Bring him in; he might be easier to crack than Thorpe.'

'Very good, sir.' He pushed his lips together. 'A thought came to me.'

'Go on.'

'None of those shots hit anybody. What happened with the woman was a pure accident.'

'Agreed.' Harper nodded.

'I paced off the distance to the head of the ginnel. It's thirty-three feet.'

Harper stared across King Street. 'What about it?'

'Let's just suppose it wasn't Mullen with the gun, and those shots were *intended* to scare and not to hit anyone, sir. It would explain why he waited until Walsh was inside, to make it look as if he was after him. That's careful shooting with a handgun at that range. We both know it's hard to be accurate if you're more than ten feet away.'

It made as much sense as anything else in all this. 'I'd been wondering about that myself. It has to be someone who knows what he's doing.'

'A target shooter, or someone with army training, perhaps.'

'Don't the army use rifles?' Harper asked. He'd seen troops marching with the weapons on their shoulders.

'Not the officers, sir.'

An officer working for Thorpe? Maybe anything was possible. A man who owed money and needed to work off his debt, perhaps. Or maybe the idea was barmy.

'I don't know. You'll have to go a long way to convince me. Ask around. See what your informers have to say.'

'Thinking about guns led me on to something else.' Ash interrupted his thoughts. 'Do you remember early last year someone broke into Harewood Barracks, where they train the Territorials?'

They'd never caught the robber. He'd stolen Webley revolvers and a box of bullets. Nothing else. The police had scrambled around for weeks, holding their breath in case the weapons were used. But there'd been nothing at all. No hint of who was responsible, and the guns had never surfaced.

'It's a bit of a stretch. Do you really think it connects to this?' Harper tried to imagine Barney Thorpe as a mastermind behind a burglary. No. It wasn't possible.

'I've no idea,' Ash replied. 'But they both involve guns. When was the last time we had any crime involving them?'

Years; they both knew that. It seemed unlikely, but it was worth asking some questions. 'Grab Bert Jones and put him through the wringer. Bring Thorpe in too, we might as well have the pair of them. Telephone me at home with any information.'

'I will, sir.'

He walked into the ginnel, thinking he could still smell cordite in the air. Turning, he had a perfect view of the hotel entrance.

There was nothing else he was going to discover here; his men had already searched it all. At least no one had been seriously hurt. Tomorrow would do.

The car was waiting, and the driver turned his head as Harper climbed in.

'Home, sir?'

'Not just yet. Town hall first.' He needed to bring the chief constable up to date.

All the clerks had long since left for the night and the cleaners had taken over, bustling round with their dusters and mops. After giving his report he came back down the stairs, footsteps ringing off the marble, said goodnight to the watchman and was walking towards the Headrow when he heard a shout. Loud enough even for his hearing. He turned to see Galt running and waving.

'I talked to Mrs Morton, sir.'

'Did she admit she'd been with Mullen?' Harper realized he was holding his breath as he waited for the answer. But what was he hoping she'd said: yes or no?

'It took a little persuasion, but yes, she did. Just as well her husband was out. She'd never have spoken to me otherwise.'

'Do you think she's telling the truth?'

'She's got no reason to lie, sir, not with Jigger Morton's temper if he finds out. She begged me to keep it quiet. And she described all the scars on Mullen's chest. They seemed to fascinate her. She told me he has one right here' – he pointed to a spot below the collar bone – 'that's perfectly round.'

'Did she, now?' He thought for a moment. Mullen could have told the truth for once. 'Come on, in the car. Metropole,' he told the driver.

'Take off your shirt and the top of your combinations,' Harper ordered.

'What?' Mullen stood, glaring. 'Why?'

'Because I told you. Just do it.'

He had eyes full of questions and resentment as he stripped. Skin as pale as a ghost, a perfect canvas for all the bruises. And a tracery of scars all across his flesh. Puckered, healed holes, white lines from knife cuts. Mullen had taken his share of violence. His history was written on his body. A tattoo on his bicep that rippled as he moved his arm: a skull with the motto *Hello Mr Death*. There were more: a heart just below his other shoulder, *Mom* inscribed beneath it. A dagger. All amateur work. He'd seen better on sailors who'd returned from the East. Still, he thought, they showed who the man really was. He might own expensive suits and clothes and think he ruled the world, but underneath he was still the raw child from Somerset Street, desperate to prove himself, and he probably always would be.

And exactly where Anthea Morton had said, an exact circle, whiter than the rest.

'You can put your clothes back on.'

'What the hell was that about?' Mullen asked as he dressed.

'Proof.'

He frowned. 'Did you find it?'

'I think I did,' Harper told him.

*   *   *

He knew they'd ring. He'd settled down at home, just starting to read the paper, and the telephone bell gave its metallic jangle.

'Deputy Chief Constable Harper.'

'It's Sissons, sir. I've been questioning Jones. He claims Thorpe sacked him as his bodyguard just a few days ago.'

Now that was interesting. It made Mullen's story about Thorpe sound more likely. 'Why?'

'He won't say, but he doesn't look happy about it.'

'Keep pressing him. Is Thorpe there, too?'

'He's with Mr Ash.'

'How does he look?'

'Stiff,' Sissons answered after a moment. 'He's moving awkwardly.'

'Let me know what happens.'

'Is that the shooting?' Annabelle asked. 'I'm surprised you're not down there with the rest of them.'

'I trained them all too well. I'd just be standing round like a spare part.' He lifted the receiver and asked the operator to connect him to Chief Constable Parker at home to give him the latest developments.

A soft, pale morning. Some high cloud, a thin haze over Leeds. The car dropped him at Millgarth. Harper found Rogers and Galt in the detectives' room, writing up reports and looking as if they'd spent the whole night there. Unshaven, wrinkled clothes, and a line of grime around their shirt collars.

'What do you have?'

'The square root of nothing, sir,' Rogers told him. 'We hammered away at Jones for hours, but we might as well have been talking to the wall. All he'd say was that he used to be Thorpe's bodyguard, but he'd been sacked and he didn't know anything else.' He rolled his eyes and ran a hand through his hair. 'A waste of time.'

'What about Thorpe?'

Galt shook his head. 'Virtually the same, sir. Mr Ash did everything, but he'd barely even admit to his name.'

Harper had dealt with Thorpe in the past. He knew exactly what the man was like. He never gave an inch. It was easy to imagine him sitting there as if he was made out of stone.

'Sissons said he was moving awkwardly.'

'Very gingerly, sir, and he had some bruises on his face. He told the super he fell.'

'Did you hear the other story, that Mullen gave him a good hiding?'

'I did,' Galt answered. 'I believe it.'

'I don't suppose you got any names from either of them?'

Rogers shook his head. 'We're rounding up some of the other people Thorpe uses this morning.'

'Do we know who took over as his bodyguard?'

'Not yet. He was at home when we found him; there was no one with him.'

Harper pushed his lips together, then said: 'Ask around; he'll have someone. And I want Sissons to go back and look at everything on the robbery from the Territorial Barracks. Circulate the information again, including the serial numbers of the pistols. Maybe we can shake something loose this time.'

'Very good, sir.'

He took an empty piece of paper and began to write a list.

Fess murder

Arson

Metropole shooting

Barracks robbery

When he finished, he pinned it to the wall. It would be right there, whenever he looked. A constant reminder of the crimes they needed to solve.

Parker paced around his large rug as he smoked a morning cigar.

'What do you think, Tom?' he asked. 'Be honest. Is Mullen behind the shooting? Or is it Thorpe? I have to talk to the reporters in a few minutes.'

'I'm almost certain it's not Mullen.'

'Almost?' The chief pounced on the word.

'Unless he has some plan that I don't understand, then I'd say it's not.'

'How about Thorpe?'

'Honestly, I don't know, sir. Someone gave Thorpe a beating. If it really was Mullen, he'd want his revenge.'

'But?'

Harper weighed his words. 'Thorpe's way is usually much more direct. This all seems far too subtle for him.'

'Maybe someone's giving him advice,' Parker said. 'It would take plenty of planning.'

'Who, though? That's what I can't see. And there's also the question of who carried out the shooting. How's the woman, by the way?'

Parker sighed with relief. 'Nothing more than a bad scratch, thank God. The Metropole said they won't charge her and her husband for their stay. They're going to ask Mullen to leave, too. Keep on top of this, Tom. You've given me a little to tell the reporters, but I'd like to have it wrapped up today if we can.'

'No promises, sir.' It sounded more hopeful than no chance.

'I know, but . . . Arthur Blake, that chap who owns that furniture business, is putting up a reward of fifty pounds for information leading to a conviction for the shooting.'

Harper raised his eyebrows. 'That's a lot of money.'

'And we both know what rewards mean. Every chancer in town will crawl out from under his rock.'

Harper pushed up the window sash in his office. The wood groaned and complained, but finally it shifted, letting in the stink of the city and the noise of the traffic along Great George Street, and a brief draught of cooler air.

He settled to work, forcing himself to read documents. But the words floated through his head without settling. As soon as he turned a page, he couldn't remember what he'd just read. After half an hour he straightened his tie and picked his hat off the hook.

'I'll be at Millgarth,' he told Miss Sharp.

'When will you be back? You have a meeting at two.'

'Cancel it for me, will you? Rearrange for tomorrow or something.'

She pursed her mouth and lifted an eyebrow. 'The shooting? You need to look after the other things, too.'

'Yes. You know, you're sounding more and more like my wife.'

The day felt close and humid as he strode up the Headrow. By the time he reached Briggate sweat was dripping under his arms. Even in a light summer suit, he was hot, fanning his face with his hat. Everyone looked red and overcooked.

A turn through Kirkgate Market, where the fishmongers had their wares displayed on ice, did little to cool him off. When he walked into Millgarth, he was thoroughly damp.

Ash was in his office, sitting back and stroking his heavy moustache as he thought.

'Penny for them,' Harper said.

'At the moment you'd get three farthings change and probably feel cheated, sir.'

'No ideas?'

'Plenty, but they don't seem to lead anywhere. There's no doubt Thorpe took a beating, even if he won't admit it.'

'Would he have used someone with a gun to have his revenge on Mullen?'

'That's the part that doesn't fit for me, sir. None of the narks have come up with a name of a pistol shooter, and Thorpe's the type who'd want to watch someone being hurt and see the pain for himself. A gun is too impersonal.'

Harper nodded. He agreed; it was more or less what he'd told the chief constable.

'That leaves two big questions, doesn't it? Who and why?'

'And that's where I'm stuck, sir.'

'This mysterious third American?'

Ash chuckled. 'It would be a good solution, wouldn't it? Shame it's not true. Mullen couldn't have set it all up himself, could he?'

Harper shook his head. 'I've had plenty of doubts about him, but I'm convinced the arson and the shooting aren't his doing. What's he been up to today? Anything unusual?'

'Over to see his father first thing. The last report I had, he'd just been to Massey's bookshop on the Headrow.'

A reader. He wouldn't have predicted that.

'Keep people on him. Twenty-four watch, same as before.'

'Still don't trust him, sir?'

'Not completely.' He paused. 'And it might be for his own safety, too. Someone appears to have it in for him.'

Mullen's leather cases lay open on the bed. He was packing quickly, with sharp, angry movements. A few books sat on the table: Jack London, Edgar Rice Burroughs, Conan Doyle.

'I shouldn't have to leave just because someone takes a shot outside the hotel.' He stopped and stared at Harper. 'It had nothing to do with me. I wasn't even here.'

'One of those shots hit another guest.'

'I'm sorry for her,' Mullen said, 'but it's not my fault.'

'You attract trouble,' Harper told him. 'No point in denying it. It's what you do.'

'Not here.' He picked up a cigarette from the ashtray and took a deep draw from it.

'Where are you going?'

'I got a room at the Queen's Hotel.' He crushed out the cigarette. 'I'll tell you now to make it easy for the guy you have trailing me.'

'I'll make sure he knows.' He leaned against the door jamb. 'Tell me, you've been insisting someone's setting you up. Who fired those shots yesterday? And the arson?'

'I don't know.' He turned, his voice raised, arms wide. 'Maybe it was Thorpe.' He stopped and turned away. Then the words started to flood out of him. 'All I can say is, I didn't do any of them. I didn't kill Louis Fess, I had nothing to do with that blaze. Someone's trying to make me look guilty. I'll tell you something else: it scares me. And I don't scare easy.'

'Then we need to find out who's responsible.'

'That's your job,' Mullen said.

Harper smiled. 'That's why I'm here.'

'It's not me. How many times do you want me to say it? Now I got to finish packing and get out of here. The manager said they won't charge me for my stay.' He snorted. 'Generous of him, huh?'

Harper walked up King Street, then cut through to Park Square, standing in the small patch of grass in the middle. A few people were sitting in the shade of the trees, talking or reading newspapers as they ate sandwiches.

This felt like an entirely different Leeds from the one that contained Davey Mullen. It was respectable and solid, tethered firmly to the ground. And his job was to keep people in places like this safe from the rest. But beyond the sensational stories in the newspapers, most of them didn't even realize another side of Leeds existed. He shook his head, followed the path through the gate in the railings, back to the town hall.

* * *

Later in the afternoon he was out of the office again, walking through town. A light breeze was blowing, enough to take the edge off the heat and blow away the worst of the soot and smoke. For once, Leeds smelled fresh and welcoming. Enjoy it while it was here, Harper thought; it would move on soon enough.

He passed the market, hearing the vendors crying their wares, six for a shilling, seven for ninepence, then crossed the road beyond Millgarth and started down Somerset Street. The bricks were black with generations of dirt and soot. Half the cobbles were missing from the road. Nearly as many broken windows as shattered dreams.

Harper knocked on the door of number twenty-five. It stood out from all the others. The woodwork was freshly painted a glossy black. It was still clean and unmarked; that spoke volumes about how quickly Davey Mullen's reputation had spread round here.

Francis Mullen was a compact version of his son. A similar stare in the eyes, the same defiant tilt of the chin. But thinner, wiry, someone who'd never known any taste of good living. Half his teeth were missing, the cheeks sunken, white stubble on the skin. He wore a grubby shirt without a collar, the sleeves rolled up to show hairless forearms.

'You're a copper.' His breath reeked of alcohol and stale smoke.

'Deputy Chief Constable Harper. I'm here about your son.'

'Arrested him again, have you? Trying to set him up for something else he hasn't done?'

'I want to see if you have any idea who's trying to make him look guilty of murder.'

'Tried Barney Thorpe?'

'We have.'

He folded his arms and leaned against the door jamb. 'Then you have your man.'

'Maybe, maybe not. Any other ideas?'

'Some. But me and our Davey, we'll take care of them.'

'No, you won't,' Harper told him. 'The police don't like people who think they can take the law into their own hands. It's not far to Millgarth. I can easily have you bounced over there every day. Do you understand?'

The man shrugged, reached into his trouser pocket and brought out a packet of Woodbines. He lit one, blowing smoke towards the sky. 'I heard what you said.'

'Well?'

'All the names went right out of my head.'

Harper stalked away, keeping his fists clenched in his pockets. Safer than staying and taking a swing at the man. On the way back to the town hall he had a word with Sergeant Mason behind the desk at Millgarth. Constables would be dragging Francis Mullen away at all hours for a while. If he wanted to be clever, he could pay the price.

ELEVEN

'Things might be starting to shift, sir,' Ash said. He and Harper stood by the window of the superintendent's office at Millgarth, watching the late afternoon crowds flood along the pavements by the outdoor market.

'Why?' He felt a brief surge of hope. 'Have you found the gun?'

'Nothing so lucky, sir. But we do have Barney Thorpe's current bodyguard in a room down the hall.'

'Who is it?'

'Teddy Duncan. You must know him. In and out of jail for assaults.'

Harper narrowed his eyes. 'I think I arrested him once. It must have been ten or fifteen years ago.'

'You probably did, sir.' Ash smiled. 'Seems like half the force has pinched him at one time or another. Galt and Sissons are questioning him now.'

'Let's see what he has to say. From what I recall, he was handy with his fists but not too clever.'

'That's him to a tee. And we have something else, too.' He gave a small, satisfied smile. 'A report of a man buying a small can of petrol a few hours before the arson at your daughter's office.'

'What?' Harper asked quickly. 'Who? Where?'

'A garage on Whitehall Road. We even have a description from the chap who served him.'

'Well?' Harper asked. He could feel the hope bubbling up inside. 'Go on.'

'Nothing like Mullen, so he's definitely out of the frame for that one. Shorter, with thinning sandy hair, moustache, a little down-at-heel.' He shrugged. 'It's better than I expected, although he can't swear to it all.'

Witnesses. Half of them weren't worth a damn; they had memories like sieves. At least this was vague enough to feel real. But as Harper searched through all the faces in his memory, he couldn't match the features to anyone. Certainly nobody they'd talked to on this case.

'Any ideas?' he asked.

'One or two, but nothing exact,' Ash replied. 'Rogers is chasing them down with Walsh. Good practice for him.'

'We need the gun from the Metropole shooting and whoever fired it.'

'I'm doing everything I can, sir.'

Harper had telephoned the heads of all the other divisions. Everyone was searching, it was a citywide hunt. The reward would keep tips coming in. Most would be useless, but they only needed one tiny spark of luck. But luck had a habit of running off just when you wanted it most.

He stared at the list he'd pinned to the wall. Only four items, but it seemed like so much.

'Let me know what they learn from Duncan. I can't recall him well, but I can't imagine him as a shooter.'

Ash chuckled. 'He'd probably end up wounding himself if he tried. Good with his fists, a piece of wood or a knife, but those are his limits.'

A brisk walk back to his office. Miss Sharp had gone for the day, leaving a fresh stack of papers on his desk. Nothing urgent; it would all still be there in the morning. No messages shouting for his attention.

He sighed and walked out, down the town hall steps, patting one of the carved lions as he passed. A warm summer afternoon. It would be perfect if it wasn't for all the crimes. But when had a copper's lot ever been different?

The car crawled to Sheepscar through the traffic. Smoke and petrol fumes in the air. He sat back and thought, trying to find some answers to all the questions. But nothing matched up. By the time the driver pulled on to Manor Street, all he felt was frustration.

'Old iron,' a voice chanted in the distance. 'Old iron.' The rag and bone man making his rounds.

'Usual time tomorrow, sir?' the driver asked.

'Make it half an hour earlier,' Harper replied. Maybe there would be some new information overnight. Maybe.

The map was spread across the entire dining table. England, Scotland, Wales, from the northern tip all the way to the end of Cornwall. Harper studied it for a moment, trying to remember the facts he'd learned in geography at school, then walked through to the kitchen.

'Planning your route for next week?'

'That's already set,' Annabelle replied. 'I'm just getting a rough idea where I'll be each day. Oh, I promised to put up a couple of marchers for the night they're in Leeds. We have those two empty rooms in the attic.'

'All right.' They'd all need somewhere to stay. Why not here?

'I'll get them aired out.'

They ate a light supper, tongue sandwiches with some lettuce, tomato and cucumber, while Annabelle traced the path of the Pilgrimage to London for him.

'It's pretty much straight south until we join up with the women from Norfolk.' She moved her finger along a line from town to town. 'But there are marches starting all over the place. Carlisle, St Austell, different parts of Wales, Manchester. I'll tell you something, though; it's going to be huge by the time we all meet up in London.'

He could see the dream and the hope in her eyes. The wish that this might make a real difference and change the mind of the government. But the men in Westminster had become too entrenched in their position. To give in now would make them look weak.

'Where are you going to sleep on the way?'

'Anywhere we can,' she said. 'People will offer beds. There'll be tents. We'll make do.'

'You in a tent?' Harper chuckled in disbelief.

'I could manage.'

'I'd pay good money to see that.'

'Cheeky beggar. Just for that, you can try to fold that map up while I wash the pots.'

*   *   *

He woke early. A tiny breeze fluttered the curtains as he eased out of bed, but the air was still balmy and full of summer. Harper washed and dressed and spread dripping on a thick slice of bread as he waited for the tea to mash.

If there had been a big breakthrough, someone would have rung him during the evening. But perhaps some tiny glimmer of light had come in overnight. Anything at all would be an improvement.

The chief needed the shooting solved. He wanted to parade someone in court, to prove that the streets were safe in Leeds. It made sense; that was his job. Once again there had been articles criticizing the police in the newspapers. But the editors trotted them out every time something bad happened. The same words, just a few variations for the differing circumstances. These days he hardly noticed them.

Harper wanted the Metropole gunman, too. Far more, though, he was after Fess's killer. That was murder. Had Mullen pulled the trigger in that one? He still couldn't say. Not with absolute certainty.

If not Mullen, then who'd done it? It was a tangled, bloody web.

He tapped the hat down on his head and walked out to Roundhay Road to wait for his driver.

'What did you squeeze out of Teddy Duncan?'

'Not much at all, sir.' Ash's voice crackled at the other end of the telephone line. 'He said he didn't know anything, and I believe him. He's not bright enough to lie convincingly.'

'Did he come up with any names?'

'None we didn't already know.'

Another brick wall. Maybe he should have gone down there and questioned the man himself. But it wouldn't have made a scrap of difference if he had nothing to tell.

'What about the man who bought the can of petrol? Any luck tracing him?'

'Rogers is working on it.'

Nothing there, either. 'Keep me informed.'

Back to the endless piles of paper on his desk. Not even a meeting to distract him this morning. By dinner time he needed to be outside, to look at something that wasn't written on a page.

Walking down Eastgate, he felt as if he'd been released. Daft, he thought. No one had forced him to become deputy chief constable. He'd worried long and hard and talked it over with

Annabelle before he took the job. If he had any regrets, they were
his own fault.

At the bottom of the hill, he turned right. Millgarth police station
was no more than a few dozen yards away. No coincidence that his
feet had led him here, Harper decided, then stopped short as four
coppers dashed out of the door and began to run.

Two more constables pushed by him as he reached for the
handle. From the desk, Sergeant Mason was shouting orders.

'What's happened?' Harper yelled.

'Somerset Street, sir.'

He felt a chill go through his body. Where Davey Mullen's father
lived.

They'd already set up a cordon around the house. He saw Galt and
Sissons questioning the neighbours. Harper pushed past the
uniforms and through the open door into number twenty-five.

Francis Mullen lay sprawled across the floor. His blood had
soaked into a tattered rag rug and pooled on the wooden boards.
Ash stood over him, rubbing the back of his hand across his chin.

'Where's the son?' Harper asked.

'We're looking for him, sir. A woman down the street heard
shouts and a scuffle and went to find the copper on the beat. By
the time he arrived, it was like this.'

'Stabbed?'

Ash nodded. 'Stomach. Looks like an upwards blow. Might have
been a long enough blade to reach the heart. Dr Lumb will be able
to tell.'

'Barney Thorpe,' Harper said. Francis Mullen had owed the man
money.

'Rogers is already on his way to bring him and Teddy Duncan
in for questioning, sir.'

A noise in the doorway made them both turn. Davey Mullen,
taking in the scene and letting out a roar as he lunged forward. Ash
moved in front of him, and a constable grabbed hold of his arms.

'I want him outside,' Harper ordered. 'Two of you, and make
sure you keep him under control.'

'Having Mullen around won't make it any easier,' Ash said. He
beckoned to one of the constables, speaking and listening in a
quiet voice.

'That's the man who's been following him,' he said after the uniform had gone. 'He was here all morning. Arrived a little after nine. Left about an hour ago and walked over to Fairburn's on Boar Lane for his dinner.'

'Before anything happened here,' Harper said.

Ash nodded. 'Well before. I never pegged him for killing his father, anyway. Did you, sir?'

'No,' But who had murdered him? Thorpe? Someone else who wanted revenge on Davey Mullen? He stared down at the old man's body. It added another question mark to the identity of Louis Fess's murderer.

'I've seen dead people before.' Davey Mullen was pacing up and down Somerset Street. He'd walk a few yards, turn and come back. Over and over and over. He was smoking, taking quick, angry drags on the cigarette. Everything about him felt taut and nervous, a man about to explode into violence.

'I know you have,' Harper said. 'If the New York police are right, you've killed a few yourself.'

Mullen shrugged. 'Maybe.'

'It's different when it's your kin. Especially close family.'

Mullen carried on walking and smoking. 'Where's Thorpe?'

'We're questioning him.'

'I'm going to kill him for it. He stabbed my da.'

Harper reached out and grabbed the man's arm, turning him until they were facing each other.

'You're not going to do a damned thing. I'm sorry about your father. But this isn't America. We're not the Wild West. You're going to let us do our job and find whoever's responsible for this. You try to handle it yourself and I'll put you in a cell. Are we clear on that?'

For a moment the world became still. It was touch and go whether Mullen would draw back his fist and throw a punch. If he tried, there were enough coppers here to put him down and drag him away before he could land a second blow.

Mullen took a breath. It passed. Harper let go and the man pulled away, smoothing the sleeve of his suit.

'Don't go in there,' Harper said. 'I mean it. It's best that you don't remember him this way. And if you see him, that's what will happen.'

'Maybe.' He started to walk again, dropping the cigarette butt on the cobbles, taking out a packet and lighting another with awkward, jerky motions. All his style and smoothness had vanished.

'We're going over to Millgarth. I need to take a statement from you.'

A small hesitation, then a nod. They began to walk side by side, a uniformed copper trailing behind.

Pray God they didn't see Thorpe, Harper thought. He'd managed to defuse this situation once. He doubted he could do it again.

The room was bare. A table, the wood scratched and gouged, four chairs. How many men had he questioned here over the years? He couldn't even begin to guess. Hundreds, definitely. The guilty, the innocent, the witnesses and families; the list stretched on and on.

'Constable, bring us two mugs of tea, please.' Once they were alone, Harper said, 'Tell me what happened this morning.'

Nothing out of the ordinary. Francis Mullen was suffering from a bad hangover. He was listless, in a mean, foul temper. Finally his son had given up and gone to eat dinner.

'I needed to get away from him. If I'd stayed we'd have ended up fighting.' He ground out a cigarette and immediately lit another.

'Has that happened before? Fighting?'

Mullen nodded. 'A time or two. Fists. Nothing too serious, but . . .'

But a father and son coming to blows? Not exactly a loving family.

'You went to Fairburn's?'

'The place on Boar Lane? Is that the name of it? I'd never paid attention. Yeah. I ate and came back. You saw the rest. One of your officers was following me the whole time. He can tell you.'

'Did you hit your father before you left?'

Mullen stared. 'What are you trying to say?'

'I'm asking a very simple question,' Harper said. 'Did you hit him?'

'No, I did not.' His voice was even and cold. His face flushed, highlighting the bruises on his skin. He held up his hands. 'See, not a graze on the knuckles. Not even a scratch. I did not hit him and I did not kill him. Is that clear enough for you?'

'Did he hit you?'

'No. He wasn't in any fit state to try.' He shook his head. 'Do you know the last thing I said to him?'

'What?'

'He was still hurting from the hangover. I told him, don't die before I come back, old man.' The pain burrowed deep in his eyes as he looked up. 'I didn't . . .' He took a deep breath. 'Thorpe. He's behind this. He killed my da.'

'You don't know that,' Harper said.

'Don't I? He wants his revenge. He set me up on Fess, on the fire and the shooting. Now he's murdered my father.' The anger was rising again in the young man's face.

'Sit here and drink your tea. I'll be back in five minutes.'

A break might take the edge off the tension.

'Where's the man who was following Mullen?' he asked one of the constables.

'Over there, sir.'

'I want you to go to Fairburn's and make sure he didn't duck out and return through any back door,' Harper told him. 'Find out what he had to eat, too.'

'Yes, sir.'

Galt was sitting in the detectives' room, copying information from a file.

'Thorpe?' Harper asked.

'The super's giving him a grilling. Walsh has Teddy Duncan. They both deny it, of course.'

Of course. He didn't expect a confession. 'They'll have alibis. I want them checked seven ways to Sunday.'

'Yes, sir. Any luck with Mullen?'

'He's not guilty. We never believed he was.' He hesitated for a second. 'Not of this, anyway. He's about ready to explode, I'm just trying to keep a lid on him.'

'You can't blame him, sir. It's his father, after all.'

'I know. But every time I think of that, I remember how many people Davey Mullen has killed.'

TWELVE

Mullen had smoked two more cigarettes, the ends squashed out in the ashtray.

'You and Thorpe,' Harper said. 'When you gave him a beating.'

'I told you before.'

'Tell me again.' Harper smiled. 'Indulge me.'

The story was the same. One or two more details to flesh it out. It was the truth – he was certain of that. And very humiliating for Thorpe, left in a puddle of his own piss with his flies open.

There was no doubt that he'd have demanded his pound of flesh for that. But would he have taken it out on Francis Mullen? Maybe; the original debt had been his. And it would send a powerful lesson.

'We're talking to people who live on Somerset Street,' Harper said. 'We should be able to find some witnesses.'

'They didn't like my da.'

'Why not?'

'He was the type who'd pick a fight with anyone when he'd had a few drinks. He probably argued with every one of them over the years.'

'This is different. He was murdered.'

'People can forget what they've seen,' Mullen said. There was absolute certainty in his voice.

Of course, he knew it was true. The man had made it happen himself. And Harper had seen the effects of intimidation. But whoever killed Francis Mullen hadn't had time to threaten any witnesses. A little luck and they'd come up with someone.

'I'll tell you this once again: you go anywhere near Thorpe or anyone associated with him, and I'll have you back here.'

Mullen shrugged and lit a cigarette.

'Do we understand each other?' Harper asked.

'I heard what you said.'

'Test me and you'll find out I don't make empty threats.'

'What will you do then? Another beating? I got to tell you, Mr Harper, your guys got nothing on the New York cops. They *really* know how to hurt a man.'

'Do what I say and it won't be a problem.'

'Is that it? I'm free to go?'

'Yes, Mr Mullen, you are. You have a funeral to arrange. Just leave the police to do their business.'

The man gave a dark look as he left, crisp, quick footsteps echoing down the hall.

The constable trailing Mullen was waiting. Before he left, he said to Harper, 'He was in Fairburn's the whole time, sir. Had the egg and chips.'

'Good. You'd better hurry. And watch yourself. He's on edge.'

Harper stretched, then went into the detectives' room. 'What have you managed to find out?'

'We have a woman who saw someone knocking on Mullen's door at dinnertime,' Galt replied.

He felt a flutter of hope in his chest. 'Reasonable description?'

Galt frowned and shook his head. 'She only saw his back. Dark suit, cap, average height, not fat. It could be anyone.'

'Did she see him come out again?'

'She wasn't looking.'

'No one else?'

'Three women at the other end of the street. They saw people come and go, but don't know where they went. They weren't paying close enough attention to remember what they looked like. Sorry, sir.'

Damn it.

'Anything more on Thorpe and Duncan?'

'They're still being questioned. But you know they'll have solid alibis.'

Of course. If they were behind the killing, they'd have made sure of that.

He unpinned his list and set it on the desk, then took out his fountain pen and added another item before replacing it on the wall.

Francis Mullen

Nothing more he could do here. Everyone knew what was needed and they'd all be pushing for answers.

'Have Superintendent Ash telephone me later.'

'Yes, sir.'

He came out into the daylight, surprised for a second that there was so much more in the world than Franny Mullen's death. Leeds was still a loud, lively place, filled with people who bustled past and paid him no mind.

His stomach reminded him that he hadn't eaten, and he took out his pocket watch. Almost four o'clock. Too late for dinner, too early for tea. He walked back to the town hall, up Eastgate and along the Headrow.

Sissons would begin digging into Francis Mullen's life, trying to discover who might hate him enough to kill him. For now, though, Thorpe and his bodyguard were the obvious suspects. Davey Mullen was innocent. This time.

But what about Fess's murder? And who was responsible for the Metropole shooting?

'Well, Tom?'

Harper sat, holding the tea in its bone china cup. Chief Constable Parker watched from the other side of the desk.

He gave a quick summary of events and his interrogation of Mullen.

'Do you think it's Thorpe?'

'My gut says yes.'

The chief nodded slowly. 'And the Metropole? Is he behind that, too?'

'Honestly, sir, I don't know. It's like I said before – Thorpe doesn't work that way. He's direct and brutal. A shooting like that would be out of character for him. I want to bring in men from other divisions to work on it. Between this Francis Mullen killing and the Fess murder, Ash and his men have their hands full.'

'That's a sensible idea,' Parker agreed. 'Do it. But I'll remind you, Tom, it's the shooting at the hotel that really concerns people. They don't give a tuppenny damn if criminals start killing each other, but they start to yell when innocent folk are hurt.'

'Of course, sir.'

Parker smiled. 'And we need to make sure they have nothing to shout about.'

The man was a good copper. It was easy to forget sometimes that he was a clever politician, too, walking the tightrope between the law, the Watch Committee, and the council.

'We're doing everything we can.'

'I know you are. You're involved in it. That's good; things will get done. Don't cut any corners, but make sure we get a result on something very soon.'

'Yes, sir.' The only thing missing from Parker's words was the threat of 'or else'.

It was a long evening. He and Ash needed to brief the three detectives brought in from the other divisions to work on the Metropole shooting. Harper stayed close as the men read through the notes, then answered their questions. It was after ten when he finally emerged from Millgarth. Smoke from the cigarettes and pipes left his eyes red and stinging.

He blinked in the darkness and set off for Sheepscar. A pleasant night, the warmth of the day only slowly fading. A brisk walk up to Vicar Lane, then out along North Street.

Across from Jews' Park, a light still burned in the workroom of Cohen and Sons. Someone else working late. But it wouldn't be Moses Cohen sewing a suit. He'd died of a heart attack two years before. Harper had grown up with him on Noble Street, not a stone's throw from here. Now it was his oldest boy, Isaac, who ran the business, training up his own son to follow behind. Time passed, Harper thought. Soon enough it would swallow him, too. It would take them all.

He chuckled at himself and shook his head. For God's sake, couldn't he find something less bloody morbid than that?

'That man.'

Mary stood in the kitchen doorway as Harper poured tea into three mugs.

'Who? Mullen, you mean? What about him?'

One sugar each for Annabelle and himself, none for Mary. He sniffed at the milk. It hadn't gone off yet. A little in each cup and stir.

'Was it his father who was killed today? I heard about it.'

He handed her the mug. 'Yes, it was,' he replied after a moment. 'Poor chap.'

'He won't bother you again. I promised you that.'

'No. I suppose he has other things on his mind.'

'Yes.' A burial and his revenge, very likely. They'd keep a close eye on Davey Mullen and rein him in before he could try anything.

'Me mam's definitely going on this Pilgrimage, isn't she?'

'Of course she is. It'll be good for her. A break from Leeds and she can spend time with all the other suffragists.'

'To remind her why she's doing it?' Mary asked.

'That's probably part of it,' he agreed, bemused. 'And it's a big celebration. Why?'

She glanced up at the ceiling and moved her gaze around. 'I don't know. This place will seem empty without her, that's all.'

He laughed. 'She's hardly going to be gone forever. It'll be a fortnight at most. Anyway, I'll still be here.'

'Yes,' Mary answered, 'but you're out at all hours.'

'Not as much as I was. It's part of the job, though. It always has been. You know that.' Harper smiled. 'Your mother told me you and Len are buying the ring on Saturday. A big event.'

'I know.' He couldn't hear any sense of joy behind her words.

'You're not getting cold feet, are you?'

'No,' she answered. But the word slipped out too quickly.

'Go on,' Harper said. 'What is it?'

'I started thinking about the idea of engagements.' She pursed her lips. 'What's the point of them? If you're going to get married, why not just do it, instead of all the palaver and spending money on a ring? What good does it do?'

'It keeps jewellers in business.' But she didn't smile at his joke. 'People have always done it. It's tradition.' He held up a hand before she could speak. 'Don't ask me why, I don't know. I feel the same way about it as you. What about Len? What does he think?'

She smiled. 'He likes the idea of putting a ring on my finger.'

'He'll do that when he marries you.'

'I know. I told him.'

'But?'

'He likes tradition. He still wants an engagement.'

'Will it really hurt that much to do it?' Harper asked. 'Will it compromise any principles?'

'No, of course not.' She took a sip of tea. 'But . . .'

'I know,' he said. 'It's a big step.'

'Yes.'

He took hold of her hand. 'For what it's worth, only do it if you feel absolutely sure.'

Her mouth curled into a smile. 'That's what my mam said, too.'

'We both want what you want for yourself.'

'I know.' She leaned forward and gave him a quick hug. 'Thank you, Da.'

Then she was gone, and he wondered if it had been some kind of test.

'Is that tea mashed yet?' Annabelle called out. 'It'll be stone cold if you leave it any longer.'

*   *   *

'We've got something on the Fess killing, sir.'

'What?' He pushed the receiver close against his ear.

'It's not much,' Ash said hesitantly. 'Sissons was out last night, talking to the prostitutes who work the Dark Arches. One admitted she heard the shot. She was close enough to Neville Street to see a man running out.'

'What did he look like? Could she tell?' Probably not, but maybe there was some tiny shred of information.

'It was dark and she only saw his back.'

Of course. Their taste of luck didn't even amount to a crumb.

'Anything more?'

'He paused when he reached the street, took his hat off for a moment. She's positive he had dark hair. No spectacles.'

'I suppose that's better than nothing. But it's still not likely to do us much good.'

'I just wanted to let you know, sir. Rogers and Galt were out until all hours. The Erin Boys decided to act up again.'

'What was it this time?'

'Beating a member of another gang. In the end he decided he didn't want to press charges.'

'It's coming on time to stamp on the Erin Boys,' Harper said.

'Once this is all over, sir. Then we'll give them our attention.'

'Very good. How are those officers we brought in doing on the Metropole shooting?'

'They're going back and questioning everyone again.'

'Most of those hotel guests will have left.'

'They'll get in touch.'

'Remind them that we need an answer very soon.'

'I will, sir. And Davey Mullen has been quiet. Visiting undertakers this morning, then he went up to Harehills Cemetery.'

'Thorpe? Duncan?'

Ash snorted. 'If their alibis were any more solid, they'd be made of concrete.'

'Lovingly constructed?'

'Very, sir. One guess is that Duncan killed Francis Mullen after Thorpe gave him the order. We've been searching, haven't come up with the knife yet—'

'It's probably down the sewer.'

'—or any bloodstained clothes. Still, we're chipping away at their stories. They'll come apart and we'll have them.'

'Just make sure Davey Mullen doesn't get close to them first.'

'Don't you worry.' A small cough. 'Speaking of Mullen, how's Miss Harper, sir? Recovered?'

'Fully. Now she's worried about shopping for an engagement ring.'

'Women, eh, sir? But I hope she'll be very happy with her young man.'

'She will. Just a few jitters.'

He'd been working for an hour, hunched over his desk with the spectacles pinching his nose, when the telephone rang again.

'Deputy Chief Constable Harper.'

'Yes, sir . . . this is Inspector Warren from Scarborough. We talked about Miss Lenton. Do you remember? The suffragette.'

He smiled at the man's diffidence. 'I remember, Inspector. Are Special Branch still there?'

'They left a couple of days ago, sir. They didn't find much, kept getting people's backs up.'

That was no surprise. 'They can be a little overbearing.'

'I wanted to bring you up to date, sir. I was talking to a couple of men down at the harbour yesterday. It seems that not long after the time Miss Lenton would have arrived here, a rowing boat took a young lady out to a yacht.'

'Do you know whose rowing boat?'

'Already talked to him, sir. She told him her name was Miss Smith, and he had no reason to believe he was doing anything wrong. He didn't know the owner of the yacht.'

'Of course not. You'd better drop the Branch a letter with the details.'

'I've already done it, sir.'

Lilian Lenton's escape had been very neatly arranged. She'd be back, he felt sure about that. For now, she'd made Special Branch look like a bunch of bumblers. But if they found her, they'd make absolutely certain she paid for that.

THIRTEEN

Harper stood in the detectives' room at Millgarth, talking to the CID officers he'd drafted in. They'd made a little progress in the Metropole shooting: one of them was in

Doncaster, interviewing a businessman who'd been in an office above King Street and seen someone running from the scene. Fingers crossed for an exact description, Harper thought.

Having three experienced men able to focus on a single crime was a luxury. Usually, detectives were spread too thin, investigating three or four or five things at once. They were hard-pressed to do real justice to anything; he knew that from years of bitter experience.

'You're doing well,' he told them. 'Keep at it and we'll soon have him.'

He turned as he heard a noise in the corridor. Rogers pushed and prodded a man towards the interview room. Harper followed and glanced through the door. A man with fair hair, a clipped moustache and a pale summer suit sat, looking confused and worried.

'Who is he?'

'He's the gentleman who bought a can of petrol not long before the arson on Albion Place, sir.' Rogers loomed over the man, big and menacing, filling out his clothes with his neck straining at his shirt collar.

'Is that right, Mr . . .?' Harper said.

'Darbyshire.' He glanced up at Rogers. 'I told your man, I needed it for an experiment.'

Darbyshire sat a little straighter. 'I tinker. I try to make things.'

'I see,' Harper said. 'What kind of things might they be?'

'All sorts. I use engines quite a bit, which was why I needed petrol. Not a great deal, that's why I only have a small can.'

Harper raised an eyebrow. 'You'd better give us the details, Mr Darbyshire.'

'Yes.' He seemed flustered. 'Yes, of course.'

He was trying to improve the efficiency of combustion engines, he claimed. To make them do more work with the same capacity. He already had a couple of patents. When he started to wander into technical talk, Harper cut him off.

'You needed the petrol to test the engines, is that what you mean?'

'Yes,' Darbyshire said, as if it was the most obvious thing in the world. 'Exactly.'

With all his facts and figures and ideas, he sounded convincing. But so many liars did.

'We're going to need to take a look at your workshop, sir. That way we can be sure you're telling us the truth.'

'But—' The man began to protest, then closed his mouth and nodded.

'Give Constable Rogers the address and the key. He'll nip over while you stay here, sir.'

At the entrance to Millgarth he took Rogers aside. 'Give the place a proper going over. I know he sounds as if he's on the level, but let's make certain.'

'Very good, sir.'

'How on earth did you manage to track him down? That was excellent work.'

The man gave a broad, proud smile. 'Thank you, sir. I just talked to a few people and they talked to a few more. You know how it goes.'

He did, but it had rarely gone that easily for him. Rogers was going to prove a very useful addition to Ash's squad.

Harper was back in his office at the town hall, trying to draft a report on CID manpower needs for 1914, when Miss Sharp tapped on the door and announced Constable Rogers.

The man seemed to fill the room, to draw in all the air and light. A handy skill for any detective; he would intimidate suspects without a word.

'I thought you'd like to know, sir, Mr Darbyshire was telling the truth. His workshop is chock full of engines. All sizes. Never seen so many in my life.'

'Let him go, then. Give him an apology and thank him for his cooperation.'

'I really thought we were getting somewhere, sir.' The man looked crestfallen.

'Plain clothes is different from being on the beat,' Harper told him. 'This was never going to be easy to solve. Most of the time our work feels like running on the spot.'

'I know, sir, but—'

'Patience.' Harper smiled. 'You've made a very good start and I'm sure it'll stay that way. But you're going to be knocked back quite a bit, too. You might as well get used to it early.'

'Yes, sir.'

'Keep on looking. You'll find the right man.'

He might find him if he was lucky, Harper thought after Rogers had left. He just hoped the man didn't become too downhearted.

*   *   *

It was almost seven when he came out of the town hall. Evening, and the Headrow was quiet. His driver waited at the kerb in the Model T.

'Millgarth,' Harper ordered. 'Wait for me once we're there. You should have time to find something to eat.'

'Thank you, sir.'

Time to catch up on the day's discoveries. For the love of God, let there be *something*.

And there was. He could see it from the glint in Walsh's eye.

'Well?' Harper asked. 'Are you going to spit it out or keep it to yourself?'

'When we questioned Barney Thorpe, he claimed he was in a pub when Francis Mullen was killed. It seems that he might have been telling us a fib.'

That was enough to catch his attention. 'Barney? God forbid he'd do anything like that. Where was he?'

The inspector looked like a cat that had just found a bowl of cream. 'From what I've been told, he was visiting a lady friend instead.'

'In two places at once,' Harper said. 'A very neat trick.'

'Especially as his missus apparently doesn't know about *this* other woman.'

He thought for a moment. 'You've always told us you have a way with the ladies. Go and have a word with her. Find out the truth.'

'Yes, sir.'

'If she admits Thorpe was with her, ask her exactly *when*. After that, drag him back in and roast him.'

Walsh grinned. 'Gladly, sir.'

Perhaps this would break down Thorpe's alibi. Harper wanted to find Francis Mullen's killer. But there were still other crimes to solve. Too damned many of them. He glanced at the list on the wall. The Metropole shooting, the Fess killing, the arson, the barracks theft.

'Davey Mullen is the connection between almost every one of them,' he said to Ash. They were standing in the warm summer darkness by Harper's car; he'd stayed far longer than he'd intended. 'I know he's not responsible for them all, but he's the common thread. Since he came to town we've had a surge of crime. Why?'

'Some people are just a magnet for trouble, sir.'

'I don't suppose we've had any more reports of a third American?'

Ash chuckled and shook his head. 'No such luck.'

Bringing in a few detectives to work on the Metropole shooting was beginning to pay off. At least they finally had a good description of a man running from the scene: the Doncaster businessman who'd seen it had a good, clear recollection. But it was nothing like Thorpe or Teddy Duncan. And the witness hadn't seen a gun in the man's hand; it could just as easily have been someone fleeing from the shots. Nowhere, once again. Every hope seemed to break apart as soon as it took shape.

The shooting was still on the front page of the *Evening Post*. Just a small piece near the bottom now, enough to keep the anger simmering. He didn't blame them. People wanted to feel safe in their city. They deserved answers. Sometimes, though, the police couldn't provide them.

You had to be an optimist if you were a copper. It was the only way to survive when you saw the worst of a place, day in and day out. Or when you spent your time dealing with people who traded in misery. But you needed to believe that you could make things better. That the police could stop some of the crime. And you kept on trying, week after week, even after you learned that you hardly made a scrap of difference. There was always the faith that one day it might all change, even though you knew deep inside that it would never happen.

'We're at the Victoria, sir.'

The car was parked on Manor Street. Annabelle's motor stood a couple of yards ahead. How long had they been here?

'Thank you. Usual time in the morning. Goodnight.'

'You look exhausted,' Annabelle said.

'I am.' With a long sigh, he settled back in the armchair and stretched out his legs. Too many thoughts were swirling through his brain.

'Remember, Mary and Len are picking out their ring tomorrow,' she said quietly. 'You'd better notice it and make a fuss.'

'I will,' he promised. Annabelle knew him far too well. When he had his mind on a case, he needed prompting to pay attention to the ordinary things in life.

'I've been making arrangements to put up the marchers from Newcastle in town,' she said.

'How many are you expecting?'

'Doesn't look like more than a couple of dozen. The numbers will be bigger as we get closer to London. We'll hold meetings everywhere we stop.' Her eyes sparkled with anticipation.

'You're going to enjoy it.'

'I am,' she agreed. Her eyes twinkled. 'We've needed something like this for a long time. Some spark.'

Mary came out of her bedroom, stretching her back and flexing the fingers in her right hand.

'What spark is that, Mam?'

'The pilgrimage. We can get people thinking about the vote again.'

'Hasn't Miss Davison's death already done that?'

His daughter was right, Harper thought. It was barely three weeks since the woman had ducked on to the racecourse during the Derby to try and put the suffragette flag on the King's horse. Instead, she'd been trampled to death. It had shocked the country. But it wouldn't change a thing in Parliament. The government would remain hard-headed. Right now, anything else would appear as capitulation. Annabelle's Pilgrimage wouldn't have any immediate effect, either. But maybe it all chipped away at the iceberg, flake by flake by flake.

'Busy week at work?' he asked Mary.

'Steady. At least it shows no sign of tailing off.'

'Big day tomorrow.'

'I know.' She beamed. She must have come to terms with whatever was troubling her. He saw Annabelle turn away to hide her smile. 'I'm surprised you remembered, Da.'

'Of course I did. You may be all grown up now, but you're still my little girl.'

'Do you think she'll be happy with Len?' Annabelle asked once they were in bed.

'Come on. You've seen them together. They love each other. And she has him wrapped around her finger.'

'Yes, but . . .' She sighed. 'I don't know. By the way, I replied to his parents. We're going over for our tea on Sunday.'

No need for him to answer; it was already arranged and he had his instructions. Very slowly, sleep arrived.

*   *   *

'Stop at Millgarth before we go to the town hall,' Harper told the driver.

Walsh was already at his desk, looking fresh with a close shave and a clean, starched collar on his shirt.

'What did Thorpe's woman friend have to say?'

He grinned. 'I think she must have had a falling out with him. Told me exactly when he was there and she'll swear to it in court.'

'Perfect. Does it mean he could have been on Somerset Street?'

He shook his head. 'The timing doesn't work, sir. But it tears his alibi down.'

Harper sighed. Damnation. 'Have you had him back in yet?'

'He's been in the cells all night, sir. Mr Ash will be talking to him soon.'

'He might not have done it himself. But let's see if he knows who's responsible.'

Harper glanced at his list. Maybe he'd be able to score through one of the items.

The news buoyed him all through the morning. Each time the telephone rang, he hoped it might be Ash with news that Thorpe had given in and admitted he'd been lying. But it was always someone else, mundane requests and pointless conversations.

He was about to leave for his dinner when the bell jangled again. As soon as he heard Ash's voice, he felt his expectations rise.

'You need to get down here, sir. As soon as possible.'

'Why?' he asked. 'What's—'

But the line was already dead.

Faster on foot. Dodging and ducking through the crowds of workers out for their dinner, squeezing between traffic on the roads. By the time he reached Millgarth he was panting and wheezing and lathered in sweat.

A line of uniformed constables formed a cordon outside the police station, keeping the curious away. They let him through and Harper stood, staring the dark, shining pool of blood on the flagstones.

'Barney Thorpe, sir. He was stabbed. It happened when he came out with his lawyer, sir.' He heard Galt's voice and turned his head to hear him more clearly. The sergeant's face was charged with anger. 'He was sticking with his alibi, kept insisting the woman was lying. He had witnesses to back him up and we couldn't break it. We had to let him go.'

'How did it happen? Who did it?' The day was warm, but he felt a chill ripple through his body.

'Don't know, sir. Whoever it was must have been waiting. He ran up to Thorpe, knifed him and took off that way.' He pointed to the open market on the far side of George Street. 'It was all over before anyone knew what had happened.'

Right outside the police station. Christ. Davey Mullen. He'd already threatened to kill Thorpe. But that was impossible; he had someone shadowing him.

'How bad is it?'

'Couldn't tell, sir. But it doesn't look good. There was plenty of blood. The wound's in his stomach. The ambulance took him just before you arrived.'

'Witnesses?' Harper asked urgently. 'There have to be some. We're right outside a police station, for God's sake. Someone must have seen something. Who's interviewing them?'

'There was only Thorpe and his lawyer, sir.'

'Then he must have seen it all.'

'We're asking questions, sir,' Galt told him quietly. 'Everyone else is hunting the man who stabbed Thorpe.'

Harper sighed and nodded. He should have known. They were capable.

'Where's Superintendent Ash?'

'In his office, sir. He's coordinating everything.'

Constables were bustling around, coming and going, every one of them wearing a stern, determined look. Harper understood why. It had happened *here*. Someone had made them look like fools. No copper was going to forgive that. They'd keep hunting until they found the man responsible.

'It's a mess,' Harper said. 'A complete bloody mess. Right on our own doorstep.'

'I know, sir, believe me. But I'm afraid I've got something that's going to make it worse.'

'What?' What the hell could be worse than this?

'Davey Mullen slipped away from the man following him this morning.'

'For Christ's sake . . .' He clenched his fists and paced around the room. 'How?'

'I don't know yet. I only found out just before Thorpe . . . we're searching for him.'

'Mullen vanishes and Thorpe is knifed.' Harper spoke slowly and clearly. 'That's hardly a coincidence. Pretty damning, isn't it? And no positive identification of the man who did the stabbing.'

'We'll know once we find him, sir.'

'Let's make it quick for once,' he snapped. 'Keep a watch on the railway stations. I don't want him trying to get out of Leeds. We need to find Mullen. Meanwhile, gather every scrap of evidence you can.'

'Yes, sir. The chief constable has already rung.'

'I'm sure he has. Use every single man. Pull them off the beats if you have to. I'll be back at five. I want to see a bulging file by then. I'd like Mullen in the interview room, too.'

'We'll do our best.'

'It happened right outside one of our own police stations, Tom,' Chief Constable Parker said. 'Right in the middle of the day. And the man who did it was able to run off and disappear.'

'Yes, sir.' He'd given Ash a scorching. Now it was his turn to be flayed. 'They're on top of things.'

'They weren't when it happened, dammit.'

'No, sir.'

'Do we at least have a suspect?'

'Yes, sir.' Time to brace himself. 'Davey Mullen. He got away from the man who was following him.'

The explosion he expected didn't happen.

'Find him.' Parker's voice was cold. 'But keep searching in case someone else is responsible. Don't go putting all your eggs in a single basket. We've been made to look like blithering idiots once today. Let's try to make sure it doesn't happen again.'

'Yes, sir.'

'I want you based down at Millgarth until we find some answers. It'll be easier than shuttling back and forth all the time.'

That made sense. Being there wouldn't feel like a hardship or exile. More like a homecoming. Ash might resent it for a little while, but he'd see it was necessary. They desperately needed to clear these cases.

And every one of them revolved around Davey Mullen.

'I spoke to the infirmary,' Parker said. 'Thorpe's in surgery. The knife did a lot of damage. There's internal bleeding.'

'What odds do they give him?'

'Fifty-fifty. That's what the doctor told me. Until we get some good news, we're going to treat it like murder.'

'Very good, sir. What about all my work here?'

'Is there likely to be anything that can't wait?'

Harper considered the pile on his desk. 'Honestly, no, sir. And Miss Sharp can handle most of it.'

'There you are. Settled. Let's wrap this up quickly.'

'I'm here until we make some arrests,' he told Ash. 'Chief's orders.'

'I'm glad to have you, sir.' He sounded sincere. All around Millgarth there was a sense of urgency, of things buzzing. 'Do you want your old desk back?'

Harper shook his head. 'All yours. I intend to be outside a lot.'

'Very good, sir.'

'Have we found Mullen yet?'

'No, sir. We're combing every inch of Leeds for him.' It sounded desperate, he thought, and Ash knew it.

Out there, free as a bloody bird. Mullen had done it. He knew it the same way he knew the sun would rise again tomorrow. He'd stabbed Barney Thorpe.

'How in God's name could he get away from our constable again? I thought you'd assigned good men to him to stop something like this.'

'I did, sir. It was Constable Howard. He's as reliable as they come. He went over on his ankle and turned it.'

'Is that true or is he just making an excuse?'

'True, sir. I've seen it; his ankle's swollen. The best he could do was hobble. Child's play for Mullen to get away from him.'

Sheer bloody misfortune.

'Do we at least have a description yet of the man who ran off after the stabbing?'

'Nothing that's worth much, sir. Cap, dark hair, suit. About the same height and colouring as Mullen.'

Damn it. They needed something more. 'What was Mullen wearing when he slipped away from our man?'

'I'll find out, sir.'

'Thorpe's lawyer was standing right next to him when it happened. He must have seen *something*.'

'He claims he was writing in his notebook when the man ran up, and then it was over so fast he didn't take much in,' Ash replied. 'I believe him. I think he was in shock.'

'Question him again. He might have remembered something in the meantime. Is anyone at the Queens Hotel in case Mullen goes back there?'

'Yes, sir.'

Harper thought for a moment. His pulse was beating a furious tattoo in his neck. Thoughts raced through his mind. 'Mullen was going around with a few people when he first arrived here.'

'Dick Harrison, Bob Turnbull, and Liam Byrne.'

'Let's have them all down here.'

Before Ash could speak, the telephone rang. Frowning, he listened to the voice on the other end, then said: 'Thank you.'

He turned to Harper. 'Thorpe's out of surgery, but it doesn't look good. The surgeon says he probably won't last the night.'

'The chief wants us to regard this as murder. Sounds like he's going to be right.'

He talked to the men on the Metropole investigation. But even as he was speaking to them, Harper watched the procession of people coming and going from the detectives' room. Millgarth had an urgency he hadn't seen in years. But no one had ever been knifed right here before.

'I'll be late,' he said when Annabelle answered the telephone at the Victoria.

'Poor man,' she said when he explained. 'Do you think Mullen did it?'

'I'm sure he did.' Not a moment's hesitation in his answer.

'There's something wrong with him,' she told him. 'I thought so when he came here.'

'We'll find him. Is Mary happy with her ring?'

'You'd think no one had ever been engaged before. Making sure everyone saw it. We had to go to the grocer up Roundhay Road so she could flaunt it.'

He laughed. With Mary, that was easy to believe. 'Tell her I'm sorry I'm not there to see.'

'You'll have plenty of chance, don't worry. They've gone to Len's to show it to his parents.'

He stood for a moment after he replaced the receiver. He remembered the little girl who was always studying, who wanted everything she did to be perfect. How had she grown up so quickly? Twenty-one? That wasn't possible. He sighed. Then someone jostled him as they passed and he was back in the here and now, surrounded by chatter and people.

He took down the list again and added two more words. Barney Thorpe.

FOURTEEN

'**S**ir?' The night sergeant's voice shook him from his thoughts. 'There's a young lady on the telephone. Says she's your daughter and that it's important.'

Panic caught him. Mullen was out there. Had he come looking for her again? Harper grabbed the receiver.

'What is it? Are you all right?' He was holding on to the edge of the desk, clutching at it as if it could keep him still.

'It's not me, Da. It's me mam.' She sounded stunned. 'I got home from Len's and she . . .'

He waited, throat dry, trying to fight down the panic. 'What?'

'She was . . . it was like she didn't know who she was or who I was. She came out of it soon after, but I don't know how long she'd been that way before I came. Then she was like nothing had happened, just laughing it off.' She was silent. 'It scared me, Da.'

'What's she doing now?'

'Lying down. I think she's asleep.'

'I'll be there in a few minutes,' he told her. How? He didn't understand. He'd only spoken to her a few hours ago. She was fine then.

'Get me a car,' he ordered, then turned to Ash. 'I need to go. It's an emergency.' The apology lay under his words. He knew he should be here, but he needed to be with his wife.

'Anything I can do, sir?' Ash's eyes clouded with concern.

'No. I don't know. Ring me later, or if anything happens.'

Come on, he thought as the car sped along North Street. Wave after wave crashed over him. Annabelle . . . suddenly Barney Thorpe and Davey Mullen hardly mattered at all.

Harper sprinted through the pub and up the stairs. A cold horror spread through his chest. Mary was pacing up and down the living room. He held her close, letting all the fright and the worry flow out with her tears. Finally, he let go and pushed open the bedroom door. Annabelle was curled up under the sheet. Eyes closed, fast asleep. She was still dressed, her hair spread across the pillow. He stood for a long time, watching, as if her resting face could tell him what was wrong.

Harper sat with Mary in the living room. They didn't speak – what was there to say? The windows were open wide, but down in Sheepscar the breeze was little more than a faint whisper, a lick and a promise, hardly strong enough to notice. He had the *Evening Post* open on his lap. It was a grotesque parody of an ordinary evening. He was reading the stories but not registering a single word.

He stood and glanced in at Annabelle again. Still sleeping, peaceful. Wake up, he thought. Please. Tell me. Tell me.

Mary stared down at the rug, biting her lip. When she looked up again, he could see the fear in her eyes. Then he noticed her ring winking in the light.

'You bought it.'

Mary brought him back to the present. She held up her hand so he could see it properly. Even this couldn't dim all the joy.

'Len let me choose it. I didn't want to go for anything big. I know he doesn't have the money.'

'I reckon that one is perfect.' He kissed the top of her head.

'She'll want something to eat when she wakes up. Some supper.'

'Yes. That's a good idea,' he told her with a smile. 'We could probably all do with something.'

She strode into the kitchen. Doing something. That was her way of dealing with things. Better than brooding. Exactly the same as her mother.

He pushed open the bedroom door again. Annabelle was lying on her back, eyes open. She managed a weak smile. 'I hope I didn't scare you.'

'You did,' he told her gently. 'Of course you did. What happened?'

'Make us a cup of tea first, will you?'

By the time he returned, she was sitting up. Mary trailed behind him, standing in the doorway as he sat on the bed and took his wife's hand. The only thing different about her was the sorrow in her face as he looked at them.

'I know what you're going to ask, and the answer is I don't know how long I was like that.' Her voice sounded fragile, wounded. 'I knew where I was, where everything should be. But I didn't know who I was or what I was doing here.' She tried to blink away the tears. 'I could move. I could walk. Mary sat me down and started talking to me. I didn't know who she was at first, then it all began to come back.' She took a drink and stared down at the mug. 'It shook me, Tom. It really did. It terrified me. It was as if there was this huge blank area, like a fog, and I couldn't see a thing.'

She began to cry, and this time she let it trickle down her cheeks.

'How do you feel now, Mam?' Mary asked.

'Right as rain. Honest, I'm fine.' She tried to smile. Her mouth curled, but it didn't reach her eyes. 'It was probably just a blip. I was tired or excited or something. It scared me, but that forty winks has seen me right.'

She was talking too much, Harper thought. Too fast. Trying to make excuses, so it seemed like nothing. But it had terrified her. Maybe it really was a blip. But he didn't think so. And neither did she.

'You should go and see the doctor.'

'I'll be fine.' Her eyes flashed. 'I told you, I already feel better.'

'It would still be a good idea.' He knew better than to try and force things.

'Da's right, Mam. I know it's probably nothing, but please let them take a look at you and make sure.'

'Monday,' she agreed reluctantly. 'I'll see how I'm feeling by then.'

Sunday, but there was going to be no rest for anyone on the force this weekend. All leave cancelled, uniform and plain clothes officers gathered at Millgarth.

Harper stood on a box in the parade ground behind the building to address them.

'Someone thinks they can do what they like in Leeds. They believe they can rub our noses in it by attacking someone just a few feet from here. Is that how you want them to treat us?' He saw the bitter looks; even with his poor hearing, he could make out the undercurrent of muttering. 'Barney Thorpe is still hanging on, but we're treating this as murder. You understand that? Murder. You've all been given your assignments. I want whoever did this. So do you, because he's laughing at every bloody one of us. I want you out there, talking to people and finding everything you can.' He raised a hand to quieten them. 'There's one man in particular we want to question. His name's Davey Mullen. His description is posted by the desk and there's an old photograph. Look at it. He hasn't changed much. One or two of you know him. He's American and he's vanished. He's dangerous. He's killed people in New York. If you spot him, blow your whistle. You do *not* try to bring him in on your own. We don't need any heroes. Use your brains. Any questions?'

He waited, but there was nothing. Harper dismissed them, picked up his hat and set out for the town hall. The chief would be in, no doubt about that. Even the brass would be working today.

He'd meant everything he said. But it all felt like empty words rattling inside his head. Next to his worry about Annabelle, he couldn't care about crime and cases. First thing that morning, Ash had tried to ask, but he'd brushed it off. All fine now. A false alarm.

He remembered how Annabelle had cuddled up to him in bed. He'd put his arm around her, keeping her close. But he couldn't protect her from something like this. What good was a husband who couldn't look after his wife?

'We're supposed to be going to Len's parents tomorrow, aren't we?' he said.

'What about it?'

'We could rearrange it.'

'No.' She was firm.

'Tell them it's because of my work. It would be true.'

'We'll go,' she insisted. 'It's nothing. And we won't tell anyone about any of this. Just keep it between the three of us.'

A blip. Nothing. And if she kept telling herself that, she might believe it.

Mary had stayed at home; she hadn't gone on her Sunday ride with the Clarions. Work was her excuse, but they all knew the real reason. To keep an eye on her mother. None of them said a word. Len would come over for his Sunday dinner. Everything perfectly normal.

Or as close as it would ever be again.

                              *   *   *

'It's all horror and outrage in the newspapers,' Parker said. He looked older, careworn and tired. 'The London ones picked it up, too. I suppose it was inevitable. All the usual things in there – *how could this happen?* – and the like. We need something to give them, Tom.'

'We don't have anything yet. Mullen's still on the run. With the number of men we have on this, we should be able to turn up something today.'

The chief kept a steady stare. 'Should? You expect or you hope? Be honest with me.'

'Hope,' Harper admitted after a small hesitation.

'What else can we do, Tom? Is there something we've missed?'

'I honestly don't believe so, sir.'

'Then carry on.' He sighed and pinched the bridge of his nose. 'Let me know what we find.'

Before returning to Millgarth he stopped at his office on the ground floor of the town hall. Already it felt musty.

He picked a report from the pile on his blotter. Miss Sharp must have taken care to place this on top. It had been sent by Ripon police. The Pilgrimage march had stopped there. It was the day of the agricultural show and the town was filled with farmers and labourers. One of the men had insulted and tried to manhandle a marcher named Miss Ida Beaver. She'd landed a blow in retaliation and sent him tumbling to the floor. The police hadn't filed any charges, but they had asked the ladies to move on from the town in order to keep the peace.

He couldn't help but smile at the idea of a woman decking a big farmer. Harper folded the paper and slid it in his jacket. Something to entertain Annabelle later.

Harper sighed. The Pilgrimage. She couldn't go; surely she'd realize that. But he knew how much it would hurt her to stay in Leeds and miss the chance. She'd been looking forward to this like a child anticipating Christmas. Yet what choice was there? What would happen if she had another episode when she was out on the road? He knew full well what she'd tell him: see what the doctor says. This time, he decided, he was going to argue the point with her.

Leeds was empty. The Sabbath, and all the businesses were closed, the streets quiet; only a pair of trams passed as he walked along the Headrow. The sky was a pale, hopeful blue, the air gently warm.

A summer of murder. Two dead, a third barely hanging on.

Had he been so completely wrong about Mullen? Was he behind everything? Could he have killed his own father? He didn't know what to think any more. They needed Davey Mullen in the interview room and answering questions. Keep hammering at him until they were certain he was telling the truth.

First they had to find him.

FIFTEEN

The mood at Millgarth had changed. He felt it as soon as he walked through the door. Hushed, sombre.

He looked at Sergeant Mason, standing behind the desk.

'Thorpe, sir. The infirmary rang; he died less than an hour ago. Didn't regain consciousness at all.'

It was definitely murder now. Three gone.

'Any other word?'

Mason pressed his lips together. 'The superintendent's men have been hauling villains in and out. That's about all I can tell you, sir.'

It looked as if every spare corner was being used for interviews. He recognized the faces of men he'd arrested over the years. Petty crooks, a few of them with a reputation for violence.

'Anything useful yet?' he asked Ash.

'Yes and no. Plenty of words and hot air.' He rubbed his thick moustache. 'You heard . . .'

'I did. No sign of Mullen?'

'None, sir. We've had all his friends here; they don't know a thing.'

'You believe them?'

'I do, more's the pity.' He sighed, then smiled. 'But we've had one piece of good news, sir.'

'What's that? We need *something*.'

'Teddy Duncan turned up the minute he heard his boss had died. Gave us chapter and verse on the Metropole shooting.'

Finally. They had that something. 'Thorpe was behind it?'

'Yes, sir. Hard to credit, isn't it?'

Hard? It was bloody impossible. This wasn't the way Barney Thorpe had ever worked. And yet it seemed to be true . . . Harper stared out of the window and exhaled slowly. Just like that, the crime was solved. So simple. But that was how it happened at times. Things could turn on a word, on someone deciding to come clean.

'Teddy's down in the cells,' Ash continued. 'He gave your Metropole squad the name of the man with the gun.'

'Who is it?'

'Nobody local. Someone called Driscoll. From Sheffield.'

'Sheffield?' He didn't understand. Why there? Maybe there was no one in Leeds who fitted the bill, but . . . 'What about Francis Mullen?' Perhaps they could kill two birds with a single stone. 'Was Thorpe behind that, too?'

'Duncan still swears it was nothing to do with them, sir.'

He sighed. 'At least we have an answer on one thing. The chief's going to be happy to hear it. May I?' He gestured at the telephone.

It relieved a little pressure. It would calm the public. But there were still three bodies and no killer. And by evening, still no sign of Mullen.

He hadn't left Leeds on a train, that was definite; there was a tight watch on the railway stations. And his father's corpse was still at the morgue, waiting to be buried. Mullen would want to take care of that; it was family. He was still here. Somewhere.

Teddy Duncan had said that Thorpe didn't even try to contact anyone nearby for the Metropole job. He'd gone straight to this man Driscoll from Sheffield; Teddy had no idea how the pair knew each other. Before he left Millgarth, Harper had telephoned the head of their CID. Tomorrow they'd have the man in custody, the gun as evidence, and he could find out the details.

Harper stretched after the driver dropped him on Roundhay Road. He'd started early, and now it was late afternoon. He felt bad that he was leaving the men to work. But today he daren't be late home.

Annabelle was bustling round, packing clothes into a small trunk as if nothing at all had happened. Mary was sitting at the table, a ledger open in front of her. She flashed him a questioning look. He answered with a small nod; he'd take care of things.

He stood by the bedroom door and watched Annabelle moving piles of clothes. She truly believed she was going.

'Anyone would think you were off on your travels for a year.'

'I need to be prepared. If all you're going to do is mither, make yourself useful and get ready. Change your collar and put on a different tie. I'm not letting Len's parents think Mary's father is a ragman.'

Home, he thought as he undid his collar stud. Nothing like it for clearing the head and making a man understand what was truly important in life.

They walked over to Cross Green.

'We don't want to turn up in a motor car and look like we're putting on airs,' Annabelle told him. Harper didn't mind. He preferred being on foot, the easy stride he'd developed during those years on the beat. It gave him a chance to see things properly, to watch.

They strolled arm in arm up through the Bank. The area seemed strangely subdued, as if a hush had descended. But by the time they reached St Hilda's Road, everything was normal; maybe he'd imagined it. It was a street of well-kept back-to-back houses, each with a tiny front yard. At number seventeen, Harper knocked on the door. He'd barely lowered his hand before it was opened by a woman with a sharp face and warm eyes.

'You must be Mary's parents. Mr and Mrs Harper. Come in.'

They were shown into the front room. The furniture smelled of beeswax and the window shone. Being treated like royalty, he thought. A man stood as they entered, burly, broad-shouldered, with short hair that was starting to turn grey.

'Harold Robinson,' he introduced himself. The man looked uncomfortable in his suit and tie, awkward and constrained. As they shook hands, Harper could feel the roughness of his palms, as tough as old leather. 'We like your lass.'

'We're fond of your Len, too,' Annabelle said. That was enough to break the ice.

A cold supper of sandwiches and cake. The women discussed the wedding. When they began, Robinson raised an eyebrow.

'I've seen your name in the paper a few times,' he said.

'Don't believe everything you read,' Harper told him with a laugh.

'Nay, I've nothing against coppers. You knew Tom Maguire, didn't you?'

'I did. I liked him.' He hadn't heard that name in a few years. The socialist who'd organized strikes. A major political figure from

Leeds who'd died of pneumonia in a room with no food or coal for heating before he could turn thirty.

'I had a lot of time for him,' Robinson said. 'He talked sense.'

'Annabelle knew him better than I did. They grew up just a few streets apart. What do you do, Mr Robinson?'

'You might as well call me Harold if we're going to be related. I'm at Hunslet Engine, same as Len. Started out stoking boilers and taught myself a few things. I'm a foreman in the foundry now.'

'I'm Tom. That must be hot work.'

'It is. But I enjoy it. And Len's going to go further than I ever did.'

'He was telling us that the company might help him with a degree.'

'Yes.' The man's eyes shone with pride. 'Wouldn't that be something, eh? Can you credit it? My lad at a university.' He looked around the room. 'Not something I ever expected, I'll tell you that. And your Mary – she's made something of herself, hasn't she?'

'I enjoyed that,' Annabelle said as they strolled back to Sheepscar. 'That Edna Robinson, she has her head on straight.'

'They seem down-to-earth.'

'I think Mary's marrying into a good family.'

'No doubt about it. None at all.' He let a long moment pass. 'About you going to the Pilgrimage? I—'

'We'll see what the doctor says tomorrow.'

Monday morning. For most people it marked the beginning of a new working week. Not for a copper, though. Glancing out of the window on the drive into town, Harper felt as if he'd lived this all too often, that he was repeating yesterday, the day before and the one before that.

Millgarth didn't help. The Sheffield coppers hadn't traced the shooter yet. Nothing like starting the day with a dose of frustration. The men all looked exhausted, but there wasn't going to be much rest until they found the killer. Or was it killers? He didn't know. He truly didn't know.

At the close of the division heads' meeting, Harper gave his update, feeling all the eyes on him. As he finished, the chief constable said, 'Are we prepared for this suffragist march, or whatever they're calling it?'

'The Great Pilgrimage,' Harper said. 'Everything's in place. They're due tomorrow. Rally in Roundhay Park in the afternoon, then a bigger one on Woodhouse Moor in the evening. We have uniforms set for both of those and the march across town.'

'Do you expect any trouble?' Parker asked.

'Not from the women, sir,' he replied. 'There was an incident in Ripon, but they didn't start that.'

'Very good.' The chief studied the glowing tip of his cigar. 'I don't need to tell you, gentlemen, that we need this Thorpe business concluded as soon as possible. We have three murders to solve, and Mullen has vanished without trace. I want it done and dusted.'

He spoke thoughtfully and didn't raise his voice, but none of them doubted it was a command. The men gathered on the town hall steps, lighting pipes and cigarettes. Another sunny day, with the thin, oily haze of industry in the air.

'Much progress, Tom?' one of them asked.

'Not enough,' he admitted, seeing their nods of understanding. They'd all worked their way up from being constables in uniform. They'd experienced every obstacle themselves. Many times over.

'What next?'

Harper looked at Ash. The big man was restless, ready to stride back to Millgarth and get on with directing everything. The last few days seemed to have aged him. His face was drawn, the lines in his skin carved deeper and sharper. Worst of all, the bright twinkle that made him appear as if he never took the world too seriously had vanished from his eyes.

'We find Mullen. If any of you come across him . . .'

He had to fight the urge to telephone the Victoria. To ask Annabelle if she'd managed to see the doctor and what he'd said. But even more, perhaps, to check on her, to be certain it hadn't happened again.

'You can't be here all the time,' she'd said over breakfast as she looked at him and Mary. 'Neither of you.'

He knew she was right.

'Anyway,' she added, 'it's probably nothing.'

Maybe. He'd find out later.

*   *   *

The police in Sheffield finally found the man involved in the Metropole shooting. Simon Driscoll. The gun was still in his pocket when they arrested him. At least there was some progress.

'What's the serial number on the weapon?' Harper asked. The line was so poor that he had to shout into the receiver to make himself heard. Through the crackles he made out the answer. It matched one stolen from Harewood Barracks.

'I want to know who sold Driscoll that pistol,' he told Ash. 'Once we get him here, squeeze him until he says.'

'Very good, sir.'

He'd dispatched two of the hotel squad to bring the prisoner back to Leeds. They had the man, but now there were even more questions. Still, he'd take his victories where he could find them.

Davey Mullen? He'd found some rock to hide under.

'Have we checked every rooming house in the city?' Harper asked Sissons.

'All of them, sir.'

'They need to go back and do it again.'

'Have you considered talking to the newspapers? If they print his description—'

'We'll have more tips from the public than we can handle, and most of them will be rubbish. It's a idea, though. If we haven't found Mullen by tonight, I'll do it tomorrow.'

If.

He pored over every report until his sight blurred, hoping there might be some little detail the others had missed. But they were good, they were thorough. Nothing had slipped through.

He took down the list from the wall and picked up his fountain pen.

Fess murder

Arson

~~Metropole shooting~~

Barracks robbery

Francis Mullen

Barney Thorpe

One thing crossed off. It was a start.

Harper went for his dinner, leaving the others to work. The privilege of rank. In the café at the market he ate the beef casserole and dumplings without noticing the taste, lost in his own thoughts and the noise rising from the stalls.

SIXTEEN

H e was in Ash's office, talking to the superintendent, when Galt tapped on the door. His face almost glowed with anticipation.

'You'll want to come and hear this, sir. We have a woman who claims she saw the Fess murder.'

'Who is she?' Harper asked, but he was already hurrying to catch the others.

She was young and nervous, fingers kneading the handle of her reticule and peering anxiously around the room. Harper stepped back, leaving Galt to ask the questions. He had a gentle, reassuring manner, trying to put her at ease.

'Thank you for coming in. You said your name's Miss Milner?'

She didn't reply, just gave a tiny nod.

'You told the sergeant at the desk you saw what happened in the Dark Arches.'

'Yes.' She was hesitant, slow to answer, too nervous to meet his eyes. 'That's right. Will I be in any trouble? You know, for being down there.'

For being a prostitute, she meant. She'd taken a risk in coming here. Some coppers might put her in court.

'No.' Galt smiled. 'We'll make sure of that.'

'Only I haven't been able to stop thinking about it,' she continued. 'It wakes me up in the night. It's given me nightmares.' She turned her head to look at Harper. 'Do you know what I mean?'

'I do,' he replied. 'Telling us might help, miss.'

'Yes. I was . . .' She didn't need to explain. They knew.

'What did you see?' Galt gently prodded her along.

'There . . . there were a man walking in from Neville Street.' She paused, trying to find the courage to continue. 'The light was behind him, so I could only see his . . . what do you call it?'

'Silhouette?'

'Yes,' she said. 'That's it, silhouette.' Another gap as she hunted for words. 'I weren't far from the entrance, but he . . . he walked right by me. Didn't even notice I were there.' She closed her eyes. 'I remember . . . he didn't seem like he were, you know, looking for a girl.'

'What happened after that?' Galt kept his voice low and soothing.

'I didn't pay him no more mind. He wun't business.' Her fingers tightened around the handle of her bag. 'Then I saw something . . . it were out of the corner of me eye. Somebody moving. I couldn't see much, mind, the man who came in was further along and there wasn't too much light from the street reaching down there.' She took a deep breath. 'But this other shape stepped out behind him. Next thing I knew there were this big boom that seemed to fill my ears, then the second man was running towards the street.'

'Did you manage to see his face?'

'Not anything proper.' She hesitated. 'He went by so quick and it were hard to see in there. But he were quite tall.' Her gaze settled on Harper. 'About your height, maybe. But in his twenties, you know, still young.'

'Could you make out anything at all? His hair colour?' Galt asked.

'Dark,' she said, then stopped and began again, more slowly. 'Leastways, I think it was dark. But there was one thing. He had a scar on his cheek. The light caught it for a second. His right cheek. Just here.' She traced a line from the edge of her eye down to just below the ear. 'Like that.'

'Are you certain about that?' Harper asked. He felt as if he could hardly breathe. The woman stared at him, lowered her head and nodded.

'Plain as day. Only for a moment, but I saw it.'

'Can you remember anything else?' Galt asked gently.

Harper had stopped listening. He looked at Ash. The superintendent nodded. They both knew a man with a face like that. In his twenties and around the same height as Harper. It wasn't Davey Mullen.

'Robbie Beckett,' he said when they were out in the corridor.

'Exactly what I was thinking, sir,' Ash agreed. 'We've had him in for assault. I think he used to be a member of the Erin Boys. He never struck me as a killer, though.'

'We'll find out. Where does he live?'

'Somewhere in Harehills, I think.'

'Send Rogers up there with three big constables and drag him

down here. They should be able to handle any trouble. Robbie can
tell us everything he knows.'

Harper returned to the town hall to let the chief know what was
happening and check his own desk for anything important. When
he arrived back at Millgarth, Beckett was in the interview room,
yelling about his rights, as if anyone might care. He looked the
worse for wear, a scrape on his cheek and a bruise that would turn
into a shiner tomorrow. The left shoulder of his jacket was torn
and flapping down, giving him a faintly ridiculous air. His face
was brick red with anger, the white scar standing out, livid.

But one glance at his eyes showed the menace.

'We're searching his house, sir,' Rogers said.

'Many problems getting him down here?'

'Nothing we couldn't handle.' The big man grinned.

'I don't suppose he's broken down and admitted it?' Harper
asked with a smile.

'Not yet.' Rogers grinned again. 'Early days, though.'

'Keep at him. He'll break. He shot Fess. Take that as read. What
I want to know is *why*, and who put him up to it. That's the
important information.'

Finally, he thought, things were beginning to move ahead again.

Harper dug through the clutter in his desk drawer until he found the
card, then he picked up the telephone receiver. He'd promised
the man he'd ring when he had news on Fess's murder. *Charles
Armstrong, Third Secretary.*

'The American Embassy in London, please.'

When the call was over, he kept his hand on the receiver until
the operator came on the line.

'The Vi—' he began. 'Never mind. I'm sorry.'

Tonight, he told himself. Tonight.

With Beckett in custody, he felt the mood shift at Millgarth. The
sense of anticipation that something was about to break. But two
hours later, nothing had changed. Beckett still raged, though his
protests were hoarse now. And they still had nothing new.

Harper was waiting for the men to arrive with the Sheffield
shooter when Sergeant Mason appeared, moving quietly through
the detectives' room.

'We've had word about someone found beaten and injured at Roundhay Park, sir,' he said quietly. 'I thought you'd want to know, what with those women marchers coming tomorrow.'

'Thank you. See what details you can find.'

That was worrying. If there was a real problem, he might need to change things for the rally the Pilgrimage suffragists had planned for the park tomorrow. They'd be arriving in Wetherby this afternoon, a few miles up the road.

Ten minutes and Mason returned. His face was pale and serious.

'They've identified the man, sir.' The sergeant took a breath. 'It's Davey Mullen. He's on his way to the infirmary now.'

Mullen? For a second, it didn't register. But even when it clicked into place he couldn't make sense of it.

'How bad is he? Did they say?'

'I don't know, sir. He's alive, that's all I got. A couple walking their dog found him in the woods at the top end of the Gorge.'

'Tell Superintendent Ash. I want him out there and that whole area searched.' The Gorge was what they called the part of the park that was overgrown with bracken and bushes; finding anything in that would be pure luck. If there was anything to find.

'What about you, sir?'

'I'll be at the hospital.'

No need to rush. That was what he told himself. The doctors would still be examining Mullen. But he still hurried through the streets, crossing the Headrow in the fine space between a handcart and a tram and cutting through to Great George Street and the infirmary.

As he walked down the corridor, the scents of carbolic and illness seemed all too familiar, like the particular way his footsteps echoed sharp and clean off the tiled walls. He knew every turn, every room.

Harper had to pace for half an hour, going back and forth until he wondered if he'd wear a groove in the floor. Then the doctor appeared, lighting a cigarette and running a hand through his thinning hair.

'That's probably the worst beating I've ever seen. Quite honestly, I'm amazed he's still alive. And it looks like he had a bit of a hammering not long ago. But from all the scars on his body, Mr Mullen has been through a lot.'

'He has. In America.'

The doctor nodded as if that explained everything. 'He's young and he's strong. He'll survive, but it's too early to say if there'll be any permanent damage. It's possible, and there might well be internal injuries that will show themselves.'

'When can I talk to him?'

'You can't,' the doctor told him. 'He has a broken jaw; I've wired it closed. He won't be saying anything for a while.'

How the hell was he going to find out who'd done this?

'His hands,' Harper said hopefully. 'Can he write?'

The doctor shook his head. 'No. There are broken bones in both hands. They were thorough.'

He exhaled slowly. 'Can I see him, at least?'

'Not for the moment. We're watching him very closely. I'm not allowing any visitors for twenty-four hours. Maybe more. He needs time and a lot of care.'

'But—'

The man cut him off. 'Those are my orders. I don't care if you don't like them. My concern is with the patient.'

For a few seconds they stared at each other. Then Harper nodded. 'I want to find out who did this to him. You can understand why I need to talk to him.'

'As soon as he's well enough, I'll tell you. But for now . . . he needs rest. *Complete* rest.'

Nothing but frustration at the hospital. He rushed back to Millgarth. The men needed some victory to stop them feeling as if they were drowning.

'Beckett's confessed to shooting Fess, sir. Took a while, but he gave it up.'

Rogers sat back on the chair with a smile. He was the only one in the detectives' office.

'Good work,' Harper told him. 'Who told him to do it? He didn't dream up the idea of shooting Fess all by himself. Where did he get the gun?'

'He claims he was offered ten pounds for the job.'

'Who did that?'

'Bert Jones. You know, sir, the man who used to be Barney Thorpe's bodyguard.'

'Oh yes,' Harper said. 'I know.'

'Beckett says he was paid half before it happened and given

the gun. He received the rest afterwards when he returned the weapon.'

All back to Thorpe again. And he was with the undertaker now, beyond any questions in this world. This case was twisting in and around itself. He'd believed Mullen was at the centre of things. It was beginning to look as though he was nothing more than a dupe himself. Why? Where was this all going?

'I sent some uniforms to bring Jones in, sir,' Rogers continued.

'We'll see what he has to say for himself. Did Beckett mention the Erin Boys at all?'

'No, sir. Says he hasn't been a member in years.'

Maybe, maybe not, he thought. 'Are all the others out at Roundhay Park?'

'Everyone except Sergeant Sissons, sir. He said he needed to talk to someone.'

'Has the man from Sheffield arrived yet?'

'No, sir.'

Once more he took out his pen.

~~Fess murder~~

Arson

~~Metropole shooting~~

Barracks robbery

Francis Mullen

Barney Thorpe

Davey Mullen

He couldn't wait any longer; he needed to get to Roundhay Park and see where Mullen had been dumped.

Through the gate in the railings on Park Lane; there was nowhere closer. Harper followed the track. On any other day, this would have been a summer stroll through the park.

The area was thick with brambles and gorse, a valley with a small, winding stream. A rough dirt track climbed higher, then down again, until he reached the coppers at a small wooden bridge over the running water. Isolated, hidden, but only about two hundred yards from the road.

'Where was he found?' Harper asked.

'By that holly bush, sir,' Galt said with a frown. 'His clothes were filthy and torn. They must have dragged him a long way from Park Lane. We found tracks and marks. It's a fair distance.'

'Why here?' Harper wondered as he looked around. There was nothing significant about the place. Just plants and dirt. 'Why all the effort to put him *here*?'

'Perhaps because it's out of the way.' He hadn't heard Ash arrive. 'That could be a message in itself.'

No. That didn't make sense. 'I don't see it. If that was the case, they could have left him out in the country. It would have been easier. Or why not simply kill him?'

Ash took a breath and shook his head. 'Honestly, I'm guessing, sir. We haven't found a blessed thing here.'

'How's Mullen, sir?' Galt asked.

'Alive. The doctor says he'll survive. Beyond that . . .' He shrugged. 'Beckett's confessed. Said Bert Jones paid him and gave him the gun.'

Ash frowned. 'Barney Thorpe.'

'Exactly.' Harper took out his pocket watch. 'We'll get the truth out of Bert. I need to go and meet the Pilgrimage women.'

'We're not going to find anything in all this,' Ash said. 'I don't think there's anything *to* find.'

'Go back to Millgarth.' They'd be more useful there.

The road wound through villages, Bardsey, Collingham, plenty of others, before the car crossed the old bridge into Wetherby and parked by the police station. Harper desperately wanted to be back in Leeds. He wanted answers from Bert Jones and this man Driscoll from Sheffield. More than any of that, he wanted to hear what the doctor had told Annabelle.

A uniformed sergeant escorted him to the campground. 'Right over there, sir. We have a constable posted, but we don't expect any trouble.'

In spite of everything Annabelle had said, he'd anticipated more of them; up to fifty, even a hundred. But all he saw were around two dozen women, their faces brown from the sun. A pair of horse-drawn caravans were drawn up, two tents pitched, small fires already burning.

The curious had gathered, asking questions or simply looking.

Miss Beaver was formidable, short but with broad shoulders, and a crisp manner. She relaxed once he explained he wanted to make sure everything went smoothly in Leeds, and introduced him to the others who'd come down with her from Newcastle. They seemed like a cheery bunch, all wondering what they'd find the next day.

Miss Beaver eyed him curiously, then said: 'There's a Mrs Harper on the welcoming committee for tomorrow. Any relation?'

'My wife,' he answered, and saw their surprise. He decided to say nothing about the idea of Annabelle going to London.

The woman's eyes lit up as soon as she began to speak about the pilgrimage. She had the zeal and the fire of a true believer. If only it was that simple, he thought, women would already have the vote.

He stayed long enough to introduce himself and be polite. The marchers wouldn't cause any problems. On the journey back to Leeds, he tried to find some rhyme or reason in the jumble of Thorpe, Jones, Beckett, and Mullen. There was no thread to grab and follow. As soon as he thought he knew what was happening, the ground shifted under his feet.

And then there was the arson. He hadn't forgotten that; he definitely hadn't forgotten that.

'Drop me at the town hall,' he instructed the driver.

'I'm stymied, sir,' Harper said. 'We keep learning more, but I feel like I'm blundering through a maze. I thought you might have an idea. Something fresh.'

Chief Constable Parker took a breath and narrowed his eyes.

'It sounds like we need to know more about Thorpe, for a start. He seems to be involved in too many things here. We'd better start finding out everything we can about him.'

'I agree.'

Parker steepled his fingers under his chin. 'There are two things in here that worry me,' he said after a moment. 'The Metropole gun came from the barracks robbery. How?'

'With a little luck, we ought to know that soon. Bert Jones should be able to tell us. After all, he was Thorpe's bodyguard for a long time.'

'How many guns were stolen?' Parker asked.

'Four.'

'We know about one. If Jones has another, that still leaves two. I'd like to find them. The other thing is Mullen.' The chief rolled the name over his tongue. 'Any idea about what happened to him?'

'None at all. And he won't be able to speak for weeks. Broken jaw.'

Parker stared at the ceiling. 'What about the murder of his father?'

'We still don't have a clue on that either. As soon as we solve one thing, another two pop up.'

'You know what I'm going to say, don't you, Tom?'

He did; he could have given the short speech himself. The newspapers were asking more and more questions, and soon the Watch Committee would be joining them.

Parker had to say it; it came with the job. But he knew full well that Harper and his men couldn't magic the answers out of thin air. Solutions took work. They took time. And they needed a healthy dose of luck, the right break at the right moment.

From the back of the car, he watched the faces he passed. Ground down after a single day of work, walking with slumped shoulders. They faded from his mind as soon as he'd passed. Only one thing was important at the moment: what the doctor had said to Annabelle.

All he could do was hope it really was something minor, a tiny lapse that wouldn't be repeated. For God's sake, Annabelle was only fifty-four. A year older than him, and he hardly felt ancient. She was active, full of life.

The driver roused him from his thoughts. 'We're here, sir.'

'Yes. Thank you. Usual time in the morning.'

At the bottom of the steps he took a breath, not sure how life might change once he reached the top. But Annabelle and Mary were sitting at the table, chattering away and laughing like the closest of friends. It lifted his heart. She wouldn't be doing that if she'd had bad news, would she?

'I was just telling her some things I'd heard about the pilgrimage.' Annabelle's face was flushed with pleasure. 'I'll dish up the food.'

No mention of the doctor as they ate. Light, easy conversation until the plates had been cleared away and they sat with cups of tea and slices of cake.

'Well?' Harper asked. 'What did he have to say?'

She stared at the tablecloth, picking up crumbs and dropping them in her saucer. 'I told him what had happened. He asked me a whole lot of questions. Was I tired, all sorts of things like that.'

'What did he say after that, Mam?'

'He's not certain. It might be something and nothing.'

'What about going to London?'

She exhaled and he could feel her disappointment. 'He thinks it's best if I stay here.' She raised her head and looked at them. 'So you're going to be stuck with me, I'm afraid.' She tried to smile, but her heart wasn't in it. 'He wants me to see someone. A doctor in Park Square who specializes in things like this. Just to be on the safe side,' she added.

'Have you made an appointment?' he asked.

She nodded. 'I telephoned this afternoon. I thought I'd better do it quickly while I had the courage.' Annabelle looked from one of them to the other. 'Day after tomorrow at three o'clock.'

'I'll come with you,' he said.

'Thank you.' She squeezed his hand.

Driscoll, the shooter from Sheffield. He'd looked a sorry specimen when Harper had marched into the interview room at Millgarth late that afternoon. Bedraggled, weary, someone who knew he'd lost everything.

'When you took those shots at the hotel, what were your instructions?'

'To wait until your man went in, then shoot. Not to hit anyone. Just to scare them.' He had the clipped speech and clear tones of someone with education and money. A lieutenant in India, according to the folder lying on the desk. Qualified as a marksman. Medals for bravery. Mentioned in dispatches. He was in his thirties, a faded soul who was never likely to see good days again.

'Who gave you the orders?' Harper asked. 'Who paid you?'

'Thorpe.' He hung his head lower and took a cigarette from the packet in his pocket. He sucked down the smoke like it was mother's milk.

'How did you know him?'

The man blinked and tried to smile. 'I bought the gun from him.'

Harper tried to keep his face still, to hide the excitement bubbling through his system. He shifted the chair a little closer to the table. 'Tell me about that,' he said. 'All of it.'

He watched as a constable led Driscoll down to the cells, then walked back to the detectives' room.

'Jones has vanished, sir,' Ash said. 'Gone on the run. I've let every division know and sent out a description to all the men on the beat.'

One more bloody thing. Harper felt as if he could punch the wall. 'Someone told him.'

'What did Driscoll have to say, sir?'

'You were spot on about him. Former officer, Indian Army, cashiered for stealing from the mess. Down on his luck. Good with a weapon, thought he might be able to rob people or hire out his services. Someone tipped him the wink that Thorpe had some guns for sale. He bought the pistol six months ago. But the Metropole was the first job he'd had and that was purely because Barney got in touch.'

'So we have Thorpe for the break-in at the barracks, too.'

'Yes.' He felt tired, bone-weary. 'And we have Jones, who was Thorpe's bodyguard, hiring Beckett to kill Fess and providing the gun. Seems I was wrong about Davey Mullen being the place where the roads all met.' He picked up a mug of tea and drank. Stone cold. 'Beckett used to be a member of the Erin Boys. Anything more on that?'

'We have a couple of informers in the gang.'

'What do they say?'

'Claim they've never seen him around, so he might be telling the truth.' He shrugged. 'That's it, sir.'

'We need to do better,' he said to the men. 'All of us.'

He took out his pen and began to write.

~~Fess murder~~

Arson

~~Metropole shooting~~

Barracks robbery

Francis Mullen

Barney Thorpe

Missing pistol

Davey Mullen

Bert Jones

He was beginning to feel as if he was drowning in violence and death.

'How did it become so complicated?' he asked the superintendent later, hearing the frustration and exhaustion in his voice. 'We've moved from Mullen behind everything to Barney Thorpe being responsible . . . do you really believe he concocted all this by himself, all because Mullen gave him a beating?'

'People have done worse for less, sir. You know that.'

'I do.' He looked at the superintendent. 'But tell me this, then: can you really see Barney coming up with anything as devious as this? Where would he have got information on Fess being in Leeds?'

'I don't know, sir,' Ash said with a grimace. 'That's the problem. I wish I did.'

SEVENTEEN

D avey Mullen was stable, the nurse said when Harper telephoned from Millgarth. But he hadn't regained consciousness yet.

Shot eleven times and survived. Beaten and dumped and still here. He shook his head in disbelief. Mullen was the man no one could kill.

Who'd done it? Who had given the order? It couldn't have been Thorpe. He was already dead, and he'd bet a pound to a penny that Mullen had killed him. Who, then?

Only eight o'clock in the morning and he already felt the deep throb of a headache.

'Bert Jones?' he asked.

'No sign, sir,' Walsh replied. 'Absolutely nothing at all. I've sent a request to every force across the country. He has a sister in Bristol, he might try down there.'

Keep hunting. It was all they could do. He glanced at the list on the wall. It read like an accusation. His failings.

'Make sure they know he's probably armed.'

'There's one other thing we haven't discussed,' Ash said.

'The arson?'

'Yes, sir. I asked Beckett; he says he doesn't know anything about it and I believe him. But I'm positive it connects to Davey Mullen.'

'It does, I've no doubt about that. I bet we'll find Thorpe was behind it somehow.'

*   *   *

At two o'clock he was sitting in the back of the motor car, watching the landscape change as the vehicle passed through Sheepscar, Harehills, the woods around Gipton and beyond the new parade of shops at Oakwood, the stone still the soft colour of honey in the sunlight.

On to the Mansion at Roundhay Park, surrounded by acre after landscaped acre. Hard to believe that fifty years ago all this had belonged to a single family. To possess so much seemed wrong, unreasonable. But now it was a park, owned by the city, free and open to everyone. Soon enough the marchers would be sitting down to tea here.

He spotted Annabelle, striding around as she checked everything and gave instructions. She had a pair of raffia roses in the red, white and green suffragist colours pinned to her hat. But what made him stop and stare was the length of her skirt. Four inches off the floor, short enough to show a little ankle. It was daring, provocative. The other women had hems the same length, too.

The constables were strolling around with pleasant smiles. This was light duty for them. A few women were beginning to gather down in the arena for the afternoon meeting. Only a dozen so far, but plenty more to come and thousands were expected at the gathering on Woodhouse Moor tonight.

He turned as he heard a ragged cheer and saw Miss Beaver and the other women appear, marching together. They looked dusty and weary. Annabelle and Isabella Ford came forward, along with Miss Meikle. Every one of them in the shorter skirts, all with sashes in the colours.

Harper kept his distance. He was here to make sure things remained peaceful, nothing more. He stood out on the terrace looking down as women and a few men trickled along the path and into the arena.

'I thought you could do with this.' Annabelle handed him a cup of tea. And very welcome. His throat was parched.

'Everything going well?' he asked.

'Like clockwork,' she told him, then twirled to show off the skirt. 'What do you think?'

'It certainly caught my attention,' he told her with admiration. 'What's the reason?'

'Orders from the top. It keeps the hems out of the dirt and it's a way to identify us. A kind of uniform.'

Harper grinned. 'Very effective.'

Annabelle's face was flushed with pleasure at the day. He leaned forward and kissed her cheek, smelling the powder on her skin.

'Happy?'

'Yes.'

'How are you feeling?'

'Fine,' she told him, but a shadow passed across her face. 'I didn't drive. Took the tram out here and Mrs Marsden's going to give me a lift to Woodhouse Moor. Don't forget we'll have two guests tonight.' A hurried kiss on his cheek and she was gone.

There were no problems. About five hundred, mainly women, stood on the grass and listened to the speeches. Long before they'd finished talking, Harper was back in the car and heading for Millgarth. The case had been gnawing away at him all afternoon.

'Well?' he asked Ash. 'Tell me we have something good.'

The superintendent sighed. 'A possible sighting of Bert Jones at Crewe Station, sir. That would make sense if he was taking the train to Bristol, sir. It's a railway hub.'

'How long ago?'

'Yesterday.'

No help at all. 'Nothing on any of the other angles?'

'Not yet. Beckett and the hotel shooter have both been placed on remand for trial,' Ash told him. 'The day hasn't been a complete waste, sir.'

'I know,' Harper agreed. 'It just feels that way. Keep them at it.'

Parker had his office windows open, pulling in all the noise and fumes of the traffic along Great George Street.

'What does your gut tell you, Tom?' he asked.

'It doesn't, sir. That's the problem.'

'Barney Thorpe is at the centre of things, isn't he?'

'I hadn't expected it, but yes,' Harper answered. 'Almost everything leads to him.'

'Do you believe this tale that it was all revenge for Davey Mullen giving him that leathering?'

'I did at first. Now . . . no, sir.'

He might have believed that Barney had directed Mullen's beating. But Thorpe was dead before that happened, and he doubted that the man's reach extended beyond the grave.

'Then we need to dig deep and find out *why* he was doing it.'

'I'll put the men on it.'

'It's not as if we have anything else,' Parker said.

That was true. They were making headway with finding the men who'd committed the crimes, but they were nowhere on the identity of whoever had ordered them.

'It's not the only place we're stumped, sir. We still haven't managed to come up with anything worthwhile on Francis Mullen's murder or the way his son was beaten and dumped.'

'It doesn't look good, Tom.'

'I know that, sir. They're pushing, believe me.'

'What about this Pilgrimage?' Parker asked. 'Everything going off well with that, at least?'

'So far, sir.' He glanced at the clock on the wall. 'They should be close to Woodhouse Moor now . . .'

'You go,' Parker told him. 'Keep an eye on things.'

First, though, he stopped at the infirmary. The constable outside Mullen's room stood to attention as soon as he spotted Harper.

'Any change?'

'No, sir. The nurses have turned him a little to stop bed sores, but that's it. He still hasn't stirred.'

He opened the door and stared for a moment. Mullen looked so young, so helpless and alone. More like a broken child than a big man.

'Let Millgarth know as soon as he regains consciousness.'

The sight preyed on his mind during the short drive. Who would want to do that to him?

His driver parked close to the Adam and Eve statues at the bottom of the moor, where a jovial uniformed sergeant was giving orders to his constables and watching them disperse around the edges of the crowd.

'Good turnout,' Harper said. 'Sergeant Darnall, isn't it?'

'Spot on, sir.' The man beamed at being remembered. 'We've got two, maybe three thousand women here. All seems good-natured so far. They even had a brass band walking with them part of the way.'

It felt like a celebration. The first speakers were up on a small platform, the crowds were cheering. The early evening sun shone, so many women together. He couldn't pick out Annabelle at first, then he saw her at the back of the dais, grinning with pleasure.

He stayed for an hour, wandering around, keeping an eye on people who stopped to watch, especially small groups of men. One bunch began to catcall; a copper hurried over and moved them on.

It was all in hand. Soon enough, things would break up. The marchers would go to their lodgings. And tomorrow they'd be on the road again. Before he went home, though, he had to return to Millgarth.

His men were working; he should be, too. Lead by example, that was what Superintendent Kendall had taught him back in the days when he was still an inspector. What would the man have thought of him rising so high? Laughed, probably. Kendall had been dead for eighteen years, but Harper remembered him clearly.

Ash was still in his office, labouring over a pile of papers.

'Well?' Harper asked.

'Not a sausage, sir.'

The chief wants us to dig deeper into Thorpe.'

A small cough. 'Begging your pardon, sir, but I've had Sissons doing just that, along with the break-in at the barracks. That's why he hasn't been with the rest of us. Early days yet.'

They were working around him, not even consulting him first. Well, why not? They all had brains; any idea was worth pursuing.

'Good. Why don't you go home and spend some time with your wife?'

For a moment, Ash frowned, as if the idea seemed wrong. Then he began to smile.

'I will, if you really don't mind, sir.'

He looked at the squad, busy in the detectives' room. 'Send them all off. A good rest and they'll come back refreshed in the morning.'

Five minutes later, he had the place to himself, going over the reports and jotting down notes. A few ideas. The list glowered down at him.

The night surprised him, full of traffic and noise, the air warm with the smell of oil and soot. Harper set out for Sheepscar, relishing the time to think as his footsteps echoed off the flagstones. By the time he reached the Victoria, he'd settled on a plan. At least he had something to begin the morning.

Annabelle and Mary sat at the table with two other women. He joined them, but not for long. A day of tramping the roads had left the marchers exhausted. All they wanted was a good wash and a long sleep.

Soon enough, Harper settled in bed next to his wife. Her head rested on his chest, hair tickling his neck. So familiar, so comforting.

'A good day?' he asked.

'Wonderful.' He could hear the pleasure in her voice.

'I know you wanted to go on—'

'Let's not talk about it,' she said. It was like a door slamming shut.

'All right.'

'I understand it's for the best,' Annabelle said, 'but . . .'

But it hurt. She'd built up the Pilgrimage in her mind, she desperately wanted to set off with the other marchers. Now life had snatched it away from her.

'I'll see them off in the morning.'

A long kiss then she rolled away to sleep.

Harper turned the crank on the Rex and stepped back sharply as the engine caught. Annabelle adjusted something on the dash and the motor's roar became an easy purr.

The women they'd put up were crammed in beside her. A smile and a wave and the car glided down the street. A short drive to Woodhouse Moor to drop them off, then back again.

'She's putting on a brave face,' Mary said.

'I know.'

'The thing is, it won't make a difference,' she said. 'They won't change the country with marches and speeches. It needs action.'

'Do you want a lift into town? My driver's here.'

EIGHTEEN

Harper leaned against the wall in Ash's office. Out on the parade ground, a sergeant was drilling constables. It looked handsome enough to watch, but for the life of him he'd never understood what it had to do with being a copper.

'Barney Thorpe,' he said. 'How much do we really know about him?'

'He had a wife and a girlfriend,' Walsh answered.

'He had his business buying and selling tat for what, fifteen years, sir?' Ash asked.

'Must be close to that,' Harper agreed. 'But we all know it was moneylending that put the brass in his pocket.'

'And he was vicious with people who didn't repay on time,' Galt said.

'You're working on it, Sissons. What else have you found?'

'Just getting started, sir.'

'Fess was killed for a reason. We know that. There was nothing random about that. It was a deliberate execution.'

'Until we catch Bert Jones we're not likely to know what that reason was, though,' Rogers said. 'I telephoned Bristol first thing this morning. They still don't have a lead on him.'

'Did Jones ever do any outside jobs when he worked for Thorpe?' Harper asked.

'None that I ever heard about.' Ash shook his head.

'So he was probably under Thorpe's orders. Why would he go after Fess?'

'The beating Davey Mullen gave Barney?' Rogers suggested.

'I don't believe that,' Harper said. It was the only reason they had, but it didn't sit right. He couldn't square it with his knowledge of Thorpe. 'But that means Barney knew *exactly* who Fess was and who we'd look at for the killing. Think about that for a moment. Any way you look at it, Mullen was set up.'

'Didn't the killing happen the night Mullen turned up at the Victoria with a gun, sir?' Walsh asked.

'It did.'

'Did we ever learn where he'd got it?'

'He said he'd brought it from America.'

Sissons stirred on his chair, looking thoughtful. 'Something I'd wondered was whether Thorpe might have been directly involved in the robbery at Harewood Barracks. The Metropole shooter's gun came from there, and he bought it from Thorpe.'

'Barney's dead. Too late to ask him now,' Harper said.

Ash had been silent the whole time. Now he looked up and said, 'Unless I've missed an awful lot, I've never heard any mention of Barney Thorpe in the same breath as a break-in. Starting out with something like the barracks doesn't sound right to me. It wasn't him.'

No. Buying and selling, violence and intimidation were Thorpe's tools. The robbery at the barracks would be far beyond Barney's skills.

'Who did it, then?' Harper asked.

'It leaves us right back where we began, sir. We never did get a whisper on it.'

'I know Teddy Duncan was only Thorpe's bodyguard for a very short time at the end, but bring him back and see what he says about all this. He told us a lot last time. He might know more.'

Ash nodded and Rogers left the room.

'Keep your minds open. And I still want to know who was responsible for that arson. It fits in with all this somewhere.'

'I still can't picture Barney Thorpe as some sort of criminal mastermind,' Ash said once the men had gone. He snorted his disbelief.

'Maybe he fooled us all,' Harper said. He pulled out his pocket watch. 'I need to make sure the Pilgrimage leaves without a hitch.'

'Is Mrs Harper going with them, sir?'

'No. She's decided to stay at home.' No reason for anyone to know why.

Ash raised an eyebrow but said nothing. 'I've read it's going to be big. Nancy saw a piece in one of the magazines.'

'That's what the women hope, anyway. Thousands of them in London.'

They were assembled on Woodhouse Moor, quite a few more of them than had arrived the day before; sixty or seventy, from the look of it. The marchers at the front looked refreshed, carrying their banners high.

Annabelle was striding around, wishing people well. She was wearing a new hat, a straw boater decorated with the red, green and white suffrage rosette.

'I'll walk into town with them to see them off then come back here and drive home. And this afternoon . . .'

The specialist.

A band struck up and the marchers began to move off.

'That's my cue.' A peck on the cheek and she hurried off as if nothing in the world was wrong.

Harper waited until the pilgrimage was out of sight, then told his driver, 'Millgarth.'

*   *   *

'Teddy Duncan is in the interview room, sir,' Walsh said. 'I thought you'd want to talk to him yourself.'

The man was hunched over, drawing deep on a cigarette cupped in his hand. He was dressed in his grubby prison uniform, and his face was haggard. His skin already had deep lines and a jail pallor.

'Enjoying Armley?' Harper asked as he sat on the other side of the table and glanced at the contents of the folder.

Duncan shrugged his reply.

'On remand for the obstruction of justice and perverting the course of justice.' He read out the charges. 'Lying to the police is never a good idea, Teddy.'

'I told you the truth as soon as Barney was dead.'

'I know you did, Teddy, and that's the problem. You have to tell us when we ask, not when it's convenient for you. You'll be spending quite a bit more time inside after your day in court.'

'I've been in prison before.'

'It gets harder as you grow older, though, doesn't it?' He watched the man's face. A few days without freedom and he looked trapped and wary. 'Wouldn't it be something if one of those charges was reduced or vanished altogether?'

Duncan's head snapped up. 'What do you mean?'

'Some co-operation. Plenty of honesty. I'm not going to lie and say you'll walk out of here a free man, but you help me and I'll put in a good word for you.'

Duncan's eyes narrowed. 'Give me a reason to trust you.'

'It's up to you.' Harper sat back. 'I'm going to ask my questions, anyway. You know I have the power to help you. It's as simple as that.'

He dangled it like bait. Harper had read the report from Armley on Teddy Duncan. He wasn't the type of old lag who fitted easily into the prison system. He'd survive, but that was all. The type who might clutch at a lifebelt. Maybe a little prodding to start him on his way.

'Go on, then. Ask. Maybe I'll answer.'

'How long did you work for Barney Thorpe?'

'Not even a week. You know that. He took me on after he got rid of Bert Jones.'

Not long enough to scratch the surface of Thorpe's businesses and contacts.

'Who else did Barney work with?'

'What do you mean?' Duncan frowned. 'He had the business and the moneylending. Everyone knows that.'

'He couldn't do it all himself. He must have had meetings with other groups, other people.'

'I don't know.' Duncan frowned again. 'He had dinner with a couple of businessmen while I was with him. That was it.'

'Nothing on the Bank?'

'The Bank?' He blinked in disbelief. 'What are you talking about? There's no money up there. I wasn't with Barney long, but I know he liked his brass.' Duncan shook his head. 'Anyway, there's that gang on the Bank.'

'The Erin Boys.'

Duncan nodded. 'Yes. Them.'

'They work with other people sometimes.'

'Not with Barney. Not while I was with him, any road. I don't see why they would. He didn't have a scrap of Irish blood in him.'

'He never mentioned them?'

'Not to me.' He swallowed. 'If we're going to keep talking, can I have a cup of tea? My throat's as rough as a cinder path.'

Harper nodded at the constable. As soon as the door closed, Duncan leaned forward.

'Are you being straight with all this? If I tell you some stuff, you'll help me?'

'That's what I said. I wasn't lying. Why?'

'There's something, but it's just between you and me. I don't want people to know I heard it.' He laid a finger along the side of his nose. 'Understand?'

'Why? Is it so dangerous?'

'Guns.'

A single word, more than enough to claim Harper's attention. He tried to keep his voice even and indifferent. His mouth was dry and he scarcely dared to breathe. 'Go on.'

'A man came, the day before he died. I didn't know him, and Barney told me to stand outside, make sure no one disturbed them. But the door didn't close properly, so I could hear them.'

'Was this the office or his house?'

'Office.'

'What did they say?' Harper asked. This was what he'd been hoping for; he could feel it. But he couldn't let Duncan realize that. He couldn't give him any lever, any advantage.

'This other bloke wanted to buy a gun. A pistol. The way he talked, he knew Barney sold them, like it was a quarter of tea from the shop or something.'

'Had you seen him before?'

Duncan shook his head. 'He wasn't from round here. Sounded Geordie, that accent they have.'

He sat back quickly as the door opened and the constable returned with a mug of tea.

'Thank you,' Harper told the bobby. 'Can you leave us for a few minutes, please?'

'Sir? Regulations—'

'I know.' He smiled. 'Just wait outside the door until I shout.'

'Very good, sir,' he agreed cautiously. A final, worried look and he left.

'This man,' Harper said to Duncan.

'Barney told him he only had one gun left.'

'One? You're absolutely certain of that?' he pressed.

'Cross my heart and hope to die. They went back and forth, but they couldn't settle on a price. The man didn't want to shell out what Barney was asking.'

'Did he say what type of gun?' Harper's mind was racing.

'A Webley. That's all I know. Couldn't tell one from another myself and I wouldn't go near them.'

'Did they reach an agreement in the end?'

'No.' He gulped at the tea. 'He left with nothing. Barney never mentioned it. And next day he was . . . well, you know.'

'How did Thorpe come to know the man who did the Metropole shooting?'

'No idea. He already knew him. I've told you all this before.'

Another five minutes brought a reasonable description of the Geordie, but Duncan had given him everything important.

The warder from Armley waited by the door. 'Will you really put in a word?' Duncan asked as he stood.

'I will.'

A nod. 'Right.' Then he was gone.

The squad gathered at twelve.

'Things have changed,' Harper told them. '*Every* bloody thing has changed. That speculation about Barney Thorpe and guns was correct. According to Teddy Duncan, he was selling Webleys. He told his mysterious buyer he had one left.' He counted the stolen weapons off on his fingers. 'There's one waiting to be sold. The Metropole shooter had one. Bert Jones is running around with a pistol, and I'll bet a pound to a penny that's the third.' He looked from face to face. 'Four were taken.'

'He could have already sold one,' Rogers said.

'I know. But we'd better hope not, because it means someone out there has it.' He gave time for that to sink in. 'Anyone have any ideas on a Geordie who'd want a gun?'

They shook their heads.

'I'll punt that up to Newcastle,' Harper said. 'They might know him.'

The telephone rang in Ash's office and he hurried off to answer it. He returned and stood with his thumbs in his waistcoat pocket, waiting until all the others were staring at him.

'That was the infirmary. Davey Mullen has regained consciousness.'

'I'll go down there,' Harper said. 'The rest of you try to work your way through this labyrinth.'

'Maybe I was wrong about Thorpe,' Ash said. 'He might have had more brains than I thought.'

'Possibly. I wish to God I knew.'

NINETEEN

With a broken jaw, Mullen couldn't talk. His hands were in plaster; he couldn't hold a pen. But there might be *some* way to communicate, a method for him to give answers to the questions roaring around Harper's skull: too bloody many of them, that was the problem. First, he needed to hammer them into some kind of order.

The Headrow was clogged with people and vehicles. It seemed to grow worse each month. Fumes from car exhausts competed with smoke from the factories. He coughed. Somewhere above it all was the sun.

Mullen tried to smile. In the end, he winced. Wires wrapped his jaw and plaster covered his arms all the way to the elbow. His flesh was bruised and battered, turning a brilliant rainbow of colours where it wasn't cut and scraped a raw, bloody red.

Yet the eyes were very much alive, flickering between fierceness and amusement.

'I'm glad to see you're still with us,' Harper said. He had too many reasons to dislike the man, but he was impressed with his determination in clinging to life.

A blink and the briefest of nods in reply.

'I know you're not able to speak, but do you know who did this to you?'

Another slight nod.

'Did they have anything to do with Barney Thorpe? I'm sure you remember him.'

No movement at all. Mullen gazed at the ceiling.

'I don't know if you heard: he died not long after you slipped away from the coppers following you. I don't suppose you'd know anything about what happened to him?'

He might as well have been talking to the wall.

The ward sister bustled in, the matron hard on her heels.

'Mr Mullen needs rest, deputy chief constable.' It wasn't a comment, it was an order, and in a hospital the matron's word was law. No point in arguing or resisting. At the door he looked back. For just a second he believed that Mullen had winked.

'I don't care if you want to talk to him,' the doctor said. 'My concern is the patient. His jaw will have to be wired shut for six weeks so it can heal.'

'And the plaster casts?' Harper asked.

'About the same length of time.' The man ran a hand through his hair. He was young, stoop-shouldered and weary, a stethoscope hanging round his neck, his tweed jacket flecked with dark stains. 'He might be able to talk a little, a *very* little, before then. But I'm going to insist that you have matron's permission for any police visit. Is that understood?'

'Yes,' Harper agreed reluctantly. How the hell was he supposed to discover who'd given Mullen his beating when he couldn't even talk to the man? He needed names, he needed evidence, and the doctor had cut off his best chance of finding them.

On the way back to Millgarth, he stopped at the town hall to brief the chief constable and visit his own office. Just a few days

since he'd been working here and already there was a growing layer
of dust on all the surfaces.

Miss Sharp brought him a thin stack of papers that needed
attention.

'Is that it?' Harper asked in astonishment. 'The pile is usually
much bigger than that.'

'I dealt with the rest,' she told him. 'I put your initials on them
and sent them on to the next person. There was nothing important,
anyway.'

Of course. Just more paperwork to fill his days.

He finished reading, made the last signature with a flourish and
slipped his fountain pen back into his pocket.

'How's your investigation, sir?' she asked.

'Slow,' he answered. 'Very slow.'

'Did Mrs Harper leave on the pilgrimage?'

'No,' he replied.

Miss Sharp looked surprised.

'She decided to stay in Leeds.'

He'd just finished his work, put the cap on his fountain pen and
blotted the last sheet, when he heard a loud tap on the door. Mary,
looking fresh and young.

'You'd better come in,' Harper said.

'I rang Millgarth and they thought you might be here. I thought
I'd take you for your dinner,' Mary told him.

Once they were outside, she asked, 'Are you sure I wasn't inter-
rupting, Da?'

Harper patted one of the stone lions at the side of the steps as
he passed. For luck – a habit he'd begun when he was a child.

'No, I don't think so. You want to talk about your mam, don't
you?'

She gave a rueful smile. 'I suppose it's obvious.'

'She might be right, you know. It could be nothing, just tiredness
or excitement.'

'Do you really believe that?'

'No.' He sighed. 'I wish it could be . . . but no. But we'll know
more later.'

'Will you tell me?'

He looked at her in astonishment. 'What? Of course we will.
Why wouldn't we?'

'I know how you two can be sometimes. I'm not a little girl, Da.'

'I know that.' He took her left hand and held it up so the sunlight caught her engagement ring. 'Believe me, I know that. We'll tell you, but for now let's keep it to the three of us.'

Mary pursed her lips, then nodded.

Park Square seemed elegant in the sunshine. He imagined the way it must have looked when it was first built, the best address in town. Now every building seemed to house a doctor or a lawyer, people with enough money to make sure the buildings were well-kept. The woodwork was painted, windows clean and sparkling in the sun.

Annabelle was in the waiting room, perched on the edge of a heavily padded chair. She was wearing the same jacket and skirt as that morning, the hem still four inches off the ground, high enough to show off the tops of her button boots and a hint of stocking as she sat. A smile flickered across her face, but it couldn't hide the tension and worry.

Exactly on the dot of three, the doctor invited them through. He had plenty of questions. Harper sat and listened. He had nothing to say; he hadn't been there when Annabelle had her episode, he hadn't seen anything similar in her before. She talked about the fog in her memory.

'Yet you knew where you were?' the doctor asked.

'Yes. I didn't even have to think about that. I could move from the kitchen to the living room. The problem was everything else. I didn't even know my own daughter.'

'Did it clear suddenly or was it gradual?'

For a second the question seemed to stump her. 'I suppose . . . gradual at first, then sudden. Like the way fog goes.'

The doctor stared down at his blotter. 'Have you had any incidents at all like this before? I don't mean just forgetting something when you go shopping or where you left your keys.'

'Once.' She looked at Harper and blushed. 'It was short, a couple of minutes after I woke up. Back in spring, the start of April. But it was over quickly and it was first thing in the morning, so I didn't think much about it.'

She'd never told him. Even if she had, she'd have laughed it off and he'd have paid it no mind.

More questions, then listening to her heart and lungs with the stethoscope, putting on the cuff and checking her blood pressure. 'Physically, you're in excellent health,' he told her.

'But?' she asked. 'Don't be delicate because I'm a woman. Am I going round the bend?'

Her question made him smile. 'No, nothing like that, Mrs Harper. If you'd described one episode, I wouldn't be concerned. But two within the space of three months gives me a very slight pause for thought. It's possible that you experienced two very mild strokes.'

'Strokes?' Her face fell.

'It's possible,' the doctor repeated, 'but I'm not entirely convinced by that. Tell me, do you know what senility is?'

'Of course,' she answered. 'I saw enough old people with it when I was a Poor Law Guardian.' Annabelle stopped, horror spreading across her face. She gripped the arms of the chair. 'Are you trying to tell me I'm going senile?'

His voice was full of reassurance. 'No. I'm not saying anything of the kind, Mrs Harper. But I want you to be aware that it can happen to people before they're old, too. Is there a history of it in your family at all?'

'I don't know. None of them lived long enough to find out.'

A dip of his head in uncomfortable acknowledgement. 'My advice would be not to push yourself too hard. And if it happens again, come back and see me.'

'If it *should* happen again, what can you do?' Harper asked. 'Is there any kind of treatment?'

'There's a German doctor, a chap named Alzheimer. He's identified some things in the brain that are related to this. In older people it's possible that strokes may be one of the causes.' A small hesitation. 'For younger people like your wife, we simply don't know. Honestly, we're still groping in the dark at the moment. And we don't have any treatments.'

'You mean there's nothing you can do?' Annabelle asked. Harper heard the sorrow in her voice.

'No,' the doctor replied. 'I'm afraid not, certainly at present. But please, you need to be aware that two instances don't mean you have this. Not by a long chalk.'

'Two guineas to be told I'm losing my mind.'

'He didn't say that.'

'Then you didn't hear the same thing as me, Tom Harper.' Her
words snapped out, bitter, angry, filled with pain.

They were in the small, grassy park at the centre of the square.
He pulled her close and held her tight. She cried, letting out the
fear and the pain. He stroked her neck and tried to soothe her, not
caring who saw them. Finally the tears passed and she wiped a hand
across her eyes.

'What are we going to do?'

At the cab rank near the bottom of Briggate, Harper helped her into
a hackney.

'Are you sure you'll be all right?'

'Of course I will.' Bravado, and they both knew it. 'I'm not an
invalid.'

'I'll try not to be late home.'

He couldn't think about it all; there was simply too much. It
might be nothing at all. That was something to hang on to. Deep
inside, though, he knew it was a vain hope. Two instances in a few
months . . . It was an illness that would never show itself in any
obvious physical way. There was no medicine to cure it. No plans
they could make, because that would be an admission that it was
real and would only grow worse.

Safer to push it to the back of his mind until it needed to come
forward again.

TWENTY

Ash raised his eyebrows as Harper entered. He shook his head
in reply.

Sissons was at his desk in the corner, hidden behind
mounds of files.

'How much of this relates to the barracks robbery?' Harper asked
him.

'This pile here, sir.' The smallest of the lot, only a foot high.

Harper scooped them up. 'I'll handle this from now on. I want
you to concentrate on Thorpe.'

'Yes, sir.' He seemed relieved by the offer. 'I've been putting together some of the connections he had. A web, really.'

'Are they all crooks?'

'A fair few of them, yes.'

'Why don't we have these men in and question them? They won't be expecting it.'

'Yes, sir.' A pause. 'I wouldn't expect too much from it. There's no evidence of anything at all.'

Harper smiled. 'It doesn't matter. Let's shake things up and see what happens.'

He read through everything on the barracks theft, scribbling a few notes, then sat back and thought for a while before going to talk to Sergeant Mason at the front desk.

'Do you have any cadets here at the moment?'

'Two, sir. Learning on the job.'

'I have something for them. Search out the records of anyone convicted of gun crime in the last twenty years, pull their files and make sure they're on my desk first thing in the morning.'

After supper, the pots washed and put away, they sat down with Mary and told her about the appointment. He let Annabelle do all the talking. But for once words didn't come easily to her, and really, there was so little to tell. Nothing definite. No answers, just more questions. Possibilities. Guesses and hopes.

In bed he held his wife close. She wasn't sleeping; her body stayed tense and tight against him.

'We'll be all right, won't we, Tom?'

'We will,' he said. 'I promise.'

He was waiting for his driver when Mary slipped out of the Victoria, locking the door behind her. 'Can you give me a lift into town, Da?'

'I imagine I can. Busy morning? You're bright and early.'

'I have to talk to some possible new clients.'

But she could take the tram for that. She wanted to talk about her mother.

'What can we do?'

'Keep our eyes open,' he told her. 'Help her when she needs it. There isn't anything more than that. And it might be nothing at all; the doctor said that.'

'Da, I'll ask you the same question I asked yesterday: do you believe it?'

'No,' he answered quietly. 'I want to, but I don't.'

The car stopped on Albion Place. She looked back at him from the pavement. For once he didn't see the bright, capable young businesswoman. In her place was a bewildered little girl.

Harper had brought home the file on Francis Mullen's killing, to see if there was anything they'd missed. They'd used the new advances, taking fingerprints all through his house. In the end, they'd managed to eliminate the dead man and his son, along with the police who'd searched the place. Two more names had popped up from records, old men who'd visited the week before the killing. But neither had been there on the day. At least a dozen more remained unidentified, and no guarantee that any of them had wielded the knife. Sometimes all these grand ideas were more hindrance than help. And no substitute for questions, a brain and wearing out a lot of shoe leather.

He'd spotted one small thing, enough to give him a sliver of hope. When the constables had questioned the neighbours on Somerset Street, one had mentioned seeing a man. It was just in passing, but they mentioned a small limp. It didn't look as if they'd ever properly followed up on it. He looked around the room. Rogers, he decided. The man had an uncanny way of tracing people.

'How do you fancy a breath of fresh air?'

The man grinned, full of the joys of being in plain clothes. 'Sounds perfect, sir. What did you have in mind?'

'We're taking a little wander. Just follow me and listen.'

Even in the gentle morning light, Somerset Street looked weary, on its uppers. The best thing would be to tear it down, Harper thought as he knocked on the door. He put the thoughts away as the handle turned.

The woman was probably in her seventies, with grey hair hidden under a thin cotton shawl. But she was sharp. She remembered exactly what she'd seen, and came out with something a little more exact than she'd originally given to the constable.

'You're certain the limp was in his right leg?' Harper asked.

'I just told you, didn't I?'

'You seem to be the only one on the street who noticed him, Mrs Foster.'

She gave him a withering glance. 'I can't help it if they're blind, can I, luv?'

'Go round and ask them all again,' he told Rogers. 'I don't expect much, but it's all we've got.'

'Do you have any idea who it might be, sir?'

'No,' Harper replied. 'I can think of three or four with limps, but none of them are killers. You've walked a beat recently – anyone spring to mind?'

'Like you, sir, one or two. I hadn't seen them as violent, but . . .' Rogers shrugged.

'Let's try and find him.' Maybe it was something, maybe it was nothing. But they'd missed it before. And it was all they had.

At Millgarth, he listened to the progress his men had made the day before. Inch by inch, a name here and there. People to track down and question. They seemed to have a sense of purpose. Of eagerness. It was enough to make him believe that the answers were only a matter of time.

Half past nine and he slipped away with Ash for the weekly meeting between the heads of each division and the chief constable.

'The men appreciate you taking over the barracks robbery angle, sir.'

'It's only fair. They're stretched tight as it is.'

'They are,' Ash agreed. 'But they'd do anything to try and please you.'

'I need to do my share, too.'

'That's what's given them the gee up, sir. You're mucking in and helping. You're one of us.'

He was tempted to go to the infirmary, to try and edge past the nurses to visit Davey Mullen. Safer not, he decided as he walked up the drive to the hospital. Someone would see him and he'd end up completely banned. Mullen couldn't talk, and from yesterday's defiant stare, he wasn't about to give up any names.

Instead, he turned around and strode back to Millgarth, ready to lose himself in the files the cadets had left for him. It occupied him all morning, whittling down the candidates until only three names remained.

But however much he willed or hoped it, none of them was a good fit. The closest was Henry Eason. He'd had a brief history with guns and burglary when he was young. But for the last ten years he'd run a business importing goods from the Empire to sell in shops. He was successful, solid, well-to-do these days, married with a growing family. Would he risk all that to take four pistols from a barracks?

In the end, he tossed the folder aside in frustration. It had been a good idea, but it hadn't worked.

'Any luck, sir?' Sissons called from across the room.

'I—'

Harper stopped as the door flew open and Ash entered, beaming as if he'd won the sweepstakes.

'Bristol police just telephoned,' he announced to the room. 'They've arrested Bert Jones, *with* the gun. Walsh, Galt, go home and pack a bag. I want you on the train to Bristol to bring him back.' He rubbed his hands together with pleasure. 'Things are moving now.'

TWENTY-ONE

'Some good news,' Harper said. 'Finally.'

The relief softened Ash's features, and the old joy was back in his eyes. 'It makes me feel better, that's a fact, sir. I was beginning to think we'd be going round in circles forever.'

The superintendent paced around the room, on edge now and unable to settle in his chair.

'We should be able to drag some information out of him tomorrow.' Harper paused. 'I don't suppose Bristol police gave you the number of that pistol?'

'No, sir.'

'Never mind. We'll find out once he's here.'

He stopped at Sissons's desk. The man was writing on a sheet of paper. 'You've been delving deep into Thorpe. Have you come across the name Henry Eason at all?'

'No, sir. It hasn't come up.'

Time to let go of that idea. They had Jones, possibly something on Francis Mullen's murder. The tide was beginning to turn in their favour. He could feel it. They had hope once again.

Harper was still working his way through the files for any other possibilities when a messenger from the chief constable arrived. He tore open the envelope and glanced at the paper.

'How would you like to go and look at papers somewhere else, Sergeant?' he asked Sissons. 'Barney Thorpe's office.'

The man's eyes glowed with pleasure. 'Yes, sir.'

'Take a pair of constables. If anything's even vaguely interesting, bring it back here. Unfortunately, it's only the office, not his house. Tear the place apart. If that gun's there, I want it.'

Parker had tried to persuade the judge to let them go everywhere, but the man had been adamant. A house was sacrosanct. A man's castle, that was the principle in law, the judge insisted; no matter that it was far from true. But never mind. They'd work around that if they had to; Harper had managed it before. He knew just how far the rules would bend before they snapped completely.

He smiled to himself. Yes, things were moving. About bloody time, too.

As he turned the corner on to Manor Street, Harper saw that Annabelle's car was gone. For a moment, he felt a sense of panic.

Upstairs, a note on the table: *You'll have to fend for yourselves tonight. Miss Ford asked me to cover a meeting in Bramley. Kate Whistler's with me, no need to worry.*

He'd just finished reading it when he heard Mary's tread on the steps.

'Fish and chips,' he said.

'Tell me something, Da.' The grease had soaked through the newspaper. It glistened on her fingers and her mouth as she ate another chip. 'Do you really believe in women having the vote?'

Where had she come up with that? 'Of course I do. I always have. Why?'

'I hear plenty of businessmen your age and they all seem opposed to it. They seem to think women can't understand politics.'

'I've lived with your mother and politics for years. I've heard all the votes for women arguments, and I've always supported them.' He stopped. 'Anyway, what do you mean about my age? Are you saying I'm old?'

She didn't reply immediately, but carefully weighed her words as she popped the last of the scraps between her lips and wadded up the paper.

'It seems to be mostly young men who support suffrage, that's all. I just wondered. And you have to admit, you're not young.'

Harper smiled to himself. No, he certainly wasn't young any more.

He'd just finished shaving, staring in the mirror as he buttoned the front collar stud of his shirt and straightened his tie. The telephone started to ring and he dashed through to the living room.

'It's Sergeant Mason at Millgarth, sir.'

'I hope you have some good news to start the morning.'

'Superintendent Ash says to tell you that we have a man with a limp in for questioning. He says you'd know what it meant.'

'I do. Thank you.'

How the devil had Rogers managed that?

As soon as he walked into Millgarth, people were smiling. He just hoped it wouldn't all end in disappointment again.

'Who did Rogers bring in?'

'Someone called Soapy Turnbull,' Ash said. 'He knew him from his time on the beat. He's questioning him now.'

Turnbull . . . he didn't recognize the name. But the time had long since passed when he knew every criminal on his patch. He was responsible for too large an area these days.

'Does he have a record?'

'Assault, grievous bodily harm, wounding . . .' Ash began. 'He's a good candidate.'

'Let me know what happens.' At the door he turned back. 'Why do people call him Soapy?'

'If you had to be anywhere near him, you'd understand, sir. I reckon Rogers deserves danger money.'

'What about Sissons? What did he find at Barney Thorpe's office?'

The corners of Ash's mouth turned down. 'He's brought back sacks full of papers. But no gun. If Thorpe had it, it's somewhere else.'

Of course. Lady Luck couldn't smile at them for long. That was too much to hope.

'When's the train due from Bristol?' Harper asked.

'Sixteen minutes past three,' Ash replied.

He glanced at the clock. The hands were crawling towards noon. All the answers Jones had to give them were hours away yet.

'Is Rogers still in with Turnbull?'

'Yes, sir. But the way the man stinks, I don't know how he can stand it.'

'I'm going over to the town hall.'

'That's excellent news on Jones,' Parker agreed. 'It'll look good in the papers. What about this other man you've brought in for questioning?'

'Turnbull? I don't know anything about that yet, sir.' And he wasn't about to guess; he'd only be tempting fate.

While he was there, he slipped downstairs to his own office. Miss Sharp was on the telephone. She held up her hand and passed him the telephone receiver.

'It's for you.'

'Ash, sir,' He sounded . . . Harper didn't know. Astonished? Dumbfounded? 'You're not going to believe this.'

'I certainly won't if you don't tell me. What's happened?'

'It's Turnbull, sir. He's admitted he murdered Francis Mullen.'

'He did what?' Now he understood the man's reaction. 'Why? Who ordered it?'

'Nobody, sir. It must be about the only thing so far where Barney Thorpe hasn't had a hand. The thing's about as mundane as you can imagine.' He heard Ash take a breath and pictured him shaking his head in disbelief. 'Mullen owed him money and Turnbull went to collect. When Mullen wouldn't pay, Turnbull pulled a knife. More to scare him than anything. Mullen dared him to use it and he did.'

Christ Almighty. Nothing sinister at all. Just a waste of a life. Pointless. In the end the answer had been simple. No deep secrets. No conspiracy. They'd been hunting for something that wasn't there, and Harper was as guilty as any of them. More; he'd been the one in charge, urging them on. For a moment he wanted to laugh at his own stupidity. With his rank, he should know better. Keep an open mind; how often had he said that to detectives over the years? But this time he'd ignored it completely, searching instead for connections that never existed.

'How much money did he owe?'

'Two shillings, sir.'

No sum at all. A life ended for that.

'At least we can clear that from the books.' He could hear the emptiness in his voice. They had the result. He should have been celebrating. But it didn't seem like a victory at all.

The matron wasn't in her office at the infirmary. Harper waited for five minutes, but when she didn't return, he strode down the corridor to Davey Mullen's room.

'Anyone been in to see him?' he asked the constable on guard.

'The nurse early on, and the doctor doing his rounds.'

He shouldn't be disturbed, then. 'Tap on the door if you see anyone coming.'

Mullen was lying on his back, head on the pillows. Awake. He turned, eyes narrowing as he saw his visitor.

'I've brought some news. I wish it was better, but I thought you'd like to know. We found the man who killed your father.'

The gaze turned to stone. His jaw moved, as he was trying to make a word, but he flinched from the pain.

'No. It was nothing to do with Thorpe. You murdered him for nothing.' No reaction at all. 'The man who did it is called Soapy Turnbull,' Harper continued. 'Have you ever heard of him?'

Mullen shook his head. Once. Twice.

'Turns out your father owed him money. Two shillings. You could have given him that out of your pocket and never even noticed.' He paused. 'I'm sorry.'

He had nothing more to say right now. Plenty of questions, but those would wait. Let Mullen take it all in.

'You've done some good work since you joined the squad,' he told Rogers.

The big man beamed. 'Thank you, sir.'

'What put you on to Turnbull?'

'I talked to a couple of men I'd known on the beat. As soon as I mentioned a limp, one of them said his name. It was a place to start, so I thought I'd ask him about Somerset Street and Francis Mullen. He just wasn't too easy to find. It took me most of the night. And when I did come across him, he needed some persuading to come down here.'

It was easy enough to imagine how Rogers had persuaded him. No matter, that was done. Turnbull would stand trial for murder.

Fess murder
Arson
Metropole shooting
Barracks robbery
Francis Mullen
Barney Thorpe
Missing pistol
Davey Mullen
Bert Jones

At first, Bert Jones refused to say a word.

'He's been like that the whole journey,' Walsh said. 'Absolutely *shtum*. Still, it makes a change to have a prisoner who's not complaining all the time.'

'Did you question him at all?'

The inspector shook his head. 'I thought we'd wait until we were back here.'

Jones was a big man, a bruiser. He seemed to fill the small room. Broad shoulders and thick wrists with plenty of dark hair peering out of the cuffs. Scarred knuckles and a thick shadow of stubble across his face. Everyone's idea of a bodyguard. No collar or tie, a cheap suit buttoned tight across his chest.

'Ready?' Harper asked.

'Completely.' Walsh smiled. 'See if we can get a peep out of him.'

'We're charging you with murder, Bert,' the inspector began. 'You know what that means, don't you?' No response. 'If the jury finds you guilty, it's the noose for you.'

'I didn't shoot him.' He had a gruff, rasping voice that sounded as if every word had been dragged over pebbles.

'No, we know that,' Walsh agreed. 'But it doesn't matter. You found the man who did, you paid him and you supplied him with the gun. That makes you guilty.'

'And the gun you were carrying when you were arrested was stolen from Harewood Barracks last year,' Harper said. 'We checked the serial number.'

Jones turned his head to look at him with no expression on his face. 'I bought it. Don't know where it came from.'

'Who sold it to you?'

'Don't remember.'

'You help us, we can help you,' Walsh said.

Jones snorted. 'What are you going to do? Make sure the drop is long enough to break my neck straight away?'

Harper stood up and left. He'd said his piece; if he stayed, he'd simply be a distraction. Better to let Walsh burrow into the man's head and twist him inside out.

He'd never seriously expected a truthful answer from Jones. He wanted to see the man, to hear him. They'd recovered two of the stolen weapons now. That was a start. The third was hidden away, either in Thorpe's home or somewhere else. They'd find it. And the fourth? He didn't have a clue. That was the one which really worried him.

Galt was writing up the report of the Bristol trip, looking uncomfortable behind a desk. Ash had sent Rogers home to sleep; he'd worked for more than twenty-four hours straight. Sissons was off somewhere. Apart from the scratch of pen on paper, the detectives' room was quiet.

Yet even with his poor hearing, Harper could identify all the other sounds around Millgarth. After so many years here, they were a part of him. The small creaks and groans of the building, the sound of footsteps on the stairs, the comings and goings in the parade ground at the back.

'Penny for them, sir,' Ash said.

'Not worth your money,' he said with a smile. 'I'm just on my way to talk to Thorpe's lawyer.'

'We've interviewed him twice. He says he never saw the face of Barney's killer.'

'Maybe I can stir something in his memory. At the moment there's nothing I can do here.'

At first it seemed like a wasted trip. A chance to sit in a plush office on Park Square with Mr Simmons, the worried, fidgeting solicitor. He'd seen his client murdered as they walked together; that would be enough to terrify anyone.

Nothing jogged his memory; it was as if his senses had frozen the moment he saw Barney Thorpe collapse on the pavement. All Simmons could recall was the blur of a dark shape hurrying past. He hadn't seen the flash of a knife or the blow.

'I'm sure you find all that unlikely, Mr Harper,' he admitted. He was a prissy man, pushing sixty, dressed in the formal clothes of the law – a black frock coat with a wing collar and black tie. Pale and thin, he looked curiously bloodless, with fine wisps of hair combed across his skull. But he was good at his work; over the decades he'd represented plenty of important people in Leeds.

'We want whoever killed Mr Thorpe.'

'So do I.' The man gave a small, sharp nod. 'I'm not hiding anything. I was checking something in my notebook and then . . .' He remained silent for a long time. 'We always imagine how we'll react, don't we?' he said thoughtfully. 'That we'll do something heroic. In the event, I discovered I was helpless. It's not a pleasant revelation. I'm sorry.'

'For what it's worth, you couldn't have saved him.'

'No.' He sighed. 'But I could have tried.'

'Are you sure there's nothing at all you can remember about the killer?'

Simmons began to shake his head, then stopped and narrowed his eyes. 'Maybe there is something. His shoes.' He was quiet for a moment. 'It just came back into my mind, right this minute. The shoes. An image, nothing more than that. Someone running, wearing a pair of brown shoes. I can't swear I saw it or if my mind's playing tricks. It might not even have been then. I'm sorry . . .'

'Please concentrate on it, sir. It's important.'

Simmons was quiet, going over it all, letting the moment play again and again. Finally he took a breath. 'I *think* it's real,' he said. 'I *think* it happened then. But in all conscience, I can't go any further than that. I certainly wouldn't swear to it in court. No competent barrister would give me the chance, anyway.'

Harper nodded. He was right. For one second he'd been close to something that might help convict Mullen. Then it was snatched away again. Just like everything else that related to the man.

'Do we have a list of everything Davey Mullen had with him?' he asked Simmons. The man knew where every piece of paper from the case was kept.

'We took an inventory of his hotel room before we put it all in storage, sir.'

'Find that for me, please.' Harper thought for a moment. 'What about the clothes he was wearing when he was taken to hospital?'

'No.' Sissons stretched out the word. 'I'm sure we don't have a record of those. We wouldn't have any need.'

Mullen had one pair of black boots and a pair of black shoes in his room. Both American made. Harper sat for a moment, then picked up his hat and strode out into the sunshine.

He wanted to know. For his own satisfaction. To settle it all in his mind.

At the infirmary, he decided to be official and wait outside the matron's office until she returned. No ducking into Mullen's room this time. Sitting on a chair, he felt like a schoolboy sent to the headmistress. She raised her eyes when she saw him.

'I hadn't expected to see you again, Deputy Chief Constable. I thought I'd made myself perfectly clear the last time.'

Good, he thought; she hadn't heard about his other visit.

'You had. But there's something I need.' He waited for her objection.

'I—'

'It's important for a murder investigation.' He cut through her words. Murder always left people quiet and uncomfortable. 'I don't want to talk to Mr Mullen. I want to take a look at his shoes.'

She stared at him sceptically. 'That's acceptable. But,' she told him, 'you'll have the ward sister with you every moment, and you will *not* attempt to talk to the patient.'

'Agreed.'

He didn't have a chance to enter the room. The nurse brought him a package wrapped in brown paper and tied with string. As he loosened the knot, Harper realized he was holding his breath.

They were scuffed and dusty, but they were right there in front of him: a pair of black shoes.

'At this rate, the squad's going to get a reputation, sir,' Ash said with a smile and the others laughed. 'Solving all these cases in a single day.'

'Two.' Harper wanted to be exact. 'And it's bloody good going.' He gave a small bow to the men. 'You've worked wonders.' He turned towards Walsh. 'That was a good, quick confession you got from Bert Jones.'

The inspector shook his head. 'All I had to do was point out the lies and contradictions in his story. Turns out that Barney Thorpe told him to arrange Fess's murder, but to hire someone and not to do it himself. That way they could avoid a trail that led back to them.'

'It didn't work that way in the end, though, did it?'

'Not quite.' Walsh was flushed with pleasure at his success.

'Why did Thorpe want Fess dead? What did Jones have to say about that?'

'He claims that Barney didn't tell him, and he didn't ask. He just did what he was told. I believe him, sir; I haven't been able to shake him on that.'

'We're solving crimes but we're finding more damned questions.'

'Never mind, sir,' Ash said. 'The rate we're moving along now, we'll have all the answers by Saturday.'

~~Fess murder~~

Arson

~~Metropole shooting~~

Barracks robbery

~~Francis Mullen~~

Barney Thorpe

Missing pistol

Davey Mullen

~~Bert Jones~~

'Good work, Tom,' Chief Constable Parker said. 'Give them my congratulations. How does it feel to be out and working again?'

'I'm enjoying it, sir,' he replied. He felt alive, the blood singing in his veins in a way it hadn't for too long.

Parker selected a cigar from the box on his desk, cut the end and lit it with a match, applying the flame evenly and carefully around the tip. He blew out the smoke and tilted his head back to watch it rise to the ceiling.

'Let's hope your luck holds and you can clear up everything else.'

TWENTY-TWO

I t was the kind of balmy evening when men took their chairs and sat outside on the pavement in their shirtsleeves to enjoy the sun. Around Sheepscar, quite a few were doing that, cradling glasses of beer, braces slipped off their shoulders to hang around their waists.

Harper nodded his greetings as he passed, then ducked into the Victoria and up the stairs. As he opened the door to the living quarters, the smell of food greeted him.

Len was on the settee, legs stretched out, reading the *Evening Post*. As soon as he saw Harper, he stood, looking embarrassed.

'Mary invited me for my supper,' he began, tripping over his words. 'I hope it's . . . She said it would be . . .'

Harper waved him back down. 'Of course it is, don't be daft. You're family now. Make yourself comfortable.'

'I thought he should have a taste of my cooking,' Mary said from the kitchen. She was deftly moving saucepans on the range. 'See what he's letting himself in for when we're married.'

'Where's your mother?'

'She said she fancied a lie-down.' Mary glanced at him and raised her eyebrows in a knowing gesture. 'And she said it would be good practice for me to cook.'

Annabelle didn't sleep during the day. They both knew that.

He was silent in the bedroom, watching her lying on the candle-wick, eyes closed. Very softly, he turned to leave.

'I'm not really sleeping,' she said, but her voice was slurred and lazy enough to make it a lie.

'Are you all right?'

'Frightened,' she answered after a moment. 'And I'm weary, Tom. All the way to my bones. I didn't feel like cooking. Besides, it'll give her a taste of the future.'

'It's ready,' Mary called from the living room.

'Getting up?'

She nodded and held out her hand.

'I really think trains will remain the way ahead,' Len said. He had a glass of best bitter in front of him, brought up from downstairs. He'd eaten well, praised his fiancée's cooking, and come out of his shell a little.

'What about aeroplanes?' Harper asked.

'They're all well and good,' Len agreed. 'But would you feel safe travelling up there?'

Ten minutes later, Annabelle began to collect the plates. 'Mary said you two were going to the pictures. We'll do the pots.'

'We?' Harper asked. 'What did your last one die of?'

'Overwork,' Annabelle said. 'Which is more than you're likely to do around here.'

'This is what it's like, lad.' He turned to Mary. 'Are you going to make Len put a pinny on?'

The young man stared hard at the rug, as if he wished the floor would swallow him.

'Why not?' For a fraction of a second, her eyes blazed. Then she saw Harper's grin, reached across and took her fiancé's hand. 'Don't mind him. My da's just having his fun. We're both going to be working. Anyway, he agrees he should do his share.'

'Yes,' Len agreed with a nod and blushed again.

'You're training him well,' he said, then winked before she could take the huff.

Once everything was clean, he read the newspapers for a few minutes, but his mind kept drifting back to the cases. Mullen, Thorpe, and the tangle surrounding them.

Two questions stood out from the rest swirling around his brain. Who wanted Louis Fess dead? Who'd contacted Thorpe to arrange it and paid him?

He wasn't going to solve it tonight. Maybe his luck would hold into tomorrow.

Mostly, though, he thought about Annabelle. A nap today. He'd need to keep a watch on her. But he didn't know how, when he was at work all day. There was nothing he could do about any of her problems. He was powerless.

He stood in Ash's office, watching the men at their desks. Walsh folded a paper, stuck it in his jacket pocket and left, Rogers behind him.

'I hate to say it, sir, but after all yesterday's success, I think we're stuck again,' Ash said. 'Banging our head against a brick wall on the rest of it.'

'Then we'll have to keep on hitting it until we break through,' Harper told him. 'We're not going to let this one fade away. We can't.'

'Yes, sir.'

'What are they hunting for today?'

'Anything,' Ash told him. 'Anything at all.'

*   *   *

He couldn't put a foot right. Harper spent the morning out and about, but no one had any answers to give him. Ash was right; their momentum had screeched to a halt.

Who would have known Fess was in Leeds? It was pure chance that the police had discovered him; that was down to Rogers's sharp ear for an accent.

Barney Thorpe. Again. They had all the papers from his office. Sissons was working his way through them, but so far nothing about guns.

Time to go through his house.

'Sissons,' he said, 'Dig yourself out from those mountains. We're taking a little trip.'

'Sir?' The sergeant looked confused.

'Don't worry, you'll love it.'

Dorothea Thorpe was still wearing black, and there was dark crepe paper draped around the frame of her husband's photograph. But it was all for appearances. She already had that spark in her eye. Barney had left her money and a good house. She'd never want for anything. Soon enough she'd be enjoying life again. A new woman would emerge.

Even if she hadn't been aware of his final mistress, she knew full well that her husband had often been unfaithful; it must have rankled and hurt. Harper could see the future in her eyes. With him gone, her time was about to begin. But she didn't know anything about his business. That was what she claimed, and he believed her. Thorpe would never trust information about money-lending and crime to a woman. Work and home were two different worlds.

'Did he keep many papers here?'

'In his library. Over there.' She pointed to a closed door and snorted. 'Well, Barney called it a library, although there's hardly a book in it. Somewhere to hide and plot, more like.'

'Would you mind if we took a look in there?' Harper tried to make it sound offhand and casual, the most ordinary thing in the world. He hoped her hatred of her husband was strong enough to give them permission. Neat, and perfectly legal.

'Help yourself.'

They cleared the first hurdle. Now for the second. 'We might want to take some things. Documents.'

'I don't care,' she said, 'as long as it doesn't stop me getting what I'm due.'

Sissons was in there for an hour. He came out carrying four heavy bags crammed with paper. His face gave nothing away. Harper said his farewells to Mrs Thorpe and remained quiet until the car was gliding down the road.

'Worthwhile?'

Sissons opened the briefcase he always carried and took out two pieces of paper.

'I have plenty to go through, but I thought you'd want to see these, sir. They don't tell us *who* wanted Fess dead, but they're still very interesting.'

A spidery scrawl of ink on paper, something written quickly. Harper put on his spectacles, slowly making out three or four words, then more. A description of Fess, as if Thorpe had jotted it down during a conversation. All the details, even the fact that the man was at Mrs Hardisty's lodging house.

He moved on to the second note.

Make sure Bert tracks down Beckett and supplies gun.

'This is good work. Another step forward, at least.'

'There's still plenty we don't know,' Sissons said. 'Who gave Thorpe that information, for a start.' He hesitated. 'I found this, too.' He drew out a Webley revolver. 'It was right at the back of the drawer,' he continued. 'Just the one. The serial number matches those stolen from the barracks.' He grinned.

Harper beamed. 'I think you just earned your pay today, Sergeant. Every penny.'

Progress. Real progress. They'd demolished that brick wall again.

'That's the third gun,' Harper said. 'I don't think the fourth one is there. They'd have been together if he'd had it.' He raised a hand to quiet the objections. 'I've been in touch with Mrs Thorpe and she's agreed to let us do a proper search. But if we assume it's not there, where the hell is it? Who's got it?'

Walsh examined the pieces of paper from Sissons's briefcase. 'Who could Barney have been talking to about Fess? A visitor?'

'No strangers came to the house in the days right before Fess was killed,' Harper said. 'I asked his wife and she doesn't remember any.'

'Did he have a telephone?'

'On the desk in his library,' Sissons said. 'But he must have been talking to someone in Britain.'

Of course. His instructions couldn't have come from a New York gang; there were no phone lines to the far side of the ocean. That meant someone else was involved. Someone closer to home.

'Rogers,' Harper said, 'you went back to talk to Mrs Hardisty. What did she have to say?'

'Very little I didn't already know, sir. But there was one gem: someone came looking for him at her place. Not asking by name, but for the American.'

'When?' Harper asked.

'The day he vanished, the way she tells it. Fess went out in the morning and never came back.'

'The same day we hauled him in here,' Ash said. 'Who was looking for him? Could she give you a description?'

Rogers smiled. 'She went one better than that, sir. She gave me a name.'

'Let me guess,' Harper interrupted. 'Bert Jones.'

'Spot on, sir. She knew his sister back when she was younger. She recognized him.'

All too often these days Leeds felt like a huge, sprawling city. But sometimes, at moments like this, it was a tiny village.

'Jones didn't mention this when you questioned him, did he?' Harper asked Walsh.

'Not a dicky bird, sir.'

'Have another session with him. Maybe you can jog his memory. Push him again on who might have paid Barney for the killing.'

The men had plenty to keep them busy tomorrow. Harper watched them all leave; only he and Ash remained as day edged towards evening.

'It's a mess, sir.'

'Half the time I feel we're getting more questions than answers,' Harper said. 'Maybe it'll seem clearer after a good night's sleep.'

'Look on the bright side: we've had some good successes. We're doing well, sir,' Ash said with a smile.

'Yes,' Harper agreed. But why didn't it seem that way?

Mary was over at Len's. Now they were engaged, not just courting, the families would become a bigger part of their lives. Last night had shown the lad fitted in well here. He'd seemed more comfortable, less on display. Just as well; they'd be seeing plenty of him in future.

Harper looked over at his wife. 'Nothing more?'

She shook her head. 'Absolutely normal. Didn't even need a little snooze.'

'Good.' He paused. 'I've been wondering. Do you think we should tell Len? He's going to have to know sooner or later.'

'Later.' Her tone made it clear there was nothing more to say on the matter.

He was in an old-fashioned hackney cab, the horse galloping out of control over bumpy ground as he bounced up and down on the seat holding on for dear life. Slowly the scene began to fade around him. Someone was shaking his shoulder.

'Telephone, Tom. It's Rogers.'

He'd been dead to the world, slept all the way through the ringing.

'Harper.' His voice was thick and groggy. He pressed the receiver against his good ear.

'I'm sorry to bother you, sir, but you need to come in. Bert Jones has escaped from Armley. And it looks like he killed Beckett before he left.'

Christ. He took a breath. 'Send a car for me.'

'It should already be waiting.'

Harper glanced at the clock on the wall. Seven minutes past three. He dressed in a rush and hurried out to Roundhay Road. The streets were empty and dark as they sped along. Almost before he knew it, the driver pulled up outside Millgarth.

The squad were all in the detectives' room, listening as Ash briefed them on what he knew. A pot of tea sat on a desk. Harper poured himself a cup as he listened.

'The best we can tell, there was a disturbance after midnight. It was arranged. A few prisoners set fire to their mattresses at the same time and the warders took them all out into the yard while the smoke cleared and everything was cleaned up. Jones must have had some kind of weapon. He took advantage of the confusion to knife Beckett in the throat.'

'How did he get out of the gaol?' Galt asked.

'We don't know yet,' Ash said after a moment. 'But he escaped. That's definite.'

'What are Armley and Wortley Division doing?' Harper asked.

'Every man they have is out looking. The chief constable's taken command there. We're watching Jones's home. And Thorpe's house, in case he decides to go there.'

'I want you to go over all his friends and associates,' Harper ordered. 'Any name you can dredge up. Go through their houses. Let them know they'll be in a cell if they help him.'

He was fully awake now, as if someone had thrown a bucket of cold water over him. The men disappeared, grim-faced and determined. Leeds had more than a quarter of a million inhabitants. Finding one determined to stay hidden was going to be a thankless task.

'Where do you want me, sir?' Ash asked.

'Right here, keeping an eye on things. I'm going to be out there myself. I don't suppose you had any revelations about any of it during the night, did you?'

'No such luck.' He gave a wistful smile. 'What about you?'

Harper shook his head.

Dawn wasn't far away. The air had a different smell, not as soft. He wanted to walk, to let his thoughts flow. Sellers were already setting up at the outdoor market, moving through the half-light with practised grace as they unloaded handcarts and laid out their goods ready for the day.

He'd been a detective for over a quarter of a century. He'd known hundreds of people, quite possibly thousands. Some of them must have had dealings with Bert Jones. But that was the problem with rank. Stuck in an office all day, he'd lost contact with so many. The old links rusted and fell apart.

Suddenly, in the middle of the pavement, he stopped. Yes, that was a good place to start. Not yet, though, he decided after looking at his watch. It was barely five o'clock; another hour or so, at least. Time for breakfast.

It didn't matter whether it was first thing in the morning or the middle of the night. Word would have passed that there was a plain clothes copper walking around the Bank. The Erin Boys were no longer the force they'd once been up here, but they still had their network of young lads who kept their eyes open.

Harper had had his moments in this place. A few pitched battles when he'd gone in with constables to arrest people. He still carried the scars. As he strolled, he could feel eyes watching him, even if he couldn't see them. His hand closed around the cosh in his pocket and he slipped the leather loop over his wrist.

Let them watch him. This was Leeds, he was a copper and he wasn't going to be cowed, no matter what area. The police kept order for honest people, and there were plenty of those on the Bank.

TWENTY-THREE

S tephen Scargill had once been married to Bert Jones's younger sister. He still was, for all Harper knew, but she'd left him years before, run off to Birmingham with a man she'd met, taking the children and leaving him all on his own.

It was ancient history, but there was no love lost between Scargill and Jones. Bert had taken his sister's part; back when the wound was still raw, it had often come to blows after the pubs closed. That was long ago now, but Harper hoped the grudge still festered, and Scargill had stayed aware of Jones.

He turned the corner on to Bread Street. Three men loitered across the road, hands in their pockets, staring at him. Trying to intimidate, to remind him he wasn't welcome.

He walked to number twenty-four and knocked on the door. Ten seconds and Scargill opened up, fully dressed and ready for work. He glanced up and down before letting Harper inside.

The man was older. What remained of his hair was grey, pomaded down against his scalp. But his body was still strong. The years of physical work showed.

'I've got ten minutes before I have to go,' Scargill said. 'You're taking your life in your hands, coming up here on your own. Must be important.'

'Bert Jones.'

He snorted. 'I could guess that. I'm not bloody simple. I thought you lot had arrested him. If you're here, something must have happened.'

'He was in Armley Gaol. Killed another prisoner and escaped overnight.'

'Well, I'm not likely to be hiding him here.' He opened his arms wide. 'Take a look around if you don't believe me.'

'Do you still know all about him?' Harper asked.

'Not the way I used to.' Scargill shrugged. 'But I can probably tell you this and that.'

'I need to ask you a few questions.'

'I told you, ten minutes. And I'll be eating while we talk. I'm not going in on an empty belly for anyone.'

Worth his time, Harper thought as he started back down the street. From up here, Leeds lay spread out before him. Haze from the chimneys, the dirty ribbon of the river and canal. Muck everywhere. Plenty of brass with it, too, for the right people.

He was aware of the man coming up behind him. A hand tried to grab his upper arm. He turned into it before the fingers could get a grip on his jacket. The man had yellow teeth and a feral grin. Brown hair cut in a short back and sides, and a cheap black suit.

'Coppers aren't welcome round here.'

Harper stared and shook his head, disappointed. 'Is that it? That's your message?'

'This is Erin Boys territory.'

'No, it's not.' The young man seemed startled by the words. 'This is Leeds. You might want to remind Johnny Dempster of that.'

Dempster. The leader of the Boys, in charge since his brother went to prison. Ambitious and greedy by all accounts, and wanting to make the gang a force on the Bank again. With himself in absolute control. But he had a brain.

'I could make you—'

He didn't have the chance to say anything more. Harper brought the cosh down on his hand. A short, vicious swing. He felt the bones break and heard the man whimper. Then he turned and walked away. Over in a second and no one had seen.

Ash sat back in his chair, fingers steepled under his chin. 'I have to say, sir, it's been worthwhile having you working back here.' He glanced at the list of names he'd just scribbled down.

'No guarantee Jones will have had contact with any of them.'

'It's still somewhere to go. We were only aware of two of these. I'll put Sissons and Galt on it.'

'Any more word from the chief?' Harper asked. 'What do they have to say over at Armley?'

'The governor has promised there'll be an inquiry into how Jones managed to escape.' His moustache twitched. They both knew what that meant. It had happened through incompetence and stupidity. Maybe corruption. They'd try to cover it up behind long words and committee meetings. 'The chief constable is still directing operations around the gaol.'

A murder and an escape meant that no one was going to be sitting in his office until Jones was back in custody. There was no doubt now that he'd hang, and he knew that as well as anyone. He had nothing to lose.

'I don't want anyone trying to tackle him alone,' Harper said. 'They all have police whistles. They can call for help.'

'Yes, sir.'

'I'm not going to give Bert Jones the satisfaction of any more bodies.'

'Did you have any trouble on the Bank, sir?'

He smiled. 'Not so as you'd notice.'

Harper visited two other men who'd once known Jones, but they had nothing to offer. He'd had his one small stroke of luck; best to be satisfied with that.

At noon he strode down Albion Place and climbed the stairs to the Harper Secretarial Agency and School. He wanted a distraction, something to take his mind off Jones and Thorpe and Mullen for a few minutes. A little joy.

Mary was in her office, going over a piece of work with another woman. So different from how she was at home. There, she was his daughter, bustling around, at ease. Here, she was a business-woman, an adult, serious, intent and professional. She knew exactly what she was doing, efficient and in control. He realized he'd never looked at her quite that way before. Then she glanced up and saw him, and instantly she was his little girl once again, gliding towards him with concern in her eyes.

'There's nothing wrong, is there? Nothing's happened to me mam?'

He laughed. 'If it has, no one's told me. I thought I'd buy you some dinner.'

'Well . . .' She glanced over her shoulder at the work piled on her desk. 'Go on, then, as long as we're quick.'

The Kardomah was just around the corner, not overrun with midday customers yet. A chance to talk without Mary's words being drowned by the hubbub of noise.

They talked about Annabelle. Mary was a woman – she saw things he'd never notice. Observations, ideas that might help. It was a conspiracy, but he felt no guilt. They both wanted the best, to be able to discuss their worries and fears.

And it was time with his daughter. To enjoy the simple pleasure of her company. Jones's escape meant he'd probably be late home, and God only knew what the next few days would bring.

By the time they parted company on Briggate, prisons and death seemed a world away. Another minute and they'd crash back into his life. For now, though, he'd take the break and be grateful.

Millgarth was bustling. The air was thick with the stink of unwashed bodies and buzzing with the hum of voices.

'They've brought in some of the people Jones knows, sir,' Sergeant Mason said from behind the front desk. 'Questioning them now.'

'Those names you gave us have been helpful, sir,' Ash said with a smile. 'At least we know the first place Jones went after he got out of Armley.'

'Where?'

'Nick Harris. He's only about half a mile from the gaol. Claims Jones turned up in the middle of the night, tossed gravel at his window to wake him. He told him to go away.'

'Do you believe him?'

'I do. Sissons noticed the gravel when they went to question him.'

'That's a start.' He nodded at the map on the wall. Ash had placed pins at the gaol and Harris's house, a piece of ribbon between them. 'Where next, do you think?'

'Anyone's guess, sir.' He gave a deep, thoughtful sigh. 'Just in case, I've warned the copper at the hospital guarding Mullen to be on his guard.'

It didn't seem likely. But better to be prepared.

Four o'clock, and the last of the men they'd brought in had walked back into the sunshine. None of them had seen Jones in months. And he was still out there. Harper stared at the map as if it might suddenly give him the answer.

The telephone rang.

'There you are, Tom.' The chief constable's voice crackled and hummed down the wire. 'Exactly who I wanted. How are things coming along?'

'Nowhere, sir. Anything in Armley?'

'Not a peep, other than that man you had. A couple of possible sightings just after dawn, but we couldn't confirm them. And nothing since.'

'Where were they?' Harper asked.

'Down through Wortley. Why?'

'I'm trying to put together a picture, sir.' Harris's house was on the way to Wortley. It fitted. But what did that give them? It was more than twelve hours ago. He could be anywhere now. Far from Leeds, if he had the chance and a scrap of sense.

'What are you thinking, Tom?'

'Trying to imagine what I'd do if I were in Jones's shoes.'

'Run like hell?' Parker laughed. But it turned into a harsh cough. 'Sorry. Too many damned cigars today. Have you seen the *Evening Post*?'

'No, sir.' He'd been too busy to buy a copy.

'They're tearing the prison governor apart. For once, no criticism of us. Just the hope we capture Jones quickly.'

By tomorrow it would have changed, and the papers would wonder why the police didn't have him back in custody yet, and they both knew it. They couldn't win.

'We'll keep pounding away, sir. Are you staying at Armley?'

'Back to the town hall, then a dinner tonight. The Lord Mayor's charity. Let me know if anything breaks.'

'I will, sir.'

The men were out, working every contact they knew, tramping the pavements with frustration rising. He remembered it all too clearly.

Harper was staring at the map once again, willing it to give him some inspiration, when Sergeant Mason knocked at the door.

'Begging your pardon, sir, but a boy just came and left this.'

An envelope, his name written on the front in a neat hand. He ripped it open and pulled out a single sheet of paper.

You've been on the Bank asking about Bert Jones. Come up and talk to me. I can help you. The lad who tried to stop you was out of order.

Dempster

'Take a look.' He passed the note to Ash.

He raised his eyebrows as he read. 'Quite something, eh, sir?'

'*Come up and talk to me.* It's like an imperial summons.' Harper shook his head and smiled. 'Maybe Dempster really does believe his Erin Boys run things up there.'

'Are you going to do it?'

Harper shrugged. 'Why not? We need information on Jones. He seems to think he has some.'

'I'd be asking myself why he's doing this, sir. I wouldn't trust him an inch.'

'I don't. And if he has something up his sleeve, I'll cut off his bloody arm.' He picked up his hat.

'If you wait until the men return, we'll come up with you, sir.'

'No. I'll be fine on my own.' He smiled, tapped the letter and put it in his pocket. 'After all, the king appears to have given me a safe conduct pass.'

The late afternoon heat clung close to the ground as he walked. Plenty of people around, none of them paying him the slightest bit of attention. But Harper knew that eyes were watching him. Marsh Lane to Mill Street, climbing up the hill. A man was lounging at the corner of Upper Cross Street, a straw hat tipped back jauntily on his head. Smoke rose from the cigarette in the corner of his mouth.

'Down along there.' He pointed over his shoulder with his thumb. 'Number five, at the far end. He's waiting for you.'

A long row of terraced houses, the bricks black from soot. The street was deserted. People who lived around here knew when it was best to stay inside. As soon as this business was over, he'd organize a force to come up here and clean out the Erin Boys once and for all. They'd let it go too long; the locals deserved better than this.

The door opened as he reached it, a big man standing aside for him. Through to the kitchen, of course. It was always the way. Life was lived in the kitchen.

Dempster was sitting at the table. He wore a pinstripe lounge suit, a light, summer weight, elegantly tailored. Fold-over collar on the shirt, a neat knot on the silk tie, a matching square tucked in the breast pocket of the jacket. He looked as fresh as if he'd just stepped out of the bath.

The man was young, still in his twenties, no more than a few years older than Mary. Short, pudgy fingers, a signet ring on one finger. He wasn't handsome, but his face had something that caught the attention. Confidence? Power? It took him a second to realize it was arrogance. Dempster was a man who expected obedience.

Harper pulled out a chair and sat across from him. 'You wanted to talk to me.'

TWENTY-FOUR

'You're looking for Bert Jones.'

'That's hardly a secret—'

'I know where he is.' Dempster hadn't moved, hands on the table in front of him.

Harper stiffened. 'Where?'

'In a moment.'

'Now.' Harper leaned forward. 'He's killed someone and escaped from Armley Gaol.'

'I know what's he's done.'

'Then you'd better tell me where he is.' He paused for a fraction of a second. 'If you really do know, that is.'

Dempster wasn't about to rise to such easy bait. He sat back. 'I could have kept quiet, had my lads take care of things.'

'Then why didn't you?' That was one thing he'd been wondering on the walk here.

'He has someone with him.'

'Who?'

'A woman. Someone he used to know. She's not sheltering him. He forced his way in and he's holding her.'

'Who is she?'

'My cousin.'

Now it made sense. If anything happened to her, Dempster could blame the police.

'Will you remember who gave you the information?' the man asked.

It was a curious turn of phrase. Harper studied Dempster's face. The man wanted to avoid responsibility, yet also claim the credit; very slick. His expression gave nothing away.

'Of course. I'm always grateful when someone helps us.'

But it didn't mean he'd owe a damned thing.

'He's on East Water Lane.'

'I know where that is. What number?'

'Four.'

'How can you be sure?'

'We have eyes all over the Bank.' It wasn't a boast, nothing more than a statement of fact. 'And like I said, the woman is a cousin of mine. She and Jones used to be close.'

Close covered plenty of sins. 'If we arrest him, I'll make sure she's not taken into custody.'

He could go that far. Maybe there was more to the story. He didn't know, and right now he didn't care. Recapturing Jones was what mattered.

'That's fair. You won't have any problems up here.'

For a second, Harper was ready to bristle. The police didn't need permission to go anywhere in Leeds. But he tamped it down and said nothing. As he stood to leave they didn't exchange handshakes. Outside, the street was quiet and warm. A dog snuffled along, picked something out of the gutter and began to chew.

'Get the men together,' he told Ash. 'We're going to need six uniforms too.'

'Very well, sir.' He gave a weary smile. 'Some good information?'

'It had better be. Jones is in a house on East Water Lane.'

'Dempster told you?'

Harper nodded. 'I think it's the truth.'

'What does he want in return?' Ash asked.

'We don't bring in the woman who lives there. His cousin.' He pressed his lips together. 'There'll be more to come later. You can bet on it.'

Harper stood by the front door of the house. The paint had weathered, all the gloss gone from the black. Rogers stood to the side, out of sight. There were coppers everywhere; Jones wasn't going to get away again.

He brought his fist down on the door, once, then a second time. No answer. No sound of anyone approaching inside. He hoped to Christ Dempster hadn't been lying. No. He couldn't be that stupid.

'Kick it in,' he ordered.

As soon as the door swung wide, crashing back against the wall, he blew his whistle and went through, keeping the cosh in his hand.

'Upstairs,' he said. There was a crash of boots as Rogers and a pair of constables thundered up to the bedrooms.

Harper wanted the kitchen, pushing through the living room then shouldering the door aside. He came to a sharp halt. Jones was standing in the corner. He had a woman by the hair, his other hand pressing a knife against her throat. Her eyes kept rolling up into her head and silent tears were running down her cheeks.

He heard someone working the back door.

'This is Harper,' he yelled. 'Stand down. Stay alert.'

Then there was silence, as if the world was holding its breath.

'You can let her go now, Bert.'

Jones shook his head. 'You'll take me back there.'

'I'll make sure you get a proper trial. A fair trial. I promise.'

'No.' His gaze was wandering round the room. He looked dishevelled, not quite focused, as if something had gone wrong in his mind.

'Why don't you release her?' Harper kept his voice calm, trying to put the man at ease. 'It'll just be you and me. We'll sit down and have a natter—'

Jones's grip on her hair tightened. She whimpered. Harper realized he didn't even know the woman's name. As long as he had her, there was nothing the police could do. They couldn't risk Jones killing her. All it would take was a single swipe of the blade across her neck.

'She can't hurt you, Bert. She's terrified.'

'I don't care.'

'She's never done anything to you. Let her go.'

Harper felt sweat trickling down his back and slick on his palms. The mood in the room wavered. The air seemed to shimmer in front of his eyes. He felt as if he hardly dared breathe. The smallest thing could tip Jones over the edge.

'Put down the knife,' he continued. 'It'll look better in court if you give yourself up. You've been around long enough to know that.'

For a moment he thought he saw a glimmer of something in the man's eyes. Doubt? Compassion? Hope? No more than a flicker, then it was gone.

'Come on, Bert, let her go. Please. Put the knife down and come out with me.'

Now there was only emptiness on his face. How could he get through to the man? How could he persuade him to surrender?

The silence pressed down, but Jones barely seemed aware of it. He raised his head and peered about the room, but whatever he was seeing didn't come from this world.

'Bert.' Harper bellowed the name at the top of his voice. For a second, the sound filled the kitchen. Jones turned his head, as if he'd only just realized someone was there.

'What do you want?'

'Let her go.' He was speaking normally again, his voice calm, making a perfectly ordinary suggestion.

'Yes.' For just a moment he stared at the woman, shocked to discover he was still holding her. With one quick movement, he pushed her away.

Harper caught her before she collapsed on the floor. His eyes never left Jones; he was ready to spring if he attacked. But the man made no move. The knife was still in his hand, but it hung down at his side; he probably didn't realize he was still armed.

Harper backed away, holding the woman. She'd passed out, a dead, awkward weight in his arms.

Rogers was waiting in the hall.

'Take her,' Harper ordered. 'There must be a neighbour who'll look after her. Stay with her. I don't think she's injured but she's definitely in shock. Get a doctor to take a look at her.'

'Very good, sir. What about Jones?'

Harper took a breath. 'We'll winkle him out in a minute. Tell the men to stand by.'

The room was airless and stifling as he walked back in. Jones didn't even follow with his eyes. He was somewhere far removed from here.

It was time to end this.

One step and then another, narrowing the distance between them. He noticed that the tap was slowly dripping into the stone sink. He let it give the rhythm to his footsteps. Jones didn't even see him. Finally he was close enough to smell the sourness of the man's breath. He began to reach for the knife, to take it away.

Suddenly, Jones let out a snarl, and slashed with the blade. Harper jumped back and brought the cosh down on the man's shoulder. One blow was enough. The knife clattered to the floor.

'Take him away.' It seemed to have lasted an eternity, but he knew it had taken no time at all. Jones was still in pain from the blow. It was easy to the coppers to push him down and lock on the handcuffs.

Harper looked around the room before he left. No damage done. Just the soft drip of the tap as he closed the door.

'Many problems, sir?' Ash asked as they strolled back to Millgarth.

'We'd better get a doctor to look at Jones. I don't know what's happened to him, but he's not right.'

'Putting it on, dò you reckon?'

'No, it's real.' He had no doubt about that. 'It could keep him from hanging. Not of sound mind.' But he wasn't the one to make that judgement. 'Who was the woman?'

'Her name's Catherine Taylor, sir. Don't know much more than that.'

'Let's find out, shall we? It might tell us more about Dempster.'

He felt deflated. All the tension, the heightened senses, they were draining away. Jones was back in custody, but somehow it felt like a hollow victory. All they were bringing back was the shell of a man. The rest . . . who knew what had happened?

'That's excellent news, Tom.' Parker was jubilant. 'Nobody injured?'

'No, sir.'

He sat in the large office at the town hall, a cup of tea in front of him. But he didn't want to eat or drink. All he craved was to go home, to disappear for a few hours and leave all this behind. To see Annabelle and make sure his own small world was still intact.

'Good police work. Inspector Ash said you faced Jones down by yourself when he had a hostage.'

It hadn't felt that way. He'd wanted to make sure Bert didn't hurt the woman. Nothing more than that. He'd never felt in real danger.

'I wouldn't call it that, sir—'

He might as well have saved his breath. 'I'm going to put you in for a commendation. You brought the whole business to an end in an admirable fashion.'

'Thank you, sir.' There was nothing else he could say.

Mary and Annabelle had finished their meal, each sitting with a currant slice. Harper took his plate from the oven and slid off the cover. Two minutes and he was caught up in the beautiful banality of family life. The typist in Mary's office who changed men the way some people changed their shirts. The woman at the bakery up Roundhay Road who insisted on telling everyone all about her husband's hernia.

He heard it all without really listening, letting the words soak through his skin. When the talk slowed, Annabelle looked at him, wondering if he wanted to say anything. He gave a quick shake of his head. After so many years, she knew. She picked some other topic from the air and began to speak.

He needed her to keep him sane. What would happen as she drifted away?

For the umpteenth time, Harper thought about Jones's face as the constables led him down to Millgarth. He had no idea where he was. He probably didn't even understand what he'd done. Just a few days before he'd been so different. What had happened in between? How had the gears disengaged in his head? Too many dark questions for the middle of the night. Not that he was ever likely to find any answers.

TWENTY-FIVE

'Stop at Millgarth,' Harper ordered the driver. 'I'll walk up to the town hall from there.'

Clouds seemed to hang on the horizon to the west, with a faint, teasing threat of rain. They needed something to damp down all the dust and clean the streets; it felt as if Leeds had been dry since the dawn of time. All the farmers would be looking to the skies and praying.

There was a buoyant mood in the detectives' room; the men sat

back, laughing and talking, still riding the wave of bringing in
Jones. Only Ash looked unhappy.

'Has Jones seen a doctor yet?' Harper asked.

'Last night, sir.' He frowned. 'He's not fit to stand trial. They'll
have him in court this morning and send him to High Royds for
assessment. The doctor thinks they'll keep him there.'

High Royds. The West Riding Lunatic Asylum. Maybe it was
the best place for him. He sighed. 'At least he's off the streets.'

'He is that, sir.' Ash hesitated for a second and gave a quick
cough. 'But I do wonder about Dempster giving us information like
that. I'd have expected him to make sure his gang took care of the
problem themselves.'

'Letting us handle it meant if anything went wrong his hands
were clean. But he's up to something. I don't know what it is yet.'

'I'm not sure if it's for him personally, or the Boys of Erin. He's
ambitious.'

Harper thought about the man he'd met, sitting at the table
as if he was the ruler of the Bank. Brimming with confidence
and arrogance. 'Both, maybe. But he's the type to put himself
first.'

'Maybe he's trying to get on our good side. You know, if he gives
us the tip about Jones, we won't look too closely at him.'

Harper shook his head. 'I don't see it. Too obvious. It wouldn't
work, anyway.'

'I wouldn't credit him with that much intelligence, sir. He's sly;
it doesn't mean he's clever.'

'He has something going on. Let's take another look at him and
the gang. There's trouble brewing. I can feel it.'

'You know we have a file on them.'

'It's been around since before I was a detective constable here.'

'I'll set Sissons on it. We're moving along with the outstanding
cases . . .'

'No,' Harper said, 'we're not.' He listed them on his fingers.
'One: who gave Davey Mullen that beating? Two: we don't have
anyone to take to court for killing Barney Thorpe. Three: what
about the arson in Mary's building? And four: there's still a gun
from the robbery that we haven't found. We're a long way from
having everything wrapped up.'

Harper took down his list. Another line through an item.

~~Fess murder~~
Arson
~~Metropole shooting~~
Barracks robbery
~~Francis Mullen~~
Barney Thorpe
Missing pistol
Davey Mullen
~~Bert Jones~~

As he walked up the Headrow he felt the first drops of rain and lifted his face to the sky. It wasn't going to be more than a light shower, but it was still welcome. He strolled on, relishing the damp and the brief coolness in the air.

'Are you back with us now, sir?' Miss Sharp asked as he settled behind his desk.

'Seems like it. Barring anything unforeseen.'

'I'd better bring you a cup of tea, then.'

The office smelled musty. He pushed up the sash on the window to air it out. It let in the smoke and soot and noise, but even that was an improvement. Miss Sharp wrinkled her mouth disapprovingly when she returned but said nothing. Tea and the morning post. Straight back into the routine.

He'd been busy for two hours, reading reports and letters, initialling documents to show he'd seen them, when Miss Sharp entered.

'Someone to see you,' she said. 'A Mr Dempster.'

Well, well, well. It hadn't taken the man long to find his way here. Perhaps he shouldn't be too surprised, after all. He thought for a moment, then said: 'Send him in.'

The same careful attention to his appearance as yesterday. The young man was fastidious. His nails were clean and carefully trimmed; you didn't often see that on a man, especially on the Bank. A different suit, a pale grey pinstripe with a starched white shirt.

'Sit down.'

'You recaptured Bert Jones.'

'We did.' Everyone in Leeds knew that by now.

'It seems you found my information useful.'

'Yes,' he acknowledged. 'I hope your – cousin, was it? – is recovering?' Ash's men had checked into her; there was nothing to tell about Catherine Taylor that they'd been able to find.

'She'll be fine. No damage done.' He ran his tongue across his lips. 'Tell me, Mr Harper, would you say that what I told you made the difference in recapturing Bert Jones?'

A very strange question. But Dempster seemed to specialize in them. What did he really want? Whatever it was, Harper was going to be wary. 'It helped, yes. As I'm sure you know, the police always appreciate people being good citizens.'

Dempster folded his hands on his lap and gave a faint smile. 'This was a little more than being a good citizen, wouldn't you say?'

'Was it? What would you call it? Helping the police is what people should do. Leeds is for everyone. All of us.'

'I was hoping you could publicly acknowledge my contribution.'

So that was it. Recognition and the idea that the coppers approved of him. Gratitude. Maybe something he could twist to make people imagine there was a partnership of some kind. Something that would give him weight and standing. A lever he might be able to use to win a council seat in time. Ash was right; Dempster was devious, but nowhere near as bright as he believed himself to be.

'If anyone asks me, I'm very happy to say we acted on information received.'

'From me.'

'We never give names, Mr Dempster. I'm sure you know that.'

The man plucked an imagined shred of lint from his sleeve. 'You could make an exception this time.'

'I'm afraid not. But I can tell you I'm grateful for what you did.' And that was all the man would receive. Nothing public, and certainly no endorsement.

Dempster sat and stared for a second, then rose in a single, flowing movement and left.

He'd been gone for almost a minute before Miss Sharp came and stood in the doorway. 'Who is he?'

'Someone who desperately wants to be somebody and thinks we should help him.'

'I don't often take against people straight off the bat,' she said, 'but there was something about him.' She gave a shudder.

Harper laughed. 'If it's any consolation, I don't think he'll be back.'

'Thank the Lord for that, at least.'

Dempster had some plan, some game in his mind. But Harper wasn't going to play. He had other things to consider.

Saturday afternoon and all the offices were closing for the week.

Still warm, though, as he began the walk back to the Victoria.

It gave him time to think without interruption. He was feeling like one of those acts at the music hall, dashing around to keep all the plates spinning on sticks without any of them crashing to the floor. And the longer it continued, the harder it became. With everything that was going on at home, how long could he keep going before it all fell around him?

For now, though, he needed to push on, to finish this. Tomorrow he'd go to the infirmary again. No doubt the matron would refuse him permission to see Davey Mullen. Still, he needed to try. That man was the key to too many things.

Sunday morning, Mary cancelled her ride with the Clarion cyclists again.

'Too much to do,' she said. 'I have to finish the accounts for the month.'

'I'm not an invalid,' Annabelle said.

'I mean it, Mam, I have plenty to keep me busy. Len's going to pop in later, once he's back from the cycling. Come out for a walk with us,' she said, as if the thought had just occurred to her.

'Give over.' But Annabelle was smiling.

At the infirmary, a few patients stood outside the hospital in their pyjamas and dressing gowns, taking in the sun as they stood and smoked.

The matron's door stood open. As he knocked, she turned and gave him a disdainful glance. 'What can I do for you, Deputy Chief Constable?' Polite, giving him the due of his rank, but without too much respect.

'Davey Mullen.'

'I gave you the answer before. I'm not allowing you to question him. He still can't speak or write. Or did you imagine some sort of miracle had happened? I can assure you it hasn't.'

He didn't let her words touch him. 'I simply wanted to know how he's progressing.'

She sniffed. 'You should know better than to ask me that. You'll need to talk to the doctor.'

Harper caught the man between wards, the same one he'd seen the other day.

'Physically, he's improving. There doesn't appear to be any internal damage.' The doctor shook his head in amazement. 'That's remarkable enough, given the hammering he took. Mr Mullen is starting to heal.'

'Could he answer questions?'

'You know he can't sp—'

'I mean nodding or shaking his head. He doesn't have to try and say a word.'

'Is it that important?'

'Yes,' Harper said. 'Truly, it is.'

The doctor took out a cigarette and lit it, closing his eyes for a moment as he sucked down the smoke. 'Come back tomorrow,' he said. 'I'll leave the order. But no more than ten minutes, and I'll make sure the nurse enforces that. Less if he becomes distressed.'

Annabelle curled against him in bed, his arm around her shoulders. It felt natural, it felt right.

'Did you go for that walk?'

'A little wander, listening to the lovebirds natter nineteen to the dozen. Made me feel like I was chaperoning them. Ruining their fun.'

'Mary wouldn't have asked if she didn't want you there.'

'We both know exactly why she asked me, and why she stayed here this morning. She wanted to keep an eye on me. The monthly accounts have always waited before.' She turned her head, and he could feel her eyes on him in the darkness. 'Did you two cook this up between you?'

'No,' he replied. It was a lie, but maybe better if she never knew the truth.

'Is this how it has to be from now on? Someone watching out for me?'

That was a question he didn't want to answer.

TWENTY-SIX

The hospital was just a short walk along Great George Street from the town hall. By nine o'clock, most people were at work, the streets quiet as Harper strode out. The air was dusty, soft with summer warmth and shimmering with soot.

The matron didn't say a word; her disapproving glare spoke volumes. But she led him along the corridor to the room. The constable outside the door hurriedly pushed his newspaper away as he saw his superior officer.

'A nurse will be here in a moment, Deputy Chief Constable. I expect you to obey what the doctor said to the letter.'

'I will. Thank you.'

'Has anyone tried to visit?' he asked the copper once the matron had gone.

'Just doctors and nurses, sir. Not many of those, to be honest. He's mostly on his own in there. I feel a bit sorry for him.'

'Don't. He'll survive.'

The nurse arrived and opened the door. Mullen turned his head, eyes widening as he saw Harper.

He was sitting up in bed. A newspaper lay open on his lap; with his arms in plaster, he couldn't hold it. No one had shaved him and now a thick, dark beard covered his cheeks and chin. It gave him a serious air, impossible to recognize as the same cocky man who'd turned up at the Victoria.

'You look as though you're improving, Mr Mullen.'

A slight shrug was his answer.

'I need to ask you a couple of things.'

Mullen inclined his head.

'Who did this to you?'

Under the beard, his mouth seemed to tighten. His gaze hardened. But no response. Harper hadn't expected an answer, but he needed to ask.

'You killed Barney Thorpe, didn't you?'

Harper saw a flicker of worry cross Mullen's face. He'd be wondering what the police had discovered. No need to let him know it was nothing at all, just suspicion, that he was free and clear. Let him stew and fret.

'Well?'

A firm shake of the head.

'Do you know the Boys of Erin?'

Mullen's eyes narrowed, but he shook his head once more. He looked at the nurse.

'Is that all, Mr Harper?' the nurse asked. 'The patient is growing tired.'

At the door, he glanced over his shoulder. Mullen was smirking.

'He's untouchable in there, sir,' Harper said. He paced around the chief constable's office, working off his anger. 'He knows it, too.'

'There's nothing we can do, Tom. It's not as if we have firm evidence against him for anything at all, is it?'

'He murdered Thorpe, I'm absolutely convinced of it.'

Parker blew smoke towards the ceiling. 'I daresay you're right. He probably did. He certainly has form. But, like I said, we have no proof, do we?'

'No. And he's not willing to tell us who beat him.'

'Then we'd better come up with the answer by ourselves. We're the police, after all. It's our job.'

'Yes, sir. But . . .'

'I do understand, Tom. It's the frustration. I've experienced it often enough, myself. Look, you and the detectives at Millgarth have worked wonders so far on all this.'

'Thank you.'

'You can crack it. I have faith.'

That was more than he had himself at the moment.

A morning of correspondence and reports in his office. Two meetings with the heads of C and D divisions about manpower. He'd slid so easily back into the routine, right down to tea and a biscuit at half past ten.

He'd just finished his work, put the cap on his fountain pen and blotted the last sheet, when the telephone rang.

'Busy, sir?' Ash asked.

'About to go for my dinner,' Harper answered. 'Why?'

'When you have a moment, you might want to come over to Millgarth, sir.'

'What have you got?'

'It can wait until you've eaten. No rush at all.'

How could he eat when temptation like that had been dangled in front of him?

'Well?' Harper asked the superintendent.

'Sissons has something.' He waved the sergeant in.

'I did a quick search on the house where we found Bert Jones. It's owned by the Boys of Erin through a company they have.'

'By the gang?' Harper asked. That didn't seem likely.

'Yes, sir.' Sissons nodded, his Adam's apple bobbing up and down. 'After I saw that, I checked a little further. In the last nine months they've bought four properties on the Bank.'

'Properties. What do you mean, exactly?'

'All houses, sir.'

'What are the addresses?'

Sissons placed a list on the table. Right there, the house where he'd met Dempster. Where they'd arrested Bert Jones.

'They're all occupied. Dempster lives in one of them, and as far as I can tell, the tenants in the others are his relatives.'

'Yes.'

'It made me wonder where they'd come up with the money for these places,' Sissons continued. 'They paid cash in every instance.'

'Do you have any answers?'

'Not yet, sir. I'm still working on that.'

'And loving every minute of it,' Harper said.

'Can't deny that, sir. The work suits me.' He grinned. 'And I'm still going through all the papers I took from Thorpe's house. There's quite a bit to look at, sir.'

'What do you make of it?' he asked after the sergeant had gone.

'Something's going on, no doubt about it,' Ash replied. 'I'm very curious about where they found the money.'

'So am I.' Harper frowned. 'We'll keep this on the back burner for now.'

'You look frazzled,' Annabelle said as he walked into the living room.

'I am.' He settled in the chair and popped his collar stud. 'When this case is over, I'm going to sleep for a week.'

Her mouth became a knowing smile. 'Do you know how many

times I've heard you say that, Tom Harper? And when it's all done and dusted, the next morning you're up and off again at the usual time.'

'Maybe so,' he admitted with a laugh.

Perfectly normal. But for how much longer?

TWENTY-SEVEN

'How are things coming along with Thorpe's papers?' he asked Sissons.

The sergeant gestured at the pile on his desk and three more on the floor. Slowly dwindling, but still daunting to anyone who didn't enjoy paperwork.

'I wouldn't have guessed he was such a stickler for detail, sir. That's good for us. It means everything's in there. But it takes an age to go through it all when I'm working on my own.'

'Anything in there about the guns?'

'Nothing. I'd have told you straight away. Sorry, sir.'

'Keep at it.' It had to be in there somewhere. Had to be.

'What do you think?' he asked Ash.

'I'm hopeful, sir,' the man answered after a little thought. 'Galt seems to think he has a tip on something.'

Harper felt a stir of possibility. 'Did he say what it was?'

'No, sir. Scared of hexing it. We'll hear if it turns into something.'

'It feels like we still have so much to do. Too much.'

'We're getting there. Bit by bit.'

'If you say so.' He sighed. 'Seems to me we're walking uphill with a force ten gale blowing in our faces.'

'Don't you worry, sir. We'll sort it out.'

'Yes.' But at the moment it was hard to feel confident about anything.

When he returned the next day there was a hushed atmosphere of study in the detectives' room at Millgarth. All of them with their heads down as they read files and made notes. It was an unusual sight.

Harper raised his eyebrows in a question as he entered Ash's office.

'I decided it would be best to have them all sifting through the rest of Thorpe's papers. It would take Sissons the rest of the year on his own.'

'How long have they been at it?' he asked.

'Since first thing, sir. They're going over every scrap with a nit comb.'

'Did Galt's tip amount to anything?'

A small shrug. 'He says he has to talk to someone else later.'

That happened. One person sent you to another. A chain. Sometimes it paid off. More often, it petered out to nothing. But it all took patience and persistence.

Out to Morley for a meeting that stretched on and on, and finally back into town, past the Jewish cemetery on Gelderd Road and through all the aching, dismal poverty that was Beeston and Holbeck, over the river to the centre of the city and the town hall. Miss Sharp had left for the day. He checked through the papers on his desk. They could all wait for tomorrow.

He was about to close the door when the telephone rang.

'Galt's tip came through,' Ash told him. 'We have a name on the arson.'

'The arson? Who is it?'

'A lad called Billy Bell. No record as an adult, but he was up for setting fires when he was a boy.'

Harper felt his heartbeat quicken. 'How old is he now?'

'Seventeen, sir.'

'Does he have any connections with anyone?'

'With Thorpe, you mean, sir? Nothing that we know of at the moment.'

'Have you brought him in?'

'Just arranging it. He's in Burmantofts. Haymount View, close by the brick works. I telephoned to ask if you want to join us, since you have a personal interest.'

'I'll meet you up there.'

He heard the pleasure in Ash's voice. 'Give us a quarter of an hour, sir.'

This was better than having to think and brood. Something to send a jolt through his system.

*   *   *

'Rogers, you and I will take the front door,' Ash said. 'Walsh and Galt at the back.'

'Where do you want me?' Harper asked.

'Come in behind us at the front. Billy lives with his father. Stephen Bell.' He glanced at Harper. 'I'm sure you remember him, sir.'

'All too well.' It explained why the superintendent wanted the whole squad here. Ten years before, Stephen Bell had knocked out two constables with his fists before another four managed to bring him down and arrest him. Not just violent, but strong.

'Two minutes to get yourselves in position,' Ash continued. 'Be ready as soon as I blow the whistle. I'll knock on the door first. If they don't answer, we'll hammer it down.'

One or two people were out and about, going to and from the corner shop or the public house. Down at the far end of the road, women sat out by their doorsteps while children played in groups on the cobbles. Two or three men had gathered together to talk and smoke near the gable end of the terrace row. The rest of the street was quiet. Together, Ash and Rogers filled the pavement; trailing behind them, he felt small.

A pause outside number eleven. Rogers brought his fist down on the door. No answer at first, then a sudden scurry of feet across the floor.

'Kick it down.'

The big boot pushed the lock back, then sent the door crashing against the wall. Ash was through, Rogers hard on his heels, running into the kitchen.

Harper moved slowly up the stairs. Two bedrooms, both of them empty, just a tangle of sheets on the bed. He checked the wardrobes. Nobody was hiding up here. Nothing that could be used to start a fire.

Bell and his father were standing in the tiny yard, both of them with wrists cuffed behind their backs. Sissons was bent over, retching and holding his stomach. Rogers had the warm flush of a good scrap on his face.

Harper stood back and looked at the prisoners. He remembered the father, a brute of a man with hair shaved down to stubble and thick, quick fists. The son was nearly as tall, but he hadn't filled out yet. He stared straight ahead, not gazing at anyone.

'Take them down to Millgarth,' Ash ordered.

It didn't take long to search the rest of the house. No small can of petrol, no pile of rags that could be used to start a blaze. He prised open the door of the small outhouse at the back of the yard.

Old tins with paint dried around the rims. Stiff, stained pieces of canvas. Then, hidden away under some ratty blankets, another can. It was rectangular, the red paint flaking away from the metal, with a short neck and a cap that screwed on tight. Harper picked it up. Half-full. He opened it up and sniffed. Petrol. Billy Bell was going to have some questions to answer.

He was sitting in the interview room, a sullen frown on his face, when Harper walked in with the petrol can.

'You didn't do a very good job of hiding it.' The young man glanced at it then turned away. 'Looks like you used just about enough to start a fire. Maybe the one on Albion Place. We know you like to get a good blaze going, Billy.'

Just a slow shake of his head in response.

Harper didn't have the patience for this. Not when it involved Mary. Certainly not with life the way it stood just now. Better to leave Billy for Walsh. He'd be able to tie the lad in knots and ease the truth out of him. By morning they'd know, though he was already convinced. Young Billy practically shone with guilt.

The real question was why he'd done it. He hadn't picked the building at random; there were plenty of easier targets in the middle of town. Someone had put him up to it. Who? And why?

'What have you charged the father with?' Harper asked.

'Assaulting a policeman,' Ash replied. 'The magistrate for him tomorrow.'

Six months. It was the standard sentence for the crime.

'Tell young Billy we might make it a lesser charge for his da if he cooperates with us.'

Ash raised an eyebrow in surprise. 'Do you think it's necessary, sir? He'll spill it all, anyway.'

'If Walsh has any problems, he can make the offer.'

'Very good, sir. I'm sure we'll have something for you by morning.'

'You will, I'm certain. That's good work by Galt. And thank you for inviting me.' He smiled. 'I enjoyed that. Clean and easy.'

'It was, although Sissons might disagree.'

TWENTY-EIGHT

Almost ten o'clock. A velvet darkness all around him as he took the familiar walk home. The brief moments of action had been a welcome release, taking everything else off his mind. But now they were over and reality was seeping back in.

He kicked a pebble down the pavement time after time until it vanished in the gutter. Counted the flagstones. Anything to occupy his brain and keep the thoughts away. It worked until he reached Manor Street and saw Annabelle's Rex Touring Car parked there.

What was going to happen to her?

'Me mam went to bed a quarter of an hour ago,' Mary said as soon as he came through the door. She was at the table, making calculations and writing figures in a ledger. 'She said she was feeling tired.'

'How was she?' Harper asked.

'Keeping herself busy,' she answered after a moment. 'One thing after another.'

'Yes,' he said. No surprise; that was Annabelle's way. 'No more incidents?'

'Nothing at all. She was fine.'

'I'm sure she is. We found the lad who set the fire.'

Her eyes widened. 'Who was he? Did he say why?'

'Just seventeen. We haven't dug up the reason yet. We will.' He sighed. 'Goodnight. Don't stay up too late.'

As he eased under the sheet he heard a single soft snore and a warm exhalation. She really was asleep.

'Town hall, sir?' his driver asked.

'Yes,' he began, then changed his mind. 'No, let's start at Millgarth. I shouldn't be too long.'

With luck, he'd have some good news to take to the chief constable.

'It only took half an hour before he admitted he'd done it,' Walsh said.

'Did he say why?'

'He claims he liked the look of the building and there was no one around. That's all.'

'Do you believe him?'

'No, sir. But I haven't managed to break him down on that yet. I'll take another crack at him this morning.'

'Did you try the offer of a lesser charge for his father?'

Walsh nodded. 'He claims there's nothing more to tell.'

'Too late now, anyway. The old man will be up before the beak. Let me know what happens.'

~~Fess murder~~
~~Arson~~
~~Metropole shooting~~
Barracks robbery
~~Francis Mullen~~
Barney Thorpe
Missing pistol
Davey Mullen
~~Bert Jones~~

'One by one you're ticking them off,' Parker said with approval.

'Still not enough, sir. We don't know who beat Davey Mullen. And there's a stolen Webley floating around out there.'

'We solved the murders. Those were the big things. We have the newspapers off our backs.'

'Maybe we do, sir, but I believe there's much more going on below the surface. We just haven't found it yet.'

The chief constable chuckled. 'You always did like a good conspiracy, Tom. Look, you've got some results. Be happy with that.'

He didn't have them *all*. That was what he'd been trying to say. No matter; he'd keep the men at Millgarth digging. Luck and solid police work had brought them this far. It might still give them the lot.

Just after half past ten a rain shower passed through Leeds. For ten minutes the heavens opened and water bounced off the pavement. He stood by the open window, relishing the damp and the freshness in the air. People passed with their umbrellas raised, but no one was huddling out of the way; they all seemed to enjoy it. After it had gone, for a few minutes the air felt cool and clean. Soon enough, though, summer returned.

He signed another form, blotted the ink and reached for the telephone as soon as it rang.

'Deputy Chief Constable Harper.'

'This is Inspector Cartwright, sir.'

Cartwright? Who? There was no Inspector Cartwright in Leeds. He waited, pressing the receiver against his ear.

'Special Branch, sir.'

Now he knew the man. He'd looked a complete fool when he allowed that suffragette Lilian Lenton to escape from right under his nose after she was released from Armley. He smiled at the memory.

'What can I do for you, Inspector?'

'We've had a report that Miss Lenton is back in England, sir. I was wondering if anyone had mentioned seeing her in Leeds at all.'

'No,' Harper said. 'I've heard nothing. But I'll contact you if there's any word.'

A report? More likely a vague, hopeful rumour, and now they were desperately rooting around to see if there was any truth in it. He shook his head. They didn't have a bloody clue.

'Has Billy's Bell rung any more?'

Ash grimaced. 'I hope you didn't spend all your dinner time thinking up that one, sir.'

'Spur of the moment.'

'I trust you'll resist next time, sir. He did give us something. The name of the man who paid him to set the fire.'

'Who was it?'

'Barney Thorpe.'

For a moment it made no sense. But then things clicked into place. Thorpe had arranged Fess's murder and the Metropole shooting. This was part of the plan to point a finger at Davey Mullen.

'Why? Did he say?'

'Bell doesn't know. Walsh kept prodding at him, but it sounds as if he's telling the truth. He was given the address and that was it.'

'That exact address? Where my daughter has her business?'

'Yes, sir.'

'How much money did Thorpe give him?'

'A pound.'

Harper let out a slow sigh. 'Was there any previous connection between Bell and Thorpe?'

'Billy's father had done a little strong-arm work for Barney. Years ago now. That's all we've been able to find.'

'See if Thorpe had a grievance against anyone in the building.'

'We're checking, sir. But I think we both know the truth.'

'Yes, but I don't see *why*. Thorpe wasn't the brains in all this. He was just another cog. He's certainly not the one behind it. Someone else is involved and we don't know who.'

'We're still searching.'

And Thorpe was no longer around to tell them.

'At least you can tell your Mary there's no chance of it happening again,' Ash said.

That was something. She'd said nothing about it lately, but they'd all had bigger things to occupy them. Still, the worry would have remained, burrowing deeper and deeper under her skin. He could take that away.

'Who'd want Mullen hanged or in jail here?' Harper asked.

'That other gang in New York is the obvious answer. The Hudson Dusters, or whatever they're called.'

'But we haven't come up with a link between them and Thorpe. Not with Thorpe and anyone on this.'

'I've been thinking, sir,' Ash said. 'We had those mysterious sightings of a third American.'

'We established that he didn't exist.'

'What if he did, sir? What if there really was another one, watching Mullen and directing Fess?'

Harper sat back on the chair, rubbing his chin and chuckling. 'You know, just this morning the chief said I was the one who liked conspiracies.'

'It would be an explanation,' Ash said.

'Then find him. Bring him here.'

Ash grinned. 'You always point out the snags, don't you, sir? The men are still going through Thorpe's papers. Maybe they'll come up with something.'

'We're going to finish this. Keep them on it. We're getting closer. I can feel it.'

'From your lips to God's ears, sir. We've had a request from the mortuary too, about the body of Mullen's father. They can't keep him much longer. They want to know what they should do with him.'

There was only one man who could make that decision, and he

was in the infirmary. This gave the ideal opportunity to talk to him once more. And one way or another, this time he'd need to answer.

The matron listened, hands perched primly in her lap.

'You've become something of a thorn in my side regarding Mr Mullen,' she said once he'd finished. 'However, in this case I think I can allow you to speak to him.' She flashed him a dark look. 'Under supervision, and *only* to talk about plans for his father's funeral. I'll send a nurse with you.'

The woman had a face like a hawk and a brusque manner. The constable on duty outside barely had time to stand and salute as she briskly pushed the door open. Mullen was trying to turn a page in the newspaper, using the cast like an awkward paw. He stopped as he saw Harper.

It didn't take long to explain the problem. Every second he was aware of the nurse's eyes on him.

'As I recall, you were looking at cemeteries to decide on somewhere to bury your father. Did you find one?'

His eyes were dark, giving nothing away. A short nod as an answer.

'Where was it?'

Mullen lifted his arms to point at his jaw. Unable to speak.

'Beckett Street?' No reply. 'Harehills?'

Another nod. Now they were getting somewhere.

'Did you purchase a plot?'

A third.

'Would you be willing to let the burial go ahead while you're still a patient in here?'

Mullen stared straight ahead for a long time, then opened his mouth. What came out was a thin croak, nothing like his proper voice, but still no doubt about the word.

'Yes.'

'I'll take care of it,' Harper promised. 'And he'll be there for you to visit once you're out of here.'

Two words this time. Unsteady but he could make them out. *Thank you.* It was worth trying one more question.

'Who did this to you?'

'That's quite enough, Deputy Chief Constable,' the nurse warned him. 'You know what the matron said.'

Mullen looked up with a faint, mocking smile.

TWENTY-NINE

'The Branch really rang you?' the chief constable said. 'To ask if we'd heard anything about this Lenton woman sneaking back into the country? You're kidding, aren't you, Tom?'

'I wish I was, sir.'

Incredulous, Parker shook his head. 'They've got some brass neck, I'll say that.'

'I told him we'd inform them if we learned anything.'

'They've probably been in touch with every force in the country. Anything to try and make themselves look better.' He waved it away. 'Enough of that. I see your arsonist confessed.'

'Yes, sir. He claims Thorpe paid him to set fire to the place.'

'Really?' Parker frowned. 'Why would Thorpe do that?'

'We're trying to find a reason.' Harper frowned. 'It seems funny that I used to think Davey Mullen was where all the strands came together. All along it was Barney Thorpe.'

'Why, though?'

'That I don't know yet. Mullen worked it out long before we did. It's why he killed Barney.'

'You *think* he killed him.'

'I'm positive he did, sir. I just can't prove it, that's all.'

'Do you think you're close?'

'I hope so,' Harper replied. 'I really hope so.'

Just the two of them at home tonight; Mary was out at the pictures with Len. The windows were open and the sounds of Sheepscar drifted in.

'Nothing more?' he asked as they ate.

'Not a wobble.' Annabelle stared at him. 'I'm starting to wonder if I made too much of it.'

'In a way, I hope you did.' He smiled but she didn't return it.

'I'm scared, Tom,' she told him in a small voice. 'I'm terrified.'

'I know,' he told her and took her hand. It didn't seem enough. But what else could he say? What must it be like, not knowing that something might be missing from your memory when you woke up in the morning? How could he begin to imagine that? It was a life sentence, but never knowing what punishment each day would bring. Of course she was petrified. Anyone would be.

'We'll get through it,' he promised. 'You and me. Together.'

The telephone bell was hammering away as he walked into his office. Not even eight o'clock; Miss Sharp wouldn't be here for another half hour. He snatched up the receiver.

'Good morning, sir.' Sissons's voice. He sounded weary, as if he'd been working all night. 'Would you have a minute to see Superintendent Ash and myself?'

'You've found something, haven't you?'

'It's something I need to show you, sir.'

'I'll be here.'

Harper paced as he waited. Sissons was as steady and reliable as a detective sergeant should be. He'd never been given to flights of fancy. Whatever he'd found was solid. Real.

It took more than quarter of an hour for them to arrive. Sissons was unshaved, the bags heavy under his eyes, and the lines around his mouth formed into deep creases as he smiled. But he looked happy as he opened his briefcase and brought out a small pile of folders.

'Do you have something tasty?'

'I think so, sir. Wait and see for yourself.'

Harper glanced at Ash. The big man gave a nod. He was convinced.

'I was going through Thorpe's business correspondence, sir, and I came across this.' He took out a single sheet of paper. 'This is something he received. It talks about providing goods to pay back some money Thorpe had lent.'

'Any specific services?'

'No, sir, and I couldn't find anything more that related to it. But there was something about it that seemed familiar. It kept worrying away at me. I was at home; I'd just had my supper when I realized what it was.' He raised his head and beamed.

'Are you going to tell us or keep it to yourself?'

'Here, sir.' He produced another piece of paper. 'You recall I was looking at the Boys buying those houses? This was in there. Do you see? The handwriting's the same. And there's something about the colour of the ink. It's an unusual shade of blue.'

Harper put on his spectacles and compared the two. No doubt – the same person had written both. The second had a signature: John Dempster. The head of the gang.

'That's good work. You've connected Thorpe and the Boys of Erin. But as far as I can see, there's nothing illegal in here.'

'No, sir. You're right. But once I'd established they were doing business, I went deeper into Thorpe's accounts.' He reached into the briefcase again, brought out a ledger and leafed through to a bookmarked page. 'Here.'

Numbers, names, Harper thought as he looked down the list.

'Is this it? Green Erin Limited?'

'That's the company Dempster formed to buy those houses. Thorpe lent them money. Not enough to pay in full for the houses, but still a decent amount. And it looks as if he wasn't charging them interest. He was a moneylender, so that's strange in itself, you have to admit.' He turned to another marked page. 'There.'

'These show the repayments on the money Thorpe lent.' A little mental arithmetic. 'It's still thirty pounds short, even without any interest.'

Sissons turned to the next page and pointed to a line.

Green Erin, debt cleared. In the next column, three cramped lines of figures.

'Take a look at the date, sir.'

'What about it?'

'It's five days after the pistols were stolen from the barracks.'

'Interesting,' he agreed. 'But on its own, it still doesn't prove anything. What do those numbers mean?'

Sissons grinned. He brought out another file, the report of the break-in at the barracks.

'Here's the beautiful part, sir. Those figures at the side that Thorpe wrote down are the serial numbers of three of the four pistols that were stolen.'

'And we have them,' Ash said. 'The two Bert Jones and the Metropole shooter used, and that third one we found at Barney's house.'

Harper went through it all once more. But it was all right there on the page.

'I can't believe he'd be stupid enough to write all that down.'

'He probably never imagined anyone would follow the trail, sir,' Sissons said. 'And he was probably right. We're lucky that Thorpe's bookkeeping was quite exact.'

'And just as well it was you going through everything. I don't think anybody else would have spotted the similarity in those inks. That's some excellent work, Sergeant.'

Sissons blushed. 'Thank you, sir.'

'It means the Boys of Erin probably still have one gun, sir,' Ash said.

'Unless they've already sold it to someone else,' Harper said and raised a hand to stop the comment. 'I know, I know, we can't tell. That means we're going to have to assume they still have it and pray we're right.'

'And they own four houses where they can keep it out of sight,' Sissons said.

There was no choice. They had to go in and find it.

'A raid on four places on the Bank,' he said, and exhaled slowly. That was going to be bloody and brutal. As it was, the police were never welcome there.

Ash smiled under his moustache. 'Perhaps we could call in the army, sir.'

He smiled back, but it wasn't too far from the truth. There were still a few streets where the police only dared to patrol in pairs, not that the force would admit it. Going in mob-handed . . . they wouldn't just be going up against the Boys of Erin, they'd be battling the whole neighbourhood.

'I need to talk to the chief,' he said. 'This is going to take a little planning. Leave all those papers here, and I want the addresses of those houses they own. Are we sure that's all they have?'

'As much as I can be, sir,' Sissons told him without hesitation. 'I've gone over it every which way.'

'How certain are you they still have that gun?' Chief Constable Parker asked.

'Four were stolen. We know they used three to help pay their debt to Barney Thorpe. We have all those. One's still out there.'

'You mean you're guessing and hoping.'

'An educated guess, sir,' Harper answered.

Parker pinched the bridge of his nose. 'Four houses? If we're going to send enough policemen into the Bank to do this properly, we're going to risk a riot. You realize that, don't you?'

'I do, sir. But it's worthwhile. The Boys of Erin have been quietly building power and flexing their muscles. We didn't know how much. This will slap them back down and let them know who runs Leeds. All of Leeds.'

Parker nodded, puffing on his cigar. 'I'll see you have all the men you need, Tom. Just make sure you find that pistol or the papers will be down on you like the wrath of God.'

'We'll do it Sunday, sir.'

'Make sure you're fully prepared.'

'We will be.'

'Clever thinking, sir,' Ash said. 'The Bank is still a very Catholic area. Always plenty of people on their way to church on a Sunday morning.'

'We'll go in at six o'clock,' Harper told him. 'Before early Mass. Most of them won't be up yet. That's what I'm hoping, anyway. We'll have one of your men running the raid at each house. I want you to oversee it all.'

'Very good, sir. Four squads. How many constables in each?'

'I think six should be enough, don't you? That will allow for any barracking from the locals.'

'It's going to take time to search each house thoroughly, sir. People will have chance to gather outside.'

'I know.'

'And we're betting everything that it's in one of those places.'

'Believe me, I'm very well aware of that. Word about what we're doing stays strictly in this squad until Sunday morning. No mentioning it to anyone else. I don't want to risk any leaks. Get Sergeant Mason to pick the uniforms. I want big, hard men. And don't tell them what they'll be doing.'

Ash grinned. 'I'm sure he can manage that. sir.'

'You'd better put them to work. We're going to be thoroughly prepared for this.'

Annabelle was in the kitchen, scraping and scouring the pots.

'Do you and Len have any plans this weekend?' Harper asked Mary.

'Nothing in particular,' she told him. 'Maybe a walk in East End

Park tomorrow afternoon after work.' She lowered her voice. 'I'm not going out with the Clarions on Sunday, I'll stay around here. Why?'

There was no reason. Just conversation, a way to lead into something else.

'That fire at your office.'

Her gaze sharpened at the words. 'What about it?'

'You were never really the victim.' He pursed his mouth. 'It had nothing to do with you at all. You were just caught in the middle. Someone was trying to make us think Mullen had done it. He was innocent. Of most of the things we had him down for, really.'

'Are you sure of that, Da?'

'Positive.'

She didn't say any more, but he sensed her relief. The worry had been there, niggling away at the back of her mind. At least he'd been able to get rid of that. In time it would be Len who'd ease her fears and listen to her worries. His little girl would have someone else to look after her.

Saturday morning. He stopped briefly at the town hall, checking his desk to make sure nothing urgent was waiting before the driver dropped him at Millgarth.

The detectives' room was busy, all the men poring over papers. Galt and Sissons had brought plans of all the houses and streets from the city clerk's office and now they were making notes of the details.

Ash had a map of the area pinned to the wall, with nothing marked on it for curious eyes to observe.

'We're going to have two wagons parked here, sir.' His thick finger pointed at a spot on York Road. We can bring anyone we arrest there and guard them. A hop, skip and a jump back here and it's out of the Bank. I'll be there, handling things.'

'How is everything else coming along?'

'We'll be ready. Mason will have the constables here at five tomorrow morning.'

'When you have everything prepared, send the men home. I want them well rested.'

'Yes, sir. They're eager.'

He could feel it; the tension crackled in the room. In the end he stayed until noon. By then he knew the layout of each of the houses, the ways in and out, the places where there might be problems.

Harper came out to a dry, dusty afternoon. He caught the tram along North Street, alighting at the bottom of Roundhay Road.

Annabelle was sitting at the table, a glass of lemonade beside her as she read the new issue of *Common Cause*.

'All about the Pilgrimage?' he asked.

'Yes.' He could hear her regret, see it on her face. She wanted to be there. Part of her probably still wondered if she'd made the right decision.

'Come on,' he told her. 'The day's too lovely to waste around here. Why don't we drive out somewhere?'

She stared at him. 'Are you sure you trust me behind the wheel, Tom Harper?'

'I've trusted you for the last twenty-three years,' he said with a smile. 'It's a bit late to stop now. Come on, put a hat on and we'll go.'

THIRTY

Tom Harper was up long before the first glimmer of light appeared on the horizon. He hadn't slept much for the last hour, anyway; he might as well be doing something useful instead of lying in bed and brooding. He moved silently through the rooms. Too much practice, too many years of doing this without waking Annabelle or Mary.

The streets were quiet. A knocker-up went from house to house with his pole, tapping on the upstairs windows to wake people who had Sunday shifts. A cart trundled towards the Leylands, the slow clop of hooves sounding a tired rhythm over the cobbles.

Harper had the cosh in his jacket pocket, and his truncheon dangled from a leather loop around his wrist. It had been presented to him the day he became a police constable, all those years ago. The heavy wood banged against his leg as he strode down the road.

He exhaled. They'd find the gun, finish all this, and break the Boys of Erin completely. He was ready.

*   *   *

Ash was already at Millgarth, going over the final details. Walsh, Galt, Sissons and Rogers were there, too, checking house plans once more, making sure everything was clear and fixed in their minds.

They worked quietly, barely a word spoken. Harper stood and watched. Everyone knew what to do. He watched their faces, the intensity behind their eyes. Preparing for battle.

Out in the yard behind the building, constables were beginning to clamber into the two wagons. It would be a tight squeeze for a few minutes as they travelled up to York Road, but it kept them out of sight.

As the vehicles creaked out of the yard, he looked at the clock. Half past five. He turned to his squad. 'Gentlemen?'

They passed Somerset Street, and Harper glanced down the road. But no one was about, no lights shining in any of the windows. The house where Francis Mullen had lived looked deserted. A moment and he let it slip away from his mind.

The early hour meant they'd have surprise on their side, a chance to start searching. The gun was in one of those houses. It had to be. As they climbed the hill in the pale light, he hoped to God he was right.

He brought out his watch. Still ten minutes before the hour. Harper gathered his men out of sight.

'Walsh, you're going in to Dempster's house. I'll be with you.' It seemed the most likely place to find the weapon. Surely he'd want to keep it close. For control and for safety.

'Yes, sir.'

'Go and gather the uniforms. They haven't been told what we're doing, so they couldn't gossip, but they'll have worked it out by now. Brief them and get them in place. As soon as the church bell rings, break down the doors.' He stared at their faces. 'Understood?'

The first peal of the bell.

'Now,' Walsh yelled, and stood aside as a burly copper threw himself at the door. Once, twice, then it began to give.

'Again,' Harper shouted, and it flew open. Two uniforms standing guard outside, two at the back, the remaining two in the house. Harper ran up the stairs and threw open the bedroom door. Dempster was sitting up in bed, scrambling for a cudgel from the floor.

'Leave it. Where's the pistol?'

He blinked, barely awake. 'What pistol? What are you on about?'
But the words were too glib, too quick. He had the gun somewhere.

'My men are searching. You're going to stay here. Sit on the chair
by the wall and don't move. You might as well enjoy what you
can of the day.'

It wasn't in any of the drawers. No hard lumps in the mattress.
Harper made his way around the room, pulling at the floorboards
to see if any were loose, checking the skirting boards.

Dempster chuckled. 'I don't know what you're doing. I don't
have a gun. Never had one.'

'The Boys of Erin sold three to Barney Thorpe. It cleared the
debt you owed him.'

'What? Prove it.'

'Barney put the serial numbers in his ledger.'

Dempster glared. The fury and the hatred shone in his eyes. 'You
won't find any gun here. There isn't one.'

'That's fine by me,' Harper told him, relishing the astonishment
on his face. 'We're looking at those three other houses Green Erin
Limited owns.'

The man did his best to hide it, but panic flickered for a
moment in his eyes. Got him.

Walsh was tearing the living room apart.

'Send a man upstairs to escort Dempster to the wagon and
gather up every scrap of paper; we'll go through it later. I don't
think the gun's here. It's in one of the other places.'

'Very good, sir.'

The streets were still quiet. He took out his watch. Quarter past
six. Fifteen minutes had flown by. Soon enough men would come
tumbling out of their houses, ready for a Sunday morning scrap.
There wasn't a cat in hell's chance of escaping from here without
a fight, but if they were quick, it might not be too bad.

The house where Dempster's cousin lived. A constable was
guarding Catherine Taylor. She was dressed, a sullen, angry
expression on her face.

'Nothing here, sir,' Sissons told him.

'Checked everywhere?'

'Every nook and cranny.'

'Then take your men and guard the other places. Take Miss
Taylor to Millgarth.'

'Yes, sir.'

Two down, two still to go. The pistol was in one of them; Dempster had made him absolutely certain of that. But time was running out.

Harper peered outside the door. Nobody in sight. He started to run down the street, on to the next house on their list. A stone hit the wall near his head, then bounced off down the cobbles. He crouched a little. A smaller target, harder to hit.

Something struck his shoulder, a sharp, fleeting pain.

It was beginning.

Two men were watching the house. He crashed between them, knocking them to the ground, and the constable stood aside to let him in.

Galt was in the kitchen, a triumphant grin on his face. 'Look what I discovered, sir.'

He held up a Webley revolver by the tip of its barrel. God, Harper thought, it was an ugly, ungainly thing. Yet the sight made him smile with pleasure. Exactly what they'd come up here to find.

'Loaded?'

'No, sir. I checked the serial number. It's from the barracks. We've got them all now.'

The man seated at the table tried to rise. A large bobby placed a hand on his shoulder and pushed him back down.

'Where was it?'

'Behind a cupboard sir.'

'I didn't know it was here,' the man said. 'I swear to God. Someone must have left it.'

'What's your name?' Harper asked.

'Charlie. Charlie Doyle.' Dempster's brother-in-law. A sheen of sweat covered his face and the stink of fear rolled off his body.

'You're going to prison, Charlie. Possession of a stolen weapon. I daresay you're a member of the Boys of Erin. They stole the guns, didn't they, so we can get you for that, too. What do you think, Mr Galt?'

'Very likely, sir. I imagine we'll find his fingerprints on the gun.'

'Take him to the wagon. You'd better watch out – we're going to have a few problems.'

The constable grinned. 'Never you worry, sir. I've had tougher than this lot for breakfast before now. Come on, you.' He took Doyle by his collar and dragged him to his feet.

'Wait a minute.' The man's voice had the furious edge of desperation. He was looking around wildly.

'What?' Harper asked.

'I can give you some information.'

'What is it?'

'What's it worth?'

He stared at Doyle in exasperation. 'You're not in a position to try and make deals.'

'That gangster. The American.' He was scrambling for the words.

'What about him?' Harper didn't want to sound too eager. But find out who'd given him that beating . . . everything wrapped up in one fell swoop. Now that would be something.

'I know who hurt him.' He was cunning, no doubt about that.

'Who?'

Doyle shook his head. 'You've got to make it worth my while.'

'I can make you wish you'd never been born if you don't tell me.'

'I want the possession of the gun charge dropped.'

He considered the bargain. Finally, he nodded. 'Only if the information brings a conviction. Otherwise, no.'

'It's the gospel truth.'

'If I had a shilling for every time a criminal said that, I'd be a millionaire by now. But if it really is true, you'll be fine, won't you? It's your choice.'

Harper could feel his heart thudding in his chest. The moment seemed to stretch out towards eternity.

'All right,' Doyle agreed. 'It was Ciaran Fox and Pat Andrews. Johnny was with them.'

'How do you know?'

Doyle swallowed. 'I drove the motor car.'

Harper wanted to ask questions. Why had they given Davey Mullen a beating? Why did they dump him in Roundhay Park? But those could wait until they were safely back at Millgarth.

'Take him to the wagon. Handcuffs and a close guard. And keep that pistol safe.'

'Fox and Andrews are living in one of the other houses, sir,' Galt said.

'That's handy.' He smiled. 'I'm on my way there now.'

More men were out on the street. He kept a tight hold on the truncheon as he came out of the house, and held the cosh in his left hand. They followed at a distance, a constant threat. But they didn't attack. Not yet.

Rogers had two men standing in the kitchen. The floor was a chaos of pots and pans.

'They weren't too keen on me searching, sir. I don't know why. It's not as if we found anything.'

'We have the gun. But it turns out these two have been very handy with their fists. They gave Davey Mullen his pasting. Put the cuffs on them and take them to the wagon.'

One of them tried to run. He hadn't gone two steps before Rogers kicked him on the knee. As he cried out in pain, a constable threw him down to the ground, turned him over and locked on the handcuffs in quick, practised movements.

'Right, are we ready? Draw your truncheons, we're likely to have a battle royal.'

'Just one moment, sir,' Rogers said. He disappeared and Harper heard feet running up the stairs.

'They're not watching the back,' he said as he returned. 'We can slip out that way.'

It bought them a few yards, nothing more. Through the yard, down the ginnel and into the street. But as soon as they turned the corner, the crowd spotted them. Shouting and baying for blood.

Harper hurried them along the cobbles, glancing over his shoulder. They didn't have a hope of escape. He took out his police whistle and gave two short blasts, then turned. One of the constables stood beside him.

'Let's show them they don't have free run of the streets, eh, sir?'

They couldn't win; it was two against twenty or more. But they could slow up the mob a little. Enough for the others to rush the prisoners to the wagons.

A fist banged him on the side of the head, hard enough to rattle his teeth. He brought the cosh down and hit something, feeling a bone crack as a man cried out in pain. One of them out of the game. But another was right there, a fist like iron thumping him in the chest to send him spinning backwards.

They were on him like a pack of animals, ready to tear him apart. Harper curled himself into a ball, one hand protecting his skull. Make yourself small, that was what he'd been told when he began on the beat. There's less they can damage that way.

It still hurt like hell. A torrent of blows, kicks from boots with steel caps. Nothing he could do to defend himself. He just needed to survive this . . .

Then it stopped. Suddenly, swiftly. For a second he was too frightened to move; it might begin again. A broad hand reached down and grabbed his wrist.

'You're all right now, sir. They've gone.'

Ash pulled him to his feet. Harper's left arm hurt, his ears were ringing, but he could stand. When he put one foot in front of another, he could walk. He could see clearly, nothing blurred in his vision. Everything seemed fine inside.

He took a breath. 'Thank you.'

Ash grinned. 'I think the lads enjoyed wading in. We kept a few of the big ones for the magistrate and threw the minnows back.'

Harper looked down. Dust and dirt all over his suit. It was ripped in two or three places. Five years old and only fit for the bin.

'We've got the gun,' he said. 'And the men who beat Mullen.' Harper shook his head. 'Almost everything solved.'

'Sir!' someone shouted. His eyes moved around, searching for the sound.

'It came from over by the wagons, I think, sir,' Ash said. He began to sprint.

As soon as he tried to run, Harper felt a searing pain in his ribs. He pressed a hand to his side, pushing down on the bone; a little better.

But only until he turned the corner on to York Road. One wagon was standing there. Two constables lay on the ground by the wheel, three others bent over them.

'They're starting to come round,' Ash said. 'Looks like they'll be fine. Sore heads, that's all.'

'Where's the other wagon?'

'On its way to Millgarth with most of the prisoners.'

Thank God for that. Then fear rose up from his belly and he tasted bile at the back of his throat.

'Most?'

'Dempster was in this one, sir. As soon as I brought men to help you, another group must have attacked here. They freed him.'

He closed his eyes and breathed slowly, willing away the stabbing pain. Dempster could be anywhere up here. Too many people would be willing to hide him. Or too frightened to refuse.

'Put the injured men in the wagon and take them to the infirmary,' he ordered. 'How many do we still have up here?'

'Probably ten, sir.'

'Then let's start searching.'

'I'm sorry, sir.'

He shook his head. 'You weren't to know they'd go this far. Nobody could. It's happened. Send someone down to Millgarth. I want this area flooded with coppers. Start a house-to-house. I want any more information we can gather.'

'Yes, sir,' Ash answered. 'Do you want to rest? We'll have men here in a quarter of an hour.'

He shook his head. 'Let's crack on. Dempster has a head start. He won't go far, though. The bastard thinks he's king of the Bank.'

He kept one hand pressed against his side. It eased the pain as he took a breath. A broken rib, he guessed. Quite likely a few. He'd had it before; he knew he'd heal. He'd got off lightly, really. But the attack on him had only been a diversion so the gang could free Dempster. Who was hiding close by, laughing at the police. He might even be in one of these houses, watching them right this minute.

The streets were dusty. Even on a day of rest, the air was heavy with the smell of the mills and the ironworks. Half an hour and he was sweating in the heat as he walked, a constable beside him, ready and wanting revenge. Moving, looking . . . searching.

He'd seen a pair of police patrols going along the roads, checking every address.

The church bells started to ring, calling people to early mass and they came out of their houses, couples and families in their Sunday best, trooping along to church. As they passed, they gave him side-long, wary glances. No surprise. With his torn, dirty clothes, people must have taken him for a tramp.

His ribs burned. Pain sliced through him every time he breathed. Nothing to be done about that for now.

'Keep your eyes open,' he told the bobby. 'With all these people around, Dempster might try to slip away.'

A young constable dashed up the street, one hand hanging on to his helmet. 'Message from Superintendent Ash, sir. Someone spotted Dempster on Berking Terrace. He's sending some of the men over there.'

Two minutes' walk away.

'Very good. Tell him I'll take command there.'

By the time he arrived, four officers were already busy, knocking and asking their questions. Mostly they got short shrift, doors closed or slammed in their faces. But one man seemed happy to talk, pointing towards Harper.

'He wants you, sir. Says he knows you.'

Up here? That didn't seem likely. At first Harper didn't recognize the face; just another old, weary man. It was only when he came closer that it clicked. Peter Richmond. Someone he hadn't seen for years, not since his time on the beat. Richmond had lived in Fidelity Court. He must have moved up here when his old home was torn down to build County Arcade. Back then, everyone knew him as the Doctor. He'd gathered a little knowledge from somewhere, and he'd mix up potions for people when they were ill. Never charged them a penny. He worked as a signalman at Marsh Lane railway station; still did, to judge by his uniform.

'Mr Richmond. I'm sorry, I don't have time to reminisce.'

The man smiled. His teeth were brown from a lifetime of smoking. 'I know that, lad. You're after Johnny Dempster. The whole neighbourhood knows. Looks like you took a hammering trying to get him, too.'

'I did.' He glanced over his shoulder at the constable. The man was itching to move on, to keep hunting.

'You going to need to strap up that rib,' Richmond said.

'Later.'

'I saw him go by. Him and two other big lads. Slipping in and out of the church crowds.'

'Which way?'

'Over towards Chantrell Place. I've seen him go over that way before. I think there's a place they use.'

'Which place? Do you know?' Harper asked. His palms were slick with sweat and his head throbbed as the pain from the kicking began to take hold.

'I can't say for certain. But there's one that's been empty for years. You can't miss it, it's a strange shape.'

'Why are you telling me?' Harper asked. It never hurt to be suspicious. On the Bank, most people didn't volunteer information.

'I had a dog. Dempster killed it because it ran towards him once. I told him it didn't bite, it just wanted to be friendly. Killed it and walked away like it was nothing. He deserves everything he gets.'

A hatred that had grown and grown in the man's mind. And now he could have his revenge.

'Thank you.'

The building on Chantrell Place stood out. Definitely a strange shape. It wasn't rectangular; one of the corners stood at an angle, as if it had been shaved away for some reason. Three of the windows were cracked, the glass covered with a fine, unbroken layer of cobwebs.

'Go and find the superintendent,' he said to the constable standing beside him. 'Tell him to bring everyone here.'

'Is Dempster in there, sir?'

'Oh, yes.' He didn't take his eyes off the building. He knew the man was here. He could smell him, taste him. Dempster was close. 'Hurry, I want them all up here as soon as they can.'

He stood, gripping the truncheon tight and pressing his hand against the broken rib. All the churchgoers had disappeared; the priest's voice drifted up the hill.

Just him. If any of the Boys of Erin were watching, they had an easy target right in front of their faces.

Harper looked around. A few old men. A couple strolling arm in arm. He could feel his heart beating so hard it might burst through his chest.

Waiting. Bloody waiting. Sometimes he felt as if he spent half his life standing around and waiting for something to happen. But Dempster was in there, and this time Harper would make sure that no one came to free him.

A low creak, and the door of the building swung wide.

Harper glanced over his shoulder. No sign of any more coppers yet. He tightened his grip on the truncheon.

Dempster came out from the shadows, two men on his heels. They were both big, built like brick walls. Brothers, by the look of them, with red hair and hard eyes. All three carried clubs and the light glistened and shone on the knife in Dempster's right hand.

'Put it down,' Harper said. The strength of his voice surprised him. 'You don't want the trouble that's going to bring. You put it on the ground now and I've never seen it.'

THIRTY-ONE

D empster took a pace forward. For half a second, Harper
believed he was going to give up. Then he turned like an
eel and started to run. The two men with him moved, trying
to block the path.

Harper was faster. He kept his eyes on Dempster. He wasn't
going to get away again. As one of the red-headed guards tried to
reach for him, Harper crashed the truncheon down on the man's
hip, hearing him shriek in pain as he fell.

He was running. Panting, grimacing from the broken rib, trying
to squeeze it down so it didn't stab him. His whole body ached
from the kicking, but Dempster was in sight. The man kept looking
back over his shoulder. You never did that. It was too easy to
stumble if you didn't watch where you were going.

Harper pushed himself harder. It all came down to this. Him
and Dempster. He wasn't gaining ground, but he wasn't falling
behind. How long could he last? Every part of his body was
screaming. A bit further. A bit more. Dempster would make a
mistake. He'd fall, do something stupid.

All Harper had to do was keep going.

Dempster was young. He had energy. But he wasn't a runner.
The only spur he had was fear.

There were a few people on the street now, men and women
who stopped to stare, a couple of boys who started to give chase
until voices called them back. Dempster still had the knife in his
hand.

The gap was starting to widen. Harper couldn't keep pace; the
pain from the rib shot through him every time his foot landed on
the pavement. But his quarry was still in sight.

The dog lunged from the ginnel, straining against the lead as
an old man tried to control it. Suddenly it was growling and
snarling around Dempster, snapping at his ankles, even as the
owner shouted out commands and attempted to drag it back to
heel. Dempster swerved, bringing his knife hilt down on the
animal's skull. It yelped and scuttled backwards. Less than a

second, but enough to slow him down and throw him off his stride. His steps were suddenly ragged and uneven.

Harper was closer now. Every breath was painful. His lungs were on fire. But he could catch the man, he was sure of it. Belief was enough to make him draw in air and keep going. He blinked away the sweat. Dempster was beginning to panic. Each of his steps seemed a fraction shorter than the one before.

Push a little harder. A yard nearer. He forced his feet down, face set, breathing hard through his mouth. Almost time to bring him down.

Two more paces. One. He launched himself at Dempster, arms outstretched. This was it. Do or die. Either he'd bring him tumbling down to the pavement or he'd miss and the man would get away.

His shoulder hit the back of Dempster's thighs and he wrapped his arms tight around his legs.

The man fell, all the breath knocked out of him. He couldn't move. Harper batted the knife from his hands and locked handcuffs around his wrists.

He sat, pressing down hard on his broken ribs, gasping for air, too exhausted to even say a word. Every part of his body ached to scream. Dempster was moaning softly, his face still red.

A good three minutes passed before Harper felt strong enough to climb to his feet. His knees hurt, his chest burned, and his head still throbbed from the pounding he'd taken.

'Get up,' he said, reaching down and grabbing Dempster by the collar. The man tried to surprise him, springing up, head lowered, ready to charge. But after so many years Harper knew all the tricks; he'd fallen for half of them when he was still green. Now he had Johnny Dempster under arrest, he wasn't about to give him the opportunity to escape again. He flicked the truncheon down. It caught Dempster on the back of the skull and sent him sprawling back to the ground.

'Don't play silly beggars.' He was tired, he wanted a bandage tight around his chest. He was sick of this whole bloody thing. 'Now get up.'

Harper put the knife in his jacket, drew out his police whistle, took a breath and blew hard. Now all he had to do was wait.

The first constable took less than a minute. He looked at Harper, then at Dempster and muttered, 'Bloody hell' under his breath. Then he let out two long, shrieking blasts on his own whistle. Five minutes and they were all there: Ash, Rogers, Walsh, Sissons, Galt, and a small troop of uniforms. They all looked the worse for wear, battered, bloody. A couple of them would have glowing shiners in the morning. But they all wore that same smile. Victory. They'd come through it, they'd won.

It was probably plastered across his face, too, Harper thought. Why not? They deserved it. They'd had to battle for this. He watched as the coppers marched Dempster away down York Road. Enough of them to stop any more rescue attempts, and all of them primed to fight.

'That building on Chantrell Place,' he said. He had to keep stopping to catch his breath. 'I want it searched. The gang probably had things in there. Papers, all sorts.'

'Very good, sir,' Ash said. 'How did you manage to find it?'

'Someone told me. A man I knew back when I was on the beat. Dempster killed his dog, so he wasn't about to do him any favours. It's ironic,' he added after a second, 'it was a dog that slowed him enough for me to catch up.'

'Not always a man's best friend.'

'Certainly not Dempster's.'

The church bell tolled eight as they strolled back towards Millgarth. He felt as if he'd already lived an entire day since he slipped out of bed. No, much more than that. A week.

At the station he drank a cup of tea and telephoned the chief constable at home to report on the raid.

'That's excellent news, Tom. You got the gun and you got the men who put Mullen in hospital. That's a fine morning's work. Give them my congratulations.'

'I will, sir. Two of ours are in the infirmary. They were guarding Dempster in the wagon when they were attacked. Keeping them in for observation overnight, but they're all right.'

'If you find whoever did that, let's throw the book at them. Meanwhile, the ones you brought in can stew in the cells. Tell the men to go home. They've earned a rest.'

'I will, sir. Thank you.'

He waited until they'd all gone, then asked the duty sergeant to telephone for his car. A soft ride over to the hospital. He was too weary to walk.

Harper sat, placid, as the doctor wound a bandage round and

round his chest, strapping him in. The tightness was comforting; it took away most of the pain and he could breathe easily again.

'You were in the wars. How's your eyesight? Any blurriness?'

'No,' he replied.

'Head aching?'

He hesitated before he replied. 'A little.'

'I'm not surprised. Someone used your skull like a football. It must be thick, there doesn't seem to be much damage. Take some aspirin powder. If the headaches persist, if you still have them tomorrow, come back here. You might have a concussion.'

And then to Mullen's room. No talking to the matron first, no permission this time. He was beyond caring what she'd allow.

Mullen looked up, surprised to see him, eyes widening a fraction at his ragged appearance.

'We've arrested the men who put you in here.'

Maybe it was childish, but he wanted to give him the news. To show him that Leeds Police could do their job. To gloat a little.

'It means you won't have any chance for revenge once you're discharged, of course,' Harper continued. 'They'll be in jail by then. Still, you'll make a fine witness, looking like that with the wires round your jaw. You won't have to say a word.'

Mullen glared and slowly shook his head. He'd hate to be dragged to court for any reason. It went deep against the grain for him.

'There's only one thing left. Who killed Barney Thorpe? Or would you like to tell me?' Mullen's face could have been carved from granite. Harper had never expected an answer. But it was always worth a try. 'The only thing waiting for you when you get out of here is a visit to your father's grave. Then you can be on the boat back to America.'

He turned and left. Maybe it had been nothing, but it felt satisfying.

Finally, the ride home. Leeds was still dirty and grim, but for one day of the week, at least, most of the chimneys weren't billowing smoke.

'Get some fresh clothes on and sit down,' Annabelle said after she'd taken a long look at him. 'Those are only fit for the bin.'

'I want to see Dempster,' Harper said.

On Sunday evening he'd taken a long soak in a hot bath with

Epsom salts, then Annabelle had wound the bandage as tight as she could. It all helped. He'd slept well, woken without too many aches, and hardly any pain when he breathed. A small, dull throb in his head, but he'd taken more aspirin powder.

'I'll have him brought up, sir,' Ash said. 'We found several stolen items at Chantrell Place. They help us tie up several burglaries. Quite a few papers, too. Sissons has started going through them. These caught my eye; you might like to take a look before you sit down with Dempster.'

A small wad of transatlantic cablegrams. Harper read through them, flipping from one to the next, then raised his eyes. 'Well, well, well.'

'We're going to be closing every bank account associated with the Boys of Erin or their leaders.'

'I'm sure they'll prove illuminating.'

Dempster looked haggard, far older than his years. A night in the cells could do that to a man. His hair was unruly, his clothes wrinkled, the collar of his shirt filthy with grime.

'You nearly managed it.'

'Bloody dog did for me.'

'If we hadn't caught you then, we'd have done it later,' Harper told him. 'Truth is you never really had much of a chance.'

Dempster shrugged. 'If that's what you want to think.'

'I know it. You and your lads are going to have a good range of charges against you: breaking into a barracks, stealing weapons, possession of a stolen gun, selling stolen pistols. And that's just a start.'

'Prove it.' Dempster sat back and folded his arms.

'We will. I told you, Barney Thorpe kept some surprisingly complete records. He even listed the serial numbers of those Webleys you sold him to pay off your debt.'

'I had nothing to do with that. And if you found a gun, it wasn't in my house.'

Harper sighed. 'Do you really think we're fools, Johnny? I've got some very good interrogators going at your boys right now. They'll be singing their hearts out to get a lighter sentence. Think about it. You know full well they will.'

All lies, but Dempster wasn't to know that. It sounded good, convincing. And once Walsh started questioning the gang members, it would be true; he'd turn them into a choir in no time at all.

'I don't believe you.'

'If that's what you want, then you can wait and see. We also have the proceeds of several burglaries found at your property on Chantrell Place—'

'That building has nothing to do with me. We were just hiding there.'

'Of course you were.' Harper leaned forward, elbows on the table. 'Take a look at me. Go on. Here, you see that smooth baby skin on my face? You must. After all, you seem to think I was born yesterday. We also have these.' He brought the cablegrams from his pocket. 'Must have cost you a fortune, telegrams back and forth to this gang in New York. They really did want to make sure Davey Mullen never went back there, didn't they? They certainly paid you enough to make sure you took care of him. When all your plans had failed, did you enjoy watching his beating?'

'I've got nothing to say. I want to see my lawyer.'

'You will, and you'll have your day in court.' He paused for a moment, then smiled. 'And when that's done, quite a few years in prison to think about it all. Whatever little power you had is over and done. The Boys of Erin are finished.'

Harper unpinned the list from the wall and studied it. Then he took out his fountain pen and scored through more lines.

~~Fess murder~~

~~Arson~~

~~Metropole shooting~~

~~Barrack robbery~~

~~Francis Mullen~~

Barney Thorpe

~~Missing pistol~~

~~Davey Mullen~~

One item left. He sighed. He knew full well who'd done it, just as he knew Thorpe's killer would walk free and go home to the other side of the ocean.

The squad were busy. Walsh and Galt were still questioning gang members. Sissons had a mountain of paper on his desk, looking as happy as a pig in a mud puddle. Rogers was writing up a report.

'You've done well,' Harper said to Ash.

'Thank you, sir. But you were right in the thick of it.'

He shook his head. 'It was all of us.' Harper pursed his mouth. 'Have we found out why they dumped Davey Mullen in the park? For the life of me, I haven't been able to work that one out.'

Ash snorted. 'Simple, really. They'd beaten him badly, they were absolutely sure he was going to die. Dempster and the others were driving out into the country. They intended to leave him there. But he was bleeding so much, all over the upholstery. Dempster told them to stop and get rid of him before there were stains every-where. As simple as that.'

He'd imagined a twisted plot to throw the police off the scent. Instead, the truth was so ordinary. So bloody *vain*. Dempster cared more about a car seat than a human life.

'At least we know,' he said with a sigh.

Half past five. Harper sat upstairs in the Kardomah. Still thirty minutes until they closed. He kept glancing towards the stairs. Two minutes and they appeared. Mary, with Len beside her. As they sat, Len tried to hide his hands with the dirt and grease ingrained in his skin. He shouldn't, Harper thought; it was good, honest grime.

A cup of tea, a slice of cake. He stared at them both.

'I don't know what ideas you've had about your wedding,' he began. Mary looked up in surprise. Len pulled back on his chair. 'Maybe you haven't considered it yet.'

'We've decided to wait,' Len told him. 'I'm almost done with my apprenticeship, but I'd like to get settled in the company and start my university course.' Mary beamed at him with pride. 'A year or more.'

'There's no rush, Da,' Mary agreed.

'True,' Harper said. 'But make sure you give us good warning and we'll give a proper do. Push the boat out.' Len looked as if he was about to speak. 'Parents of the bride. Our prerogative.'

'Thank you.' Len seemed to fall over the words.

'Are you going to be putting money away to save for a house?'

Most people never owned anywhere of their own. Certainly not a young couple. That was for the wealthy. But Mary's business was doing well, and they were ambitious.

'We've been saving for a while now,' Mary told him.

'Then I tell you what. Before the wedding, I'll sit down with you, see what you have and give you the rest to buy a house. Just small, nothing fancy. Don't set your sights on a mansion. But you'll need a place of your own.'

A stunned silence, Then Mary narrowed her eyes as she stared at him. 'I don't know what to say, Da.'

'No need to say anything,' he said.

'Thank you, Mr Harper.' Poor Len looked to be in shock.

'My mam doesn't know about this, does she?' Mary asked.

He shook his head. 'No, and don't you go telling her yet. We have money. And my rank pays well. What's the point of it if I can't spoil my daughter and son-in-law?' He raised his teacup in a toast.

THIRTY-TWO

'**M**akes me wish I'd stayed with it,' Annabelle said as she closed her copy of *Common Cause*. Page after page about the suffragist gathering in Hyde Park. All the thousands of women who travelled from every part of the country to show their feelings, to be a part of it. 'It must have been something to see, Tom. To be a part of *that*.'

He looked at her. He'd taken to watching her. Not all the time, just hidden little glances now and then, making sure she was all right. She'd shown no more signs of any lapses. Her mind was as sharp as it had always been.

'It would,' he agreed. It was true. 'But you know—'

'Yes.' She cut him off with a small, sad smile. 'Staying in Leeds was the right thing to do. But even so . . .'

'There'll be other chances, Mam,' Mary said. She was sitting at the table, checking figures and writing them in a ledger. A responsible business owner. Just the day before she'd picked up another new client, handling all the correspondence for a small clothing company on Camp Road run by a man named Burton. Her business was growing week by week. 'I tell you what, when we get the vote, you and me will go down to London and celebrate. Drink champagne outside Downing Street.'

'I'll be happy enough if that's next year,' Annabelle told her. She stood, using her hands to push herself up from the seat; old bones. 'I'll make us a cup of tea, shall I?'

'Is Mr Mullen still in hospital?' Mary asked. What had prompted that out of the blue? Harper wondered.

'Yes,' he replied. 'I don't know what he imagined his homecoming would be like, but it turned into something very different.'

It felt strange to spend the entire day in his own office at the town hall. Miss Sharp had kept things ticking over sweetly while he'd been working at Millgarth. No mountains of documents and reports awaited him. Only a small stack of paper he'd worked through by eleven o'clock.

Harper sat back in his chair and stared out of the window. The good weather continued. Probably the farmers were clamouring for rain, but no one else was complaining.

The telephone rang and he reached for it.

'It's Sergeant Roberts from Morley, sir. My inspector thought I should give you a ring.'

Very curious, he thought. 'What is it?'

'A woman came in a few minutes ago. She swears she's seen Lilian Lenton, that suffragette who did a runner.'

'Where? How did she know it was Miss Lenton?'

'It was on Queen Street, sir. She was just strolling along, apparently. And her picture was all over the papers when she vanished. You must remember that.'

That was true. He took a deep breath. 'I want your men to keep their eyes peeled. And you did right to let me know.'

Should he wait, he wondered after the sergeant hung up? No, better not. After all, the inspector from the Branch had asked him to ring if he had information about Miss Lenton. It was probably no more than someone's imagination, but he'd be doing his duty.

'Scotland Yard in London, please,' Harper said as the operator came on the line.

Harper turned his head as he heard a tap on the door. Chief Constable Parker, and behind him a tall, dour man in a suit and glasses.

'Tom, do you have a few minutes?' he asked. His voice was dark and serious. 'There's someone I'd like you to meet. This is Mr Quinn from the Home Office. I think we both need to listen to him. He wants to talk about war.'

*   *   *

War. The very last word he wanted to hear. He remembered the last one in South Africa, back at the turn of the century. He hoped to God there wouldn't be another. No mention in the papers, no articles beating the drums. It seemed unlikely. But Quinn had sounded convincing. He had facts and figures to back up his ideas.

Conflict was no more than a faint possibility, he admitted, but the country needed to prepare. The chief seemed to be taking it seriously. A year, maybe two, and young men might be going off to fight the Germans.

'The country isn't looking for it,' Quinn said. 'I don't believe the Germans are, either. The important thing is that we're prepared in case it happens.'

He was going around England, talking to police forces. It made sense. Dozens of coppers in Leeds were in the army reserve. They'd be called up if something happened and the police would be desperately short-handed.

'We're urging everyone to begin recruiting special constables,' Quinn said. 'At the very least, to have a recruiting programme in place. Just in case.' He placed a hard emphasis on the last three words. 'And of course, we'll hope that none of this is necessary.'

Hands in his pockets, Harper walked slowly home in the evening sun. They'd discuss it in the morning, Parker had said. Go home and think about what they needed.

One more thing, another dark cloud gathering on the horizon. A boy ran by, pushing an empty cart. He had a smile plastered across his face. Done for the day, no responsibilities, no troubles.

'War,' Annabelle said. 'Do you think he's right?'

'I don't know,' Harper told her. 'I hope to God he's not. If it happened, Len would join the army.'

She reached for his hand across the table. 'Do you really think so?'

'Yes.' Of course he would. All the young men would be lining up to fight for King and country, to prove themselves and show how patriotic they were. It would spread like a madness.

They heard the footsteps on the stairs, then Mary burst through the door, bright and smiling. Annabelle flashed him a warning with her eyes: not a word. There was no need; he wasn't about to mention it to her.

An hour passed, a warm weather supper of brown bread with

cheese and apples. Annabelle disappeared into the kitchen with the plates. He opened up the *Evening Post* and began to read. Mary vanished into her room.

For now, at least, they had peace.

August, 1913

Harper stood on the platform at Leeds station. His ribs had almost healed, the bones knitting together by themselves. Hardly any pain at all now. Davey Mullen watched as the porter wheeled his trunk back to the luggage van. A small leather suitcase sat by his feet.

He'd recovered well, with a few more scars to add to all the others on his body. He'd been discharged from the hospital the day before, and bought himself a haircut and a good, close shave to get rid of his beard before taking a hackney to Harehills cemetery. Mullen had spent an hour there, walking around and viewing the ground where his father was buried. He was pale from being indoors for so long, but his eyes sparkled and he still had that light, mocking smile.

'We took your revenge for you,' Harper said. 'They'll all be in prison for a long time.'

Dempster had been given seven years, the others five or less. At least the Bank would be quiet for a while.

Mullen shrugged. 'That's fine. Saves me the effort.'

'I'm sorry about your father.' The man who'd killed him had swung from the scaffold.

'Me, too. But I don't think I'll be coming back to Leeds. There's nothing here for me now.'

That was good news. His visit had brought too many deaths, too much trouble.

Harper studied the man's face before asking his question. 'I've got no evidence at all. But I want to know, just for myself: did you kill Barney Thorpe?'

Mullen gave a soft chuckle. 'How many times have you asked me that? Do you really think I'd admit anything to a cop? I'm not saying more than that.'

Was it a confession? He'd hoped for more. But this was as far as he could go.

'Do you know who ordered all the things that happened?' Harper asked. 'Fess's killing, those shots at the Metropole, the arson, your beating?'

'I figured it out. I had plenty of time to think in the hospital. It had to be the Hudson Dusters working with that gang here. I'd taken care of the ones who shot me. They believed they could finish me off over here.'

'That makes sense,' Harper agreed. He took the sheaf of transatlantic cablegrams from his pocket. 'Read those. The Boys of Erin had them.'

Mullen raised a questioning eyebrow. As he glanced from one to the next, his mouth tightened and his eyes grew darker. He finished and handed them back.

'The Gophers,' Harper said. 'Your own gang. They wanted you out of the way.'

'They're going to get a shock when I show up. Especially Jacky goddamned Nolan. He's the one who sent those telegrams. Those are his initials on each one.'

'He thought you'd go home and try to take over the gang. Easier to have you hung or in prison here.' Harper waved the papers. 'We've told the New York police about it all, and that you're on your way.'

'You really think they can do a thing?' The whistle sounded and Mullen climbed on board. 'I wish you well, Mr Harper. No need to worry. I told you, you won't be seeing me again.'

Harper watched until the train began to pull away from the platform. Mullen stood at the carriage door, staring back. As they moved away, he made a stabbing motion with his arm and smiled. Then he was gone.

Admission or taunt? He'd never know. Not now.

Summer was starting to wane. The first cool days of September. He'd eaten his lunch sitting on a bench in Park Square, glancing up at the leaves just beginning to turn on the trees.

Back to the office. The telephone rang as he put his hat on the rack.

'Harper.'

'Walsh here, sir.'

'Yes, Inspector, what can I do for you?

'We've just received a cable from the New York police. Someone called Nolan was shot dead on the street last night. He's—'

'Mullen told me who he was.'

'They took our friend into custody. He has a solid alibi.'

'No big surprise, is it?'

'Not at all, sir. I thought you'd like to know.'

But it was New York's problem, not his.

He glanced up from the paper. Annabelle seemed to have been in the kitchen for a long time. He picked up the teapot. Empty. Time for a fresh brew.

She was standing by the sink, staring at . . . he couldn't tell what she could see. Annabelle didn't turn as he entered; she didn't even notice. She was lost somewhere in her own mind. Softly, he spoke her name. Nothing.

Sweet God.

Harper laid an arm around her shoulders and guided her back into the living room, until she was settled in her chair. She still had no idea he was there. A full minute passed before something seemed to change in her face. It came alive again. She blinked, and her mouth moved.

Annabelle saw him kneeling in front of her, looked around to see the room she'd known for years, and her expression fell as she understood what had happened.

'How long?' she asked.

'Just a few minutes. You're fine now.'

She brought her hands up to cover her eyes. 'I'm not, Tom. I'm not fine. Not fine at all.'

The tears began and he pulled her close. What could he say? There weren't any words that would make it right. There was no way to heal this. It was here, it would return again and again. The episodes would probably become longer in time. That was what the doctor had said. At some point she'd wander off into her own world and never return.

In the office on Park Square, when he'd listened to the physician, it hadn't seemed quite real. It was something that might happen to someone else. Now, seeing it for himself, he realized he was completely helpless. There was nothing he could do to fight this. Nothing any of them could do, apart from stand and watch.

'Come on,' he told her. 'Come with me and we'll make that cup of tea.'

Something routine and familiar. A task she'd been doing since she was a little child. It seemed to help. She moved without thinking, the pot, the tea caddy, the kettle. By the time it was mashing she was more like herself again. But the sorrow in her eyes was enough to make him weep.

'I could see you. But I didn't know who you were. I didn't who I was. I knew what room I was in. I just . . . I don't know. I can't explain it.'

'It's over.'

'For the moment.'

'And I'm here with you.'

They had no choice. They'd keep going and face it together.

AFTERWORD

The Great Pilgrimage did happen, more or less as described here. Suffragist women (as opposed to suffragettes) did start on routes from different parts of the country and converge on Hyde Park. From first step to London rally, it took six weeks, and one group of marchers did stop overnight in Leeds, with meetings in Roundhay Park and on Woodhouse Moor. Jane Robinson's book *The Great Pilgrimage* (Black Swan, 2018) gives a very full account.

Davey Mullen is very loosely based on Owen 'Owney' Madden. He did start out on Somerset Street in Leeds. Some accounts have the family moving to Wigan as the father searched for work. But his mother did move to New York, initially to stay with her sister, and a year later sent for her two sons. Her husband remained in England; he may or may not have lived until 1932. Owen grew up in Hell's Kitchen, belonged to a gang called the Gophers and developed a deadly reputation. He really was shot eleven times outside a dancehall, and he did recover to exact his revenge. Prohibition was good to him. He ended up owning the famous Cotton Club and eventually retired to Hot Springs, Arkansas, where he died peacefully in 1965. Supposedly he had a life-long love of the *Yorkshire Post*. There's no record of him ever returning to Leeds, however.

Lilian Lenton existed, and was released from Armley Gaol under the Cat and Mouse Act. Her brazen escape from Chapel Allerton is well chronicled in Jill Liddington's *Rebel Girls* (Virago, 2006). She did return to England and was re-arrested.

I'm grateful to all the staff at Severn House for their faith, especially Kate Lyall Grant, who gives the green light to my books, and my editor, Sara Porter. But the entire team do such a great job, and have kept going through lockdowns and the pandemic. You're all remarkable.

Thanks, too, to Lynne Patrick. She's dug down and corrected my ideas and spellings for over ten years now, as well as pointing out the errors of my ways when needed. A friend and editor, and appreciated on every level.

And it would be impossible not to thank my partner, Penny. She puts up with me constantly thinking about the book I'm writing, acting as a sounding board and first reader. How she's done it for so long is a constant source of amazement.

Finally, thanks to all the staff in bookshops and libraries. They're the lifeblood of it all. And then, every one of you who reads one of my books. Thank you.